The Solace of Bay Leaves

The Solace of Bay Leaves

A SPICE SHOP MYSTERY

BY LESLIE BUDEWITZ

SEVENTH STREET BOOKS®

Published 2020 by Seventh Street Books®

This is a work of fiction. Characters, organizations, products, locales, and events portrayed in this novel either are products of the author's imagination or are used fictitiously. Any similarities to real persons, living or dead, is coincidental and not intended by the author.

Cover images © Shutterstock
Cover design by Jennifer Do
Cover design © Start Science Fiction

Inquiries should be addressed to
Start Science Fiction
221 River Street, 9th Floor
Hoboken, NJ 07030

Phone: 212-431-5455
www.seventhstreetbooks.com

10 9 8 7 6 5 4 3 2

ISBN: 978-1-64506-017-8 (paperback)
ISBN: 978-1-64506-018-5 (ebook)

Printed in the United States of America

For my Circle sisters

*who model bringing peace and creativity
to this chaotic world.*

*Jordonna, Jules, Marsha, Rebecca,
Nancy, Sue, Maggie, and Carla*

Ingredients for a Killer Blend

a.k.a. The Cast

THE SEATTLE SPICE SHOP STAFF

Pepper Reece—Mistress of Spice
Sandra Piniella—assistant manager and mix master
Cayenne Cooper—salesclerk with a secret
Matt Kemp—salesclerk and retail wiz
Reed Locke—part-time salesclerk, full-time student
Kristen Gardiner—part-time salesclerk, Pepper's BFF
Arf—an Airedale, the King of Terriers

THE FLICK CHICKS

Pepper
Kristen
Laurel Halloran—widowed restaurateur and houseboat dweller
Seetha Sharma—massage therapist
Aimee McGillvray—vintage shop owner

IN MONTLAKE

Bruce Ellingson—bond broker who went for broke
Deanna Ellingson—neighborhood real estate agent
Cody Ellingson—their son
Maddie Petrosian—Pepper and Kristen's childhood pal
Jake Byrd—aspiring developer

MARKET MERCHANTS, RESIDENTS, AND FRIENDS

Nate Seward—the fisherman
Glenn Abbott—neighbor and city councilman
Misty the Baker—guardian of Market tradition
Jamie Ackerman—painter and Market newcomer

THE LAW

Detective Michael Tracy—homicide
Detective Shawn Armstrong—homicide
Officer Tag Buhner—on the bike beat, Pepper's former husband
Special Agent Meg Greer—FBI

One

Legend says that in the late 1950s, aspiring rocker Jimi Hendrix often met friends in Seattle's Pike Place Market and played late into the night, on the steps in front of a passage called Ghost Alley.

"THIS IS MAGIC," NATE WHISPERED TO ME AS THE WAITER poured our wine. "I can't believe I've never been here."

I smiled my thanks to the waiter. There are pockets of magic in every city, and since Nate and I got together a few months ago, we'd made a point of exploring them. The glow of new love adds its own magic to the mix, and we'd made a point of enjoying that, too. But this was our first evening at Jazz Alley.

Across the dark, gleaming table, Eric Gardiner raised his glass, catching a flicker of light. His wife Kristen, my BFF since before we were born, raised hers. Nate and I followed suit. "Cheers," Eric said. "Great to finally have a Friday night out, the four of us."

I heard my phone buzzing in the small beaded bag at my hip. I ignored it. No interruptions tonight. Besides, the Spice Shop was already closed. Nobody needed me for anything important.

"How you scored seats for the dinner show," I said, "don't even tell me. She always sells out the house." Diane Schuur, one of Seattle's best-loved musicians, wouldn't take the stage until after plates were cleared, but the promise and the wine had already begun to work their spell.

"What looks good?" Nate scanned the menu. Fish scores high in Seattle restaurants, but as a commercial fisherman, Nate is picky about his *pesce*, not to mention his salmon, crab, and halibut.

"The crab or sole," I mused, "and Key lime pie. I had it once in Florida and ever since, I've thought that's what vacation tastes like."

On the floor between us, Kristen's phone buzzed in her purse. A flash of worry flitted across her face and she fished for the bag, then snuck a peek under the table. Cell phones were frowned upon here, with good reason. But they'd left their girls home alone, so I didn't blame her.

She held it out for me to see. The text wasn't from one of her young teenagers, bored or ticked off at the other. It was from our good friend, Laurel Halloran.

Detective Tracy is in my living room, I read. *FBI on the way.*

"The girls are fine," Kristen told her husband, showing him the screen as she nudged him to slide over and let her out.

"It's Laurel," I told Nate. "Something's up. Be right back."

I followed Kristen down the hallway to the women's room. Inside, we huddled in the corner and she made the call, her blond head next to my dark one, the phone between us. This was not a place, or a topic, for speaker phone.

"They have new evidence," Laurel said, her voice barely a whisper. She lives on a houseboat on Lake Union, and short of closing herself in her own bathroom, there aren't many places to hide. And like most cops, Detective Michael Tracy seemed to possess almost super-human hearing. "He won't tell me what it is until the FBI agent gets here. What do I do?"

Kristen's eyes met mine.

"Put the coffee on," I said.

THE cool damp that had hung in the air most of the day had turned liquid in the short time we'd been inside. Eric pulled the SUV into the alley behind the club, close to the rear door, so we managed to avoid getting soaked.

No such luck at the docks. I hadn't brought a coat, not expecting to be outside for more than the door-to-door dash. It was Friday night and everyone in the Lake Union houseboat community must have been home, watching movies or reading as the wind and rain lashed their windows, unaware of the ghosts lurking outside their doors. Kristen had found a folding umbrella under the front passenger seat, and Eric held it above us as we stood near the giant golden willow, where Nate unlatched the weathered wooden gate.

"Excuse me," a female voice called. "Do you live here? Do you know where I can find Laurel Halloran?"

In the bluish light from the lamp skewered to a post on the mailbox rack, each box a different color, I saw a trim woman in a dark, hip-length jacket, jeans, and low-heeled boots striding toward us. She held a black umbrella.

Nothing about her screamed "FBI," but I knew.

"This way," I said, grabbing the rail alongside the short flight of steps to the dock where Laurel's houseboat was moored. Technically, it's a floating home, since it isn't actually seaworthy, but no one calls them that. Damp wood can be slippery and one misstep can lead to disaster.

Four sets of footsteps followed me, introductions deferred. Normally, when I duck beneath the willow's graceful branches, my tensions melt away, as if the tree guards an invisible gate through which stress cannot pass. That's why Laurel moved here after her husband's murder three years ago. She'd sold their beloved Montlake home, and she and Gabe, then fifteen, had set about settling into a new neighborhood. Still close to his school and friends, but a world apart from worry.

Not tonight.

Across the lake, lights glowed along the shore. Headlights whizzed by on Westlake Avenue, winking off and on as they passed the narrow gaps between buildings. More lights clustered at the north end of the lake where sailing yachts and working ships waited for repairs. On the hill above them—Seattle is a city of water and hills—the industrial figures of Gasworks Park stood watch.

Laurel's sapphire blue door faced an empty slip. Instead of a boat, she keeps a pair of yellow kayaks, now lashed to the side of the house. Friends with boats, or neighbors with seafaring visitors, are free to tie up any time. Colorful planters flank the door, including an oak half barrel holding a bay tree. Herbs and edible flowers fill smaller pots, befitting a chef who runs a deli and catering company. The rain had washed away most of the fish and diesel odor that clings to the lakefront, and I caught a whiff of bay and mint.

I took a deep breath, knocked, and walked in. "Laurel, we're here. And we've brought company," I called. Despite my accidental involvement in several crimes over the past year, I had never before encountered an FBI agent in the course of his or professional pursuits. Nor had I met one in my long career working HR for a big law firm, before I bought the spice shop, or in my thirteen-year marriage to a cop.

"Special Agent Meg Greer," the woman said to me after umbrellas had been leaned in the corner, coats and jackets shed, and we'd all shaken like the damp dogs we'd become. Her green eyes assessed me as she held out her hand, her reddish curls frizzy from the moist air.

"Pepper Reece," I replied. My Pied Piper routine must have signaled me leader of the pack. Or maybe it was the long "thank God you're here" hug from Laurel. Introductions were made. Detective Tracy had not met Nate or Greer.

"Is there a reason you thought you needed to call a lawyer?" the detective asked Laurel, tilting his head at Eric.

Laurel wrapped her arms around herself, gripping her elbows. "I called my two best friends," she said. "Kristen just happens to be married to one of the most highly respected attorneys in the city."

"And the other comes with a man who can pour coffee," Nate said. "Smells done. I'll bring it out." I watched with gratitude as my fisherman, tall, dark, handsome, and efficient, disappeared into the tiny galley.

"Looks like we broke up a double date," Tracy said, running a hand over his close-cropped hair. He's a short man with medium brown skin whose ever-present camel hair sport coat strains across his stomach when it's buttoned. Though we'd met a few times at police department functions when I was married, our first professional contact had come just over a year ago when a man died on the doorstep of Seattle Spice, the shop I run in Pike Place Market. Tracy and his then partner had caught the case and quickly focused on one of my employees. Thanks to my intervention, and a bit of four-footed luck, justice had been done.

I sank onto the soft butterscotch leather couch and Laurel

perched beside me, clutching a framed photo of smiling, sandy-haired Patrick Halloran. "Detective, as much as I enjoy seeing you," I said, "we're cold and wet and hungry, and we walked out of Jazz Alley before the music even started. What's this about?"

Tracy and Special Agent Greer sat in matching chairs opposite us. On TV, FBI agents all wear suits or tactical gear, but I suppose in real life, they try to blend in. And Greer could easily have been off duty when summoned to join the party, relaxing in her black jeans and black turtleneck. Just add the gun now holstered at her hip and go.

Tracy cleared his throat. Patrick Halloran's murder was officially an active investigation, and he called Laurel every few months to touch base and reassure her that the murder was still on their minds. But with no new leads, the search had come to a dead end.

Dead end. I cringed at the term. Honestly, before I found myself repeatedly dragged into murder investigations, I had no idea how many death- and crime-related phrases we use every day.

"As we told Mrs. Halloran," Tracy said now, "preliminary ballistics received late this afternoon indicate a match between a handgun used in a shooting Thursday morning and Mr. Halloran's murder."

"What? The shooting in Montlake?" I leaned forward. Nate set a heavy tray on the rattan ottoman, and returned a moment later with a stainless steel vacuum pot.

"When Mrs. Halloran said she wanted to call you, I agreed because we know your friendship," Tracy said. "And we know this is a shock."

Last winter, Laurel and I had found the body of an up-and-coming young chef. In that encounter, and others, I thought Tracy had come to see me as helpful. But he might not want to admit that in front of the FBI.

If Tracy could be subtle, I could be humble.

"Same gun, same neighborhood," Eric said from his post by the French doors leading to the deck, one arm around Kristen's shoulders. She looked as stunned as I felt. "Any other connection between the crimes or the victims that you know of?"

"They were acquainted," Tracy said.

"Who?" I asked. "Who is he? How is he?"

"Is anybody going to pour that coffee, or are we just going to let the smell torture us?"

Our questions were reasonable, but clearly, Tracy wasn't ready to answer. Such is the power of Vitamin C. Laurel poured and I passed out cups and saucers, along with a plate of almond biscotti from Ripe, her downtown deli. I forced myself not to fall on them like a starving hyena.

Up to this point, Special Agent Greer had said nothing more than her name and that she was pleased to meet us. When we all had coffee, doctored to taste, and a cookie, she spoke. "I'm here because Mr. Halloran was an Assistant United States Attorney, which makes his murder a federal offense."

"But only if he was murdered because of his official duties," Eric interjected. "Making this a joint investigation. Is the new victim also a federal employee?"

"No," Greer said. "Unfortunately, she's not in any condition to talk to us."

"She?" That surprised me. "Who is she?"

Tracy slipped a plastic sleeve out of the inside pocket of his jacket and handed it to Laurel. I stretched an arm behind her and peered over her shoulder.

"Ohmygod." My hand flew to my mouth.

"You know her?" Tracy asked.

But when I raised my head to answer, I didn't look at him. I looked at Kristen.

"It's Maddie Petrosian."

Two

Burning coffee grounds mixed with bay leaves is said to repel almost any bug.

"NOT THAT I SHOULD BE SURPRISED," DETECTIVE TRACY SAID. "But this is Seattle, not Mount Podunk. Suppose you tell me how you know Ms. Petrosian."

"Is she okay?" I asked him. "Tell me she's okay. How did we not know?" I asked Kristen.

"It's a relief to see that the SPD can keep some secrets," Tracy replied. "She's still unconscious. Head shot. The docs repaired an intracranial bleed. They won't know if there's any lasting damage until she wakes up. In the meantime, we have no witnesses and little to go on."

I'd spent part of my childhood in Montlake, so when the nightly news mentioned a shooting in the old grocery on Twenty-Fourth East, my ears had perked up. But the report had been short on detail and hadn't named the victim.

"How did we not know?" I asked Kristen again.

"I wondered why Tim wasn't at soccer practice," she said. "He called when we were getting ready tonight, but I didn't answer and he didn't leave a message. I'll text him now."

"Might be good to hear what the detective has to say first," Eric suggested.

"Wait." Greer held up a hand, her gaze darting from me

to Kristen and back. "You knew both the first victim *and* the second?"

I felt myself flush, as though I'd been accused of wrongdoing and the explanation, simple as it was, would only make things sound worse.

"We went to school with Maddie, from kindergarten on," I replied, then glanced at Nate, his face creased with confusion. "Kristen sees more of her than I do. I never knew Pat Halloran. He died before we became friends with Laurel."

"You knew Pat, though, didn't you? From cases you'd had?" Kristen asked Eric, who nodded. She turned her attention back to Greer. "Maddie's kids and our girls are close in age. They go to the same schools. We see Maddie and Tim, her husband, at soccer games and school events. And we've been to their place on Whidbey Island."

"As I recall," Tracy said. "From when Mr. Halloran was killed."

Maddie Petrosian had been the Golden Girl in our class. Her great-grandparents survived the Armenian genocide and immigrated to Seattle, where they worked their tails off and amassed a fortune, mostly in real estate. Made sense for people driven from their homes to value land in their new country. Maddie and I both went to Seattle University after high school, but unlike me, she'd been a serious student. I dropped out after junior year, then stumbled into a career in HR at a prominent law firm, eventually finding my true calling in retail. Maddie, on the other hand, was magna cum everything. She went on to get an MBA, graduated first in her class, married the man who finished second, and took over the family business.

She was everything I wasn't. And impossible to dislike.

"Her name's in the file," Tracy said to Greer. "In the interviews with the Neighbors United folks."

So Greer was new on the case. New in town, too?

"As to why you didn't know, we kept her name quiet at her husband's request, until he could reach her mother," Tracy continued. "She's in Europe on some kind of tour, and he didn't want her to hear the news from someone else. We released the name to the press this evening."

Next to me on the couch, Laurel was bouncing her knee up and down. I put out a hand and stilled it.

"So does the same gun mean the same killer went after both my husband and Maddie Petrosian?" she asked. "Why? That doesn't make any sense."

I had to agree. How could a shooting yesterday morning be connected to a murder three years ago?

"That's the obvious explanation," Tracy replied. "But it's early yet."

"The newspaper called it an interrupted burglary. Is that really what happened?" I asked. "That grocery's been closed for ages. Oh, is that the one she bought to redevelop?"

Tracy shot me a "you should know better" look. And I did. I'd been married to a cop. "Interrupted burglary" is code for when the police suspect attempted murder but don't want to say so.

"It doesn't make any sense," Laurel repeated. "Maddie's a developer. Pat was a prosecutor who volunteered his spare time with a community group trying to protect the neighborhood against overzealous developers. They were on opposite sides. What could anyone hope to gain from shooting them both?" She looked from Tracy to Greer and back, but got no answer.

Finally, Eric asked, "So what's next?"

"Crime scene evidence," Tracy replied. "You wouldn't believe the dust and junk in a vacant grocery. Canvass the neighborhood. Trace the gun. Ms. Petrosian's shooting is a tragedy, and it is our immediate focus. But it's also giving us new evidence on your husband's case, Mrs. Halloran. We'll be revisiting every lead. He was one of our own."

When one of their own was attacked, every law enforcement officer kicked into high gear to solve the crime. Maybe now, they could.

"That's where the FBI comes in," Greer said. "We're conducting a thorough investigation into a person of interest, and dedicating extensive resources into reevaluating other evidence in light of this recent incident. Working closely with the SPD, of course."

"That means the project's on hold for now, right?" I said. "Who still wanted it stopped? Who didn't accept the newest proposal?"

"We're looking into that," Tracy said, "although it's hard to see how that might circle back to Mr. Halloran."

If Pat's killing was not related to his work as a prosecutor, but stemmed from his volunteer work or his personal life, then it wasn't a federal case. But until that was disproved, the FBI would take the lead. Not because they were pushy or grabby, but because that was the law. And while Mike Tracy was grumpy and suffered fools not one whit, he would do whatever it took to solve this case.

"We'll keep you posted, Mrs. Halloran," Greer said, standing to leave. "Thank you for your hospitality."

She rose, as did Mike Tracy. He buttoned his jacket and glanced at Kristen and me. "Don't suppose I can keep you two away from your old friends, now can I?"

"Not a chance," I said.

He grunted—he grunts a lot—and gestured to the Special Agent. "After you." Then he turned back and plucked a cookie off the tray.

NATE closed the houseboat's door behind the officers. I felt badly for him—he had no idea what was going on.

But then, neither did the rest of us.

Laurel sank back, eyes closed. She's a striking woman, at five nine, a couple of inches taller than me, and at fifty-five, a dozen years older. We are hair opposites—mine is short, dark, and spiky, while hers is a cascade of gray-brown curls that falls well below her shoulders. But at the moment, I suspected my face mirrored the expression of sadness mingled with shock that hers bore.

"We should leave you alone."

"No." Her dark eyes flew open. "Oh. You missed dinner. And the music."

"We're fine," I said reflexively, but she'd already jumped up. Besides being a chef, she's mother to a teenage boy, though he was safely away at college. Hungry people spur her into action.

I picked up the framed photograph she'd clutched throughout our conversation with Tracy and Greer. Pat had been a nice-looking man with a friendly, open face. Not a head-turner, but a man you'd smile at on the street. His sandy-red hair was as curly as Laurel's, and he had the hazel eyes, fair skin, and smattering of freckles that went with his Irish name.

I set the photo on the table, picked up the coffee tray, and followed Laurel into the kitchen. It's tiny but efficient, with a built-in dining booth, and within minutes, I'd poured us all glasses of pinot noir, and Laurel had served up mixed greens dressed with a basil vinaigrette and bowls of pasta with olive oil and garlic, sprinkled with parsley so fresh it was practically still growing. Eric had found Diane Schuur on his playlist and his phone serenaded us from the windowsill.

Laurel slid in next to Kristen, a glass of wine in hand. "Maybe, finally, we'll get answers."

After a few bites, my blood sugar stabilized and I could begin to think again. I set my fork down.

"So was Maddie the target, or in the wrong place at the wrong time?" I mused.

"I just sent Tim a text," Kristen said to me. "When do you want to go to the hospital tomorrow? Coma means ICU, so we might not be able to see her, but we can at least talk with him in person."

"You'll have to go without me," I said. "I am swamped at the shop."

"I need to call Gabe," Laurel said. "Friday nights are game nights. I don't even know if they won." Gabe was a freshman at Notre Dame, on a soccer scholarship.

"Call him in the morning," Kristen said. "Let him enjoy Friday night. Besides, you don't know anything yet."

"Pat always said"—Laurel's voice broke, then recovered. "He always insisted that we would not keep secrets from our son. When Pat was fifteen, his father was badly injured on the job. His mother didn't tell the kids how hurt he was, that for a while, they weren't sure he'd live. They found out from an aunt. It made the ordeal even worse, and fueled a rabid hatred for secrets."

Fifteen. The same age Gabe had been when Pat died.

"Did his dad recover?" Nate asked.

"Mostly, but he never went back to work. Pat and his brother gave up sports and got jobs. He went to college and law school on academic scholarships, not the soccer scholarship he'd dreamed of."

Kristen and I exchanged glances. We knew too well the power of family secrets. Her parents and mine had shared one for decades, and when it came to light a few months ago, it had nearly destroyed our friendship.

The exhaustion was beginning to show on Laurel's face. I

picked up plates and slid out of the booth, then beckoned to Nate. In the living room, voice low, I said "I want to stay with her overnight. Could you head home and take care of the dog?"

Nate's official residence, to the extent that he has one, is a gillnetter called the *Thalassa*, docked at Fisherman's Terminal, but since his unexpected return from Alaska a few weeks ago, he'd spent most nights at my loft.

"How 'bout I stay, too? I could call an Uber, but you know Eric will insist on running me back to your place, and I'd rather let them go straight home. I'll call Glenn to take the dog."

I put my hand on his chest, feeling the steady beat of his heart. "How do you always know exactly what to do?"

"YOU'RE going to get involved, aren't you?" Nate said as he slid between the sheets in Gabe's old room, on the houseboat's upper level. As Laurel had predicted, we'd found Snowball, the stray dock cat who adopted Gabe when they moved in, fast asleep on his bed. She barely opened an eye when I scooped her up and put her on the desk chair, atop a blue-and-green Seattle Sounders seat cushion. Gabe worshipped the city's pro soccer team.

"I don't know that there's anything to get involved in. But I'll do whatever Laurel needs. And Maddie."

"What happened? To Pat, I mean. All I've ever heard is that he was shot at home while Laurel and Gabe were away and the case has never been solved."

"That's the gist of it." I laid my shimmery blue velvet dress over the back of the chair. "Soccer team trip. Pat was supposed to go, but at the last minute, he needed to work so Laurel went instead. I never met him, but everybody says he was a great guy."

"Well, sure," Nate said. "I wouldn't expect Laurel to marry a schmuck."

"Why not? I did." Although my ex hadn't started out that way. Schmuckdom had crept up on him.

Wisely, Nate ignored that. "They honestly never had a serious suspect? But they thought he was killed in the line of duty, or whatever it's called? Because of his work, I mean."

"Not that I ever heard. And yes, killed because he was a federal prosecutor. Laurel's never said much about the case, and I haven't pressed her. My impression is they were focused on someone he'd been investigating who had a grudge against him. I knew they talked to Maddie, and to Kristen and Eric, but that's it."

"Why talk to them? Because of this development you and Laurel mentioned?"

"Yeah. On Twenty-Fourth, in Montlake, there's a block of commercial buildings, though it's pretty quiet these days. A developer had a plan to knock down the old corner grocery and put up one of those modern monstrosities. Pat was the spokesman for the neighborhood group that opposed it."

The corner grocery that my brother and I had biked to for ice cream bars on hot summer days had been empty for ages, and it needed more than updating—one of those gray 1960s boxes that had been ugly from Day One. Like every other vacant or underused corner in the city, it was a prime target for a modern mixed-use development. That's the new buzz word in urban design—retail on the ground floor, offices or apartments upstairs. After living blocks from Pike Place Market the last few years and seeing how well mixed-use works downtown, I'm a fan, when it's done right.

"So it was Maddie's project?"

Laurel had found a Sounders T-shirt for me and I pulled it on. "Honestly, I never knew the details of her role—investor, property manager, or what. The police talked with her and the other developer, but they both had alibis. She and Tim were up on Whidbey with Eric and Kristen and the kids."

"Were the developers actually suspects?"

"Not that I ever heard. Just dotting the i's and crossing the t's. Anyway, I guess the other developer backed out and nothing happened for a while. Years. But then Maddie got the project moving again and finalized plans for the corner just in the last few weeks. It's way scaled back, from what I heard." I knew most of this from Kristen. Maddie and I didn't see each other often; she didn't have much time to spend with friends.

"So the neighbors got what they wanted, but Pat didn't live to see the victory."

"It's all so sad." I climbed in beside him. Never in a million years would I tell a professional fisherman that sleeping on a boat makes me dizzy. Nate slipped an arm beneath my shoulders and pulled me close, and I let the wind and water have their way.

Three

Known simply as "small lake" or "small water" to the Puget Sound Salish and other indigenous peoples, Lake Union earned its modern name at an 1854 Fourth of July picnic, when Seattle city father Thomas Mercer predicted it would someday link saltwater to fresh.

"PEPPER, I HAVE TO TELL YOU THIS. I HAVE TO TELL SOMEONE, and those detectives will think I'm crazy." Laurel set a plate of toast and a jar of strawberry jam on her kitchen table.

I inched my coffee closer. It was my first cup of the day, and from Laurel's tone, I suspected I was going to need every ounce. It's common to crave intimacy after news of tragedy, and Nate and I had made a few waves of our own last night. I'd slept well, but not nearly long enough.

"If you want me to leave . . ." Nate said.

"No, no. She'd tell you anyway."

"I would not—" I started to protest. "Yeah, I probably would."

She sat across from us. "About ten days ago, I had a dream. A nightmare." She threaded her fingers through the handle of her coffee mug. "By the time I saw Pat—in real life, I mean, when I saw his body in the morgue—he'd been gone for hours. That beautiful light that shone from his eyes—it was gone. It wasn't my Pat anymore. But in the dream, I saw it all play out. I saw someone stand in our mudroom and lift a gun—a handgun, I don't know guns—and take aim. I heard the shot, I saw the blood, saw him fall, and then . . . it all went black."

"Could you see who it was? A man or a woman? How tall?" I felt Nate push his leg against mine, the signal unmistakable. He was right. She didn't need me peppering her with questions she couldn't answer.

"No. He was shot in the mudroom, though he managed to crawl outside—we had a little bitty back deck—and call for help. That's where the neighbor found him." She stared at her hands. "Then—then the next morning, Gabe called. He woke up screaming, scared his roommate half to death. He'd had the same nightmare. Except, in his dream, it wasn't Pat being shot."

Despite hot coffee and the warmth of the tiny kitchen, I felt a chill, afraid of what she would say next. And then she said it.

"It was me."

Outside, the rain pelted the windows. Nate took my hand. The cat's tail swept my bare leg as she strode by, headed for her own breakfast.

"He said . . ." Laurel swallowed and continued. "He said it felt so real that he called just to hear my voice." She lifted her gaze to mine. "It was like it was a warning. Why is this happening now, right as we're coming up on the anniversary?"

"That's why, don't you think?" Nate asked. "Anniversaries can be pretty powerful. Dreams, too."

I had never heard Nate mention any interest in dreams. So much we didn't know about each other yet.

Though I don't have children—by the time my ex decided he was ready, my biological clock had run down—I've got a healthy dose of what Kristen calls "Universal Mother Energy," and I channeled it now to make sure Laurel ate. I scrambled eggs and between bites, she told us more about Pat. How the long battle his parents fought to get compensation for his father's injuries led Pat to become a lawyer and his brother a doctor. How Pat had encouraged her to open her catering company, and later Ripe, serving fresh food fast in a city addicted to both. How they took the kayaks down to the wetlands on weekends, and how he coached Gabe's youth soccer team, but managed to keep from becoming an obnoxious sports dad as Gabe moved up the ranks.

How he never missed a game and happily ate takeout from Ripe for days on end.

"I think that's why I'm so proud of Gabe, bouncing back after Pat's death. He's his father's son, through and through."

"Pat sounds like a terrific guy," Nate said. "I wish I'd known him."

Laurel gave him a grateful smile. But I was stuck on an incongruent fact: The man who never missed a game had begged off the team trip claiming he had to work, and yet there was no evidence clearly tying his murder to his work. Maddie's shooting with the same gun made that seem even less likely.

The same gun didn't mean the same shooter. But the odds of a murder weapon showing up in someone else's hands, who used it to shoot a woman the murder victim had known, only blocks away, in a building that had been the subject of a dispute . . .

Well, those odds were odd.

And Mike Tracy had taught me that when something looks odd, take a closer look.

THE Uber picked us up at the willow tree. The bus runs down Eastlake, but no way was I going to hike up the hill and wait in the rain in high-heeled boots and a velvet dress, even with a borrowed coat.

"When's the food tour coming through?" Nate asked once we were in the car. "Will they cancel with this rain? Although it looks like it's tapering off."

"Eleven-thirty, fingers crossed. We're the appetizers before lunch. The Market's pretty popular in the rain—so much of it is under cover. But you never know."

"I suppose it makes tourists feel like they got a taste of the real Seattle," he replied.

"They said it rained all the time up here," our driver piped up. "I didn't believe 'em." He grinned at me through the rear-view mirror.

"Where did you move from?"

"Southern California," he replied, and the old song popped into my head.

Then the light changed and he hit the gas. Traffic wasn't heavy this early on a Saturday morning, but skirting through South Lake Union, home to Amazon, and winding down to Western, between the Market and the waterfront, navigating hills and one-way streets, required a driver's attention. I was glad it was his job, not mine. He zipped past an old redbrick building, the upper story partially covered by ghost signs, those faded reminders of businesses long gone. Such a contrast to the sleek glass and metal structures nearby. Minutes later, we reached my building.

"Musta been a great night," our driver said as Nate held the door for me, "from the way you two are dressed. Get some rest." Had we been in last night's clothes for any other reason, I'd have laughed along with him.

Inside, we reclaimed Arf from my neighbor. "He's been walked and fed," Glenn said with a wink. "Don't let him tell you otherwise."

Arf is a courtly gentleman, an Airedale terrier about five years old. But when it comes to food and treats, he'll lie with his big brown eyes. "Don't worry. I'm on to his tricks. Thanks again."

"I don't suppose you can take the dog," I said to Nate once we were in the loft. It's classic industrial style, a mix of redbrick, old wood, and twelve-foot-high windows, and I adore it. "Today will be crazy, not to mention wet."

"Wish I could, but I'll be on the boat all day, working on the engine, if I'm going to go fishing next week."

"Seems like you're always working on something or other." I hung Laurel's coat on a hook by the door and sat to peel off my boots.

"Because something or other is always breaking. It's like farming. You wanta grow wheat or apples, but you've got to be a mechanic, too."

"And a philosopher." I swatted him on his adorable backside and headed for the shower.

As the hot water warmed me, I thought about Laurel and Patrick. About the devastation untimely death leaves behind. I'd thought it was discovering a body on my doorstep thirteen months ago that set me to a life of crime, as my mother puts it. But maybe I'd started down that path earlier. Maybe it was the inevitable result of my childhood in a communal house that wore its motto, PRAY FOR PEACE AND WORK FOR JUSTICE, on the bumper sticker of the van used to pick up day-old doughnuts and bruised bananas and put them to good use in a free meal program. Of being hauled to this rally and that parade by parents who met during an antiwar protest, he a tall vet wearing his Army jacket, she the hippie chick he rescued from an oncoming truck.

Or maybe it was the example of Brother Cadfael, the crime-solving medieval monk in the books by Ellis Peters. A man whose very life blended work and prayer as easily as he blended tonics and teas for the community he served. He grew herbs, I sold spice. Though I was no monk, that was for sure.

I pulled on my shop uniform—stretchy black pants and a black T-shirt with our logo, a shaker spilling salt into the ocean. Nate took his turn in the shower, then I snapped Arf into his rain jacket, and the three of us descended to the parking garage and piled into my ancient Saab, Nate at the wheel.

"I know you love the Mustang," Nate said, "but this is a better car for driving hills in the rain." The dark blue 1967 Mustang was my father's baby, handed over to me when my parents left for Costa Rica and now in dry dock for the winter.

He pulled up to the curb at First and Pike. I gave him a kiss, then another.

"Stay safe, you maniac boat mechanic."

"And you, crazy spice queen."

A moment later, my dog and I stood on the corner, he in his yellow slicker, me in my red coat and red-plaid rain boots, looking across First Avenue at the entrance to Pike Place Market. My happy place.

Wondering why on earth Special Agent Meg Greer was standing on the opposite corner, staring at me.

Four

More than fifty years ago, according to the Seattle Times, a thief fled from Pike Place Market into the Great Northern railway tunnel and was never seen again.

THE LIGHTS CHANGED AND FOOT TRAFFIC SURGED INTO THE all-way intersection. By the time Arf and I crossed, Greer had vanished. Had I imagined her? Had she slipped into the Atrium, the corner building anchored by the Italian grocer? Or disappeared down one of the Market's many passages and back alleys?

It was nearly eight thirty and the bakeries and coffee counters were beacons of light in the gloom. Or more precisely, beacons of caffeine and sugar. Stores with doors, like mine, were still closed, but the cobbles on the main thoroughfare, the L-shaped Pike Place, glistened as trucks and vans made their deliveries. At the daystalls, men and women in rain gear unloaded buckets of flowers and crates of produce. The drizzle dampened the sounds of the Market, but not its energy.

But the coffee I'd downed at the houseboat had worn off, and as my caffeine levels plunged, so did my mood.

I started coming to the Market as a kid, tagging along on my mother's weekly shopping trips. The sample cups of tea at the Spice Shop were as much a treat as the mini doughnuts we picked up from the Daily Dozen.

Even so, when I stumbled over my husband and a parking enforcement officer practically plugging each other's meters in a downtown restaurant, just before scandal destroyed the law firm where I worked and took my HR job with it, all within months of my fortieth birthday, I never expected to find solace in bay leaves. But crazy as it sounded at the time, buying Seattle Spice may have been the smartest thing I ever did.

Today, though . . . Despite the bustle in the streets and my determination to sound upbeat when Nate asked about the rain, I worried. Saturday is our busiest day, but locals might stay home if the drops turned to torrents. Tourists could shop or stroll through the city's museums instead of getting drenched down here. Every food tour guide had a Plan B to keep the clients warm and well-fed elsewhere.

I'd been counting on a good October. The next big step for the business was to expand our production facility, with full-time staff and pricy new grinders and packaging equipment. To make it fly, we needed strong fourth quarter financials. Fall cooking and Christmas baking were the ticket.

The Market is so alluring in autumn, when the last of the fall produce and flowers fill the stalls. Not to mention Halloween. Where else can you buy warty gourds, fresh pumpkins, ghost peppers, and a Dracula costume in one shopping trip?

But worry is a retailer's ritual. As the news of Maddie's shooting and its possible link to Pat's murder soaked in, my sense of dread grew. Add in Laurel's nightmare and her questions, and I had to ask: *Why now?*

And what next?

Arf's leash looped through my hand, I bought a paper at the newsstand and stuffed it in my striped jute tote. Squeezed by the stacks of papers and magazines waiting to be unpacked and threaded my way down the congested aisle, patted Rachel the brass pig, the official Market mascot, and got in line at my favorite bakery.

Minutes later, the counter woman handed me a cinnamon roll and a nonfat double latte. I stood beside a column topped with a Victorian cast-iron capital, one of the features that prompt visitors to ask why modern architects don't do that, and took the first sip. Instant attitude adjustment. You could make a fortune selling this stuff.

As Mr. Starbucks and Mr. Folgers well knew.

Across Pike Place, the produce seller and the old lady from the Asian market were jawing at each other, each pointing at a pile of flattened cardboard boxes, then at the other's storefront and back at the boxes. I didn't say everyone in the Market always gets along. Then my dog and I headed into the Arcade, where I traded a wrinkled ten for a giant bouquet of sunflowers, a riot of red and yellow. We dashed across the cobbles to the shop and unlocked the front door.

I paused on the threshold to breathe it all in. Cinnamon and cardamom, ginger and nutmeg, cumin, cloves, and garlic. Spice in all its variety, the stuff of my life.

When new customers walk in, they often describe, unprompted, a memory evoked by scent: a fragrant stew, their grandmother's apple pie, a day exploring the lavender fields in the south of France. There's a reason for that. The same part of the limbic brain that detects smells also houses memory. They are physically linked.

Call it magic, for short.

I set my bounty on the counter and unhooked Arf. He let me wipe his feet and run a towel over his tan legs and tail; happily, the slicker had kept his head and the wiry grizzled fur on his back, called a saddle, dry. I gave him a rawhide chew bone, which he carried to his bed behind the front counter. Official Market policy says no dogs, but no one pays any attention, and the Market Master carries treats in his pocket. After I hung our coats and stashed my tote in the office, roughly the size of your standard refrigerator, I found a vase for the flowers. Even the worst grouch can't help but smile at sunflowers, especially on a rainy day.

But before the day came rushing in, I had reading to do. I took the newspaper and my breakfast to the mixing nook, a small booth where we conduct taste tests. Flipped pages, the only sounds the ticking of the railroad clock beside the front door and my dog chewing.

On the front page of the local section, I found a short update on the shooting. As Tracy had predicted, Maddie was named now, described as a property investor who had apparently surprised an intruder. No pictures, no other details. No mention of Pat Halloran's murder, though the annual recap would run soon. If the link between the two cases was public by then, the story would be front page news.

I let the last sip of coffee linger on my tongue, bitter mixed with sweet.

Then it was time to get to work. The staff arrived earlier than usual to prep. Food tours are all the rage with tourists and locals who trust an expert to find the best of the city's food and drink. Some focus on wine, or chocolate, or sushi. The Market tours give guests a close-up with merchants and vendors, and a taste of history. Guests buy tickets, so we're not paying kickbacks to the tour operators. And they shop. A group of eight or ten can easily drop several hundred dollars on spices, tea, and books, and order more online when they get home.

Sandra's husband had driven her to work today, and I helped him haul in a cooler filled with appetizers. Cayenne set up the serving table and warming trays for the stuffed mushrooms and baked paprika cheese, with help from Reed, our college kid computer whiz. Paprika cheese is an invention of one of our favorite customers, and he'd been thrilled to hear we planned to serve it today. All week, we'd been serving our new chai—a spice blend or *masala* brewed with strong black Assam tea and vegan coconut cream. But today it was back to our signature tea, and Matt started the first batch brewing in the giant electric kettle that looks like a Russian samovar. The scent of cinnamon and cardamom filled the air. We'd go through vats of the stuff—the colder and wetter the weather, the more we serve. And the more we sell.

"Trial run for the anniversary party," Sandra said.

In two weeks, we'd be marking the end of my second year as Mistress of Spice. Was it shallow to celebrate something so trivial with Laurel's more ominous anniversary on the horizon? Life is full of difficult juxtapositions. Besides, Laurel would never begrudge me a celebration, or a glass of champagne.

"And you said it wouldn't last," I replied. The corner of Sandra's mouth twitched. The shop's long-time assistant manager, she hadn't been sure about me when I went from loyal customer to owner. But we make a great team, feeding on each other's ideas.

"I'm happy to help you cook as long as I get free samples," her husband said, then kissed her goodbye.

"Taking bets," I called. "What samples will be most popular?"

Five people, five opinions. I rolled my eyes.

Cayenne brought out the decorative gourds she and I had found at the farm stalls. Nothing jazzes up a buffet like goblin eggs and speckled gremlins.

"Feeling up to a full shift?" I asked quietly. This was her first day back after an extensive bout of testing related to her multiple sclerosis. She hadn't shared last summer's diagnosis with the rest of the staff yet, and I'd honored her request for privacy.

She nodded, the roll of red-and-black braids on top of her head bobbing. "The tests confirm that it's the remissive type. How long remission will last, we don't know—it could be months or years. But the rain is a relief."

Turns out that hot, dry weather aggravates MS. And Seattle had just endured one of the hottest summers on record. "Then let it pour."

Matt finished setting up the tea cart. He and Cayenne joined the staff last spring, and they couldn't be more different. She's a trained chef who, at thirty, had never held a job outside the kitchen, but longed to trade the stress of restaurant work for a more normal life. She helps Sandra and me create the recipes we give our customers, and she had begun to experiment with developing new blends. In contrast, Matt's a retail whiz with a talent for handling difficult customers, but he'd never worked in the food business. He happily takes on the heavy jobs like wrestling a hot tea kettle or breaking down boxes and hauling out the recycling. The two of them clashed last summer when what she called "her clumsy spell"—losing her balance and dropping things—had tested his patience. But equilibrium had been restored, for now.

"Sandra and I will herd the tour guests and keep the table stocked," I told the staff. "Other customers could be tempted to crash the party, so let's give them their own treat. Cayenne, would you find a bowl for these?" I handed her a bag of our spiced glazed nuts and pretzel mix—I'd whipped up a double batch earlier in the week for exactly this purpose.

"Good thinking, boss," she said, using Sandra's nickname for me.

"I have my moments."

Then I gave the display of seasonal blends a once-over. It looked good—heavy on fall faves, along with the chai *masala* and baking blends. We pack our blends in small bags and containers with custom labels, but also keep bulk supplies behind the front counter. A rack mounted on the end of the cookbook shelves holds our signature recipes, including a few highlighting the featured blends.

Moments before our ten o'clock opening, Sandra pulled me aside. "What's up, boss? Not your usual sparky self."

"Laurel got some news yesterday," I said. "About her husband's murder."

"A break in the case?" Sandra asked. Laurel is a good customer and the staff all like her. Though Sandra isn't part of Flick Chicks, my weekly movie night with Kristen, Laurel, and two other friends, she always enjoys hearing about the movie and the food, and giving me ideas for what to serve when it's my turn.

"Cross your fingers," I said. Then it was time to unlock the door. I packed up my troubles in my old kit bag, whatever that is, and prepared to smile, smile, smile.

THE rain gods were in a good mood, pulling back the clouds in time for the tour guide to give the Market trek the go-ahead. Now, ten people crowded around as I told the story of Seattle Spice. Then Sandra described the process of developing our blends. Some, she said, are updates of classics, like our pie spice, poultry blend, and curries. Others were prompted by recipes we've dug up. A few are pure invention.

"Questions?" I asked.

Sure enough, the first question was the one we get most often. "How long should you keep spices?" a woman in a stylish black raincoat asked.

"A year is a good general rule," I said. "Whole spices last longer than ground, so a grinder is a good investment. Make sure you store your spices in tightly closed containers, out of the light and heat. Taste them occasionally. If you're not sure, replace it. Don't try to make up for the age of a spice by using more—some flavors may be fine, but others may go off. If it's worth using, it's worth using fresh."

"Those grape, cheese, and prosciutto skewers are fabulous," another woman said, her accent screaming Texas. "What did you use to marinate that mozzarella?"

"Olive oil and our Italian herb blend," I said. "We also used it in the stuffed mushrooms. You've got recipes for everything we served today in your gift bags, along with a discount coupon for our Spice of the Month Club, and a special treat—a bag of our Glazed Spiced Nuts."

"I never thought of putting herbs in shortbread," the woman in the black raincoat said. "You're setting my imagination spinning."

"Mission accomplished," I replied. "Thank you for coming in. The staff will help you any way we can. And remember, it really is okay to play with your food."

They laughed and dispersed, perusing our displays, flipping through books, and eyeing spice and tea accessories. Sandra offered shopping baskets.

I bent over to pick up a dropped napkin, a custom design featuring our shop logo.

A pair of black bike shoes strode into view, attached to a very fine pair of legs clad in black riding tights. I straightened and found myself staring at Officer Thomas Alan "Tag" Buhner of the Seattle Police Department's bicycle patrol.

I felt my pleasant retail expression wobble as I watched the man I'd once loved take off his helmet and fix his gaze on me. "I heard."

I swallowed hard and nodded. "Come sit. Tea?"

He looked down at the tiny rivulets forming on the floor from his cleated shoes.

"Don't worry about it. Days like this, we have to mop the floor every couple of hours anyway." I poured two cups of spice tea. Sandra was packing up the leftovers from the food tour and offered Tag the cookie tray. He took two gingersnaps, and we slid into the nook, facing each other.

He bit into the cookie. "If you'd made these when we were married . . ."

"Don't, Tag. Not even as a joke." He meant the black pepper, my signature ingredient—we can't call it a secret since we hand out copies of the recipe by the hundreds. But figuring out years earlier what it does to a gingersnap would not have saved our marriage.

"Sorry," he said, and reached for his tea.

It's inevitable that Tag and I run into each other frequently. Downtown, including the Market, had been his beat for years, long before I bought the loft on Western, a few blocks away, and later, the shop. But if he thought I'd invaded his territory, he'd never let on. Actually, I think he likes the chance to keep an eye on me.

He sipped and watched, with that maddening expression that mixes focus and indifference. Nonattachment, as my yoga teacher would say, if I managed to make it to class. With Nate back on land, I didn't want to leave home that early. Told myself I was stretching parts yoga didn't reach.

"So, what's the working theory on how Maddie Petrosian's shooting is related to Pat Halloran's murder? And why now?"

"Even if I knew, I couldn't tell you. You know that." He took another bite and spoke with his mouth full. "But the link could give us a break. Everybody's fired up."

"But in the meantime? Is Laurel in danger?" *Oh.* Was I? Was that why Meg Greer had been watching me?

And why Tag just happened to stop by?

"Hey, do you know this Special Agent Meg Greer? What makes them so special anyway?"

"Met her, but that's all. Transferred here last summer from somewhere back east. She'll bring a fresh perspective, which is good," he said. "The term 'Special Agent' dates to the early twentieth century, when the automobile changed the nature of crime. The FBI needed authority to make arrests across state lines, but Congress and the states were afraid of a power grab. So 'special' actually means 'limited.' The FBI's jurisdiction is limited to federal crimes, even when they cross state lines."

Tag is more than a pretty face.

"Don't tell anyone I told you," he said, "but she might be running a Mr. Big operation."

"A what?"

"A sting, sort of. They set up a fake crime ring and lure the suspect to join the fun. Then, after he's hooked, they tell him the head guy will only trust him if he tells them about similar crimes he's participated in in the past. Like a job interview, where you brag on your past accomplishments. Makes them feel all big and important." He balled up the used napkin and made a free throw into the trash basket. "Hence the name, Mr. Big."

I had never heard of such a thing. "Ohhh. Who's the target?"

"That, I don't know. I don't officially know anything."

The retort was tempting, but I bit my tongue.

"I gotta go," he said. "Just wanted to touch base." He slid toward the edge of the bench, then turned to face me, gloves in one hand, the other flat on the table. "Pepper, we've got a second chance to get this guy, whoever he is, and we're going to get him. Or her."

I breathed in and breathed out.

"Trust Mike Tracy," Tag urged.

Not long ago, that would have been the last thing Tag told me. But he and Tracy had cleared the air between them. Like Tracy, Tag saw Pat Halloran's murder as an attack on the brotherhood, and sisterhood, of crime-fighters.

The door opened and a gaggle of chatty tourists surged in.

What possessed me, I couldn't say, but when we stood, I kissed his cheek. "Stay safe," I whispered.

"You, too," he said. Then he plucked another cookie from the tray and was gone.

After the whirlwind, I surveyed the leftovers. Not enough for staff lunch, my Saturday treat, so I called the piroshky place and made an order. Traded my black clogs and apron for my rain gear, then bundled Arf into his slicker and hooked up his leash.

We wound our way through the crowds to Victor Steinbrueck Park, named for the architect credited with saving the Market from urban removal in 1971. Arf pooped and I scooped. Ordinarily, we pause at the wrought iron railing, designed by Steinbrueck himself, to enjoy the westerly view of Puget Sound and the Olympics. No point today—it was all mist and mush.

We turned back, the lure of hot dough filled with seasoned meat and veggies lighting a fire in my belly. When we reached the original Starbucks, I glanced inside. No matter what the weather, the place is always packed with coffee pilgrims.

And who should I see sitting at the counter inside the front window, nursing a white paper cup with the familiar green-and-white logo, but Special Agent Meg Greer.

Five

One man's smelly Polish market is another man's fragrant reminder of home.

—Emily Badger, "In Praise of Smelly Places"

ARF CAME TO ME A YEAR AGO THROUGH A MARKET RESIDENT named Sam, who'd acquired him under circumstances that I never fully understood. When a series of unfortunate events made clear that Sam would be better off returning to his family in Memphis, I agreed to take the dog. Where he'd gotten his training was part of the mystery, but Arf had a way of knowing what I wanted him to do before I did.

Now, he came to heel without instruction, poised to move on or turn, depending on my signal.

Problem was, I hadn't a clue.

Had Greer seen me through the steam clouding the window or the clusters of people crowding the narrow sidewalk? She might have spotted me ten minutes earlier, when we first walked by. Why was she in the Market this morning? The FBI office is way down on Third Avenue. She could have found a cup of coffee a lot closer, and without getting wet.

I'd thought, this morning when Nate dropped me off, that she was watching me. But there was no reason for that, was there?

Paranoia is not usually one of my vices.

Don't be silly, Pep. She's new in town and taking the day to explore the city.

Right. She's got a day off the day after new evidence surfaces in a major case the field office she's just joined has been unable to solve for three years.

No. Special Agent Meg Greer was in the Market on this soggy Saturday for a reason. A reason other than enjoying a taste of Seattle's famous coffee. Since she had no reason to watch me, she had to be watching someone else. Or meeting someone. Did it have to do with the special operation Tag had mentioned?

That had to be it.

I left the cover of the coffee line, Arf at my side, and glanced at the window. Saw Greer and let a pleasant expression of recognition cross my face. Waved and kept going, as if nothing out of the ordinary had happened.

At the piroshky bakery, I held the door for a woman on her way out, the hot, yeasty aroma kicking my salivary glands into gear. The sweet treats were tempting—their poppy seed cinnamon rolls are simply fab, and when doughnuts die and go to heaven, they hope to come back as cream cheese *vatrushka* topped with marionberries.

If you still want one later . . . The stalling tactic usually works. Besides, we had half a tray of cookies back at the shop, although Tag had put a dent in them.

I'd ordered a mix of the classics—potato and cheese, beef and onion—and modern variations with spinach and chicken curry. They were boxed up and ready to go, and Arf and I were back on the street in no time.

I couldn't help myself. I had to know who Greer was meeting. I detoured back to Starbucks and in my most casual spy manner, glanced inside. She was gone.

No sign of her on the street, either. Didn't matter. If she wanted to find me, she knew where to look. I opened the box and slipped out an egg and spinach piroshky, eating as I walked. It might not be traditional, but it hit the spot.

The Spice Shop was jammed. I should have guessed the threat of rain wouldn't slow people down. My first week on the job, two years ago, a near-cyclone hit. Though it rained heavily, we were spared the flooding and power outages the forecasters had predicted, and most Seattleites went about their business, damp but undeterred.

"To your bed," I told Arf and he wove between the humans to his hideout. I delivered the box of piroshky to the nook, ditched my coat, and grabbed my apron.

"The recipe calls for Turkish bay, absolutely do not use California bay," a customer asked me. "What's the difference? Why the dire warning?"

"Cookbook drama," I replied. "California bay, *laurus australas*, is more intense. Save it for dishes that cook quickly. For a soup or a stew, you want Turkish bay, *laurus nobilis*. It gives stock that rich, warm flavor. Our *bouquet garni* uses crushed Turkish bay for just that reason."

"*Laurus nobilis*," she said. "Sounds so regal."

I opened two jars and showed her the leaves. "Same color and basic shape, but the California leaves are longer and narrower. I'd offer a sample, but dried bay has about as much flavor as the inside of a cereal box. It needs the heat of cooking to release its potential."

"Sold," she said. "I trust you."

Behind the counter, I weighed and bagged the bay leaves. The customer added a tin of *bouquet garni* and several other blends to her shopping basket. Inches away, Arf snored softly, one back foot twitching, as if he were running in his dreams.

"That's a lot of cayenne," I said when the next customer gave me her order.

"I mix it into honey and warm water every morning," she replied. "Keeps my blood pressure down."

"Glad to hear it," I said. We stay away from medical advice, since none of us has any formal training, but we happily sell cayenne, turmeric, and garlic to customers with medicinal purposes in mind.

Late afternoon, a lull hit. I settled into the nook with the last of the piroshky, and wondered if Kristen and Eric had succeeded in storming the hospital's gates. I slid my phone out of my apron pocket and sent Kristen a text asking about Maddie. Other questions ricocheted around my brain. Who found her? Who called the police? The Montlake business district is only a block long; surely people would be worried; surely they'd be talking. No matter what their opinion on the redevelopment Maddie proposed, they had to be worried. When anything happens in the Market, we all rally around each other. My phone buzzed with Kristen's reply. *ICU. Family only.* I thumbed back. *Would they tell you anything? Did you see Tim?*

Dot dot dot, as she read and answered. *Saw Tim for a minute. No visitors. Still in a coma but he's optimistic.*

Though Kristen and I had spoken nearly every day of our lives—forty-three years and counting—we also had our own circles of friends. She was a lot closer to Maddie than I was—they lived in the same neighborhood, and their kids' activities intersected. Both she and Maddie lived a more financially comfortable life than I'd ever known. Not that Kristen's parents hadn't been deeply committed to the peace and justice community in which she and I were raised—they'd made the grand home Kristen's mother had inherited its center for years. My parents had come to the communal life from the working class, and if my brother and I had strayed from our hippie roots, they did at least show.

But in this rare moment of late-afternoon quiet, the shock of everything I'd learned in the last twenty-four hours had me disoriented. Mentally dizzy. I knew, from life with Tag and my own recent encounters with crime, that tragedy doesn't always happen to "other people."

Sometimes it happens to people we know and love. People we employ or work with. People we may not see every day but who are part of our lives. I'd been raised to believe we're obligated to help those around us when they're in trouble.

And this was big trouble.

Thank God, I replied. *Keep me posted.* Pat had been shot in his home, Maddie in a vacant building she owned. One in the evening; the other in the morning. Seattle averages less than twenty homicides a year, making it one of the safer big cities. But shootings occur for other reasons, too. Over the years, the police had investigated numerous incidents for a possible tie to Pat's murder and found nothing.

Both cases were initially described as an interrupted burglary, but I thought that was just cop talk. Nothing had been taken from the Hallorans' house. And what would a burglar have hoped to find in the corner grocery that had sold its last Slim Jim and quart of milk ages ago?

Tracy had said the task force was taking another look at everyone they'd questioned in Pat's case, reconsidering every lead. They were scouring his case files again, searching for someone carrying a grudge. I'd been on the receiving end of several interrogations over the years. It's no fun.

Though he'd mentioned another canvass, I wasn't sure Tracy would pay enough attention to the neighbors' concerns, especially the owners of the nearby businesses. He'd ask who they'd seen and what they'd heard, sure, but would he ask what worried them? What they feared and what kept them up at night? What their customers were saying. How business had been affected. What they knew that might shed light on the connection between Maddie and Pat. Questions like that were my forte.

I hesitated to call Tim. He needed to focus on Maddie and the kids. Who else could I talk to?

Almost time to close. First, though, I wanted to check on Laurel.

"Aimee and Seetha are here," she said when I asked how she was. "We took a long walk and now I'm cooking."

Flick Chicks pals. Good company and good eaters. They'd keep Laurel occupied.

"Perfect. If I know them, they brought lots of wine."

"They did. I'll need extra coffee tomorrow."

Tomorrow. Sunday. "We're still on then? You choose."

She named the place, and while I wondered about the wisdom of returning to the old neighborhood, I kept my mouth shut. For the moment.

I clicked off the line and locked the doors, then joined Matt and Sandra behind the counter. He was cleaning out the samovar and she was restocking spice bags.

"The food tour could not have gone better," I said. "Thanks for all your work."

"I loved doing it. And Cayenne's cookies—my goodness, that girl can bake. Paul's picking me up," Sandra said, referring to her husband, whom she calls Mr. Right to distinguish him from his predecessor, Mr. What Was I Thinking. "We're going to the Pink Door for a drink and dinner. Join us?"

"I'm going, too," Matt said. "I've never been there."

I would have loved to see his reaction to the place, although I doubted they'd stay late enough for the cabaret show or the aerialists' performance. But not tonight. "It's tempting, but I am otherwise engaged."

Sandra gave me a wicked grin. "'Lord, lead me not into temptation. I can find it myself.' That kind of temptation?"

I felt the heat rise up my neck and cheeks and she laughed. "Good to see you happy, boss. You and Nate are perfect together."

"Let's send some of those leftovers home with Matt," I called as she headed toward the back of the shop.

"Already on it," she called.

Matt lived up north, not far from Sandra, and they often rode the same bus. If he had a girlfriend or nearby family, he'd never mentioned them in my hearing.

"Thanks," he said, sounding surprised. He set the samovar's insert upside down to drain, wiped his hands, and turned to me. "Pepper, can I ask? What's going on with Cayenne? Is she okay?"

The question I'd been dreading. It had been Matt's impatience with Cayenne's clumsiness last summer that led her to tell me she'd been diagnosed with multiple sclerosis. She'd asked me to keep it to myself for now, and I'd agreed. She was still able to do the major functions of the job, which was what the law counted. And she did a great job, which counted to me.

I bit my lower lip, then exhaled. "All I can say is that I appreciate how you've all been willing to shuffle the schedule to accommodate her. But you don't need to worry."

"Ahh, I was right," he said in a knowing voice. "Pregnant. That's awesome." Grinning, he pulled the wheeled bucket out from under the industrial sink and began filling it. While he mopped, I ran the till and counted the change. Cayenne's medical condition was her business and no one else's, but keeping the secret was putting me in a difficult position. I hadn't actually misled my other employees—they were managing that on their own—but I'd let them draw the wrong conclusions, and that made me uncomfortable.

But it was still a relief to dodge that bullet. So to speak. For the moment, anyway.

Then Sandra's husband arrived and the three of them headed out to dinner. I bundled up for the walk home. It was funny to see my regal dog—Airedales are known as the King of Terriers for a reason—in the yellow slicker that reminded me of the Morton Salt girl. I grabbed my tote, a baguette and a bottle of Viognier poking out.

No sign of Meg Greer on our way through the Market. I hoped she'd found who she was looking for.

The aroma of fish stew simmering in a tangy sauce—our lemon-dill seafood blend, if my nose wasn't mistaken—filled the wide stairwell leading to my loft. I half expected to see the neighbors clustered outside my door, clutching bowls and begging, "Please, sir. Might I have some more?"

Food, glorious food! started playing in my head.

Great. I'd given myself an earworm. From *Oliver Twist*, no less. Oh, well. It could have been worse. It could have been the theme from *The Mickey Mouse Club*, which hit all the wrong notes in my brain, over and over and over.

"Smells like heaven," I said after Arf and I had fought our way through the imaginary crowd of hungry children and were safely inside the loft.

"Looks like heaven, now that you're here," Nate replied and I nearly swooned. Is there anything so gorgeous as a man standing in your kitchen wearing an apron and brandishing a spoon?

Well, yes, there is. And I was reasonably sure of getting that sight later.

I fed Arf, then slipped into the bedroom for a quick change. By the end of the day, my comfy shop clothes tend to reek of paprika and other spicery. Friends say their noses tell them when I've arrived—I carry the shop aromas with me like Pigpen in the old Peanuts comic strip carried a cloud of dust.

In the bedroom, the trio of neon lips I'd bought at Aimee's shop last summer glowed against the original redbrick wall. Beneath them sat the beautiful cypress *tansu*, a Japanese step chest I'd fallen for, also in her shop. Not long, coincidentally, after I'd fallen for the fisherman now tossing a salad in my kitchen. I'd hoped he'd leave a few things in the drawers, and they were filling up. His green cargo pants lay on the floor and I draped them over the low-back wooden chair in the corner, a find from an antiquing trip with Kristen.

I pulled on navy leggings and a pink cotton tunic and padded, barefoot, out to the main room.

"Sit," Nate told me and slid a glass of wine across the butcher block counter. I sat, as directed, on a barstool scored on a different junking jaunt.

"You get the whatever it was fixed?"

He glowered, but not at me. "Needs a part we couldn't make or scrounge up on a Saturday. On a better note, got the catch report from Bron. Going strong. He figures they've got another two or three weeks. He should be home early next month."

Bronson Seward, his younger brother and fishing partner, whom I hadn't met yet. They co-owned one boat for Puget Sound, the increasingly troublesome *Thalassa*, and another, *The Kenai Princess*, based in Dutch Harbor, Alaska. A larger boat, the *Princess* required a crew, which meant they fished as late in the season as they could to make sure the men got a decent share. "You'll like my little brother, I promise."

"But will he return the favor?" My friends and family had taken to Nate immediately. Even Tag liked him, which made me nervous at first.

"Oh, yes," he said and I swear, his green eyes twinkled. "Oh, yes."

I sipped while he stirred, and told him about the day in the shop, the successful food tour, and what little news Kristen had gleaned about Maddie.

"I've never heard you mention her until all this happened."

"Kristen's closer to her than I am. For lots of reasons." Friendships change. Sometimes we make choices that trigger those changes. Sometimes we let our envy and regret get in the way. "In college, end of sophomore year, one of our professors recommended several students for internships with a big nonprofit. Maddie and I both worked there, in different divisions. End of summer, they offered me a paid position during the school year."

He gave the soup another stir, then put the lid on the pot and stood across the counter from me, listening closely.

"My parents didn't have extra money, so the job was a big help." I paused to sip my wine. "Midyear, I dropped out of school. That meant the end of the job, which was okay. I grew up surrounded by social service work and by then I knew it wasn't for me. It did give me a taste of HR, and later, a woman I met there helped me get the law firm job. So it worked out, for me."

"What does this have to do with Maddie?" he asked.

"What I didn't know was that Maddie had applied for the school year job, too, but they hired me. When I quit, she reapplied, but they didn't want to fill the spot midyear. It was for a junior—they didn't want someone about to graduate—so she was out of luck for the next year, too. She didn't need the job—she just really wanted to work in that field." I tightened my grip on my glass. "So basically, I took the opportunity she'd desperately wanted and wasted it. After graduation, she started working for her dad in the family business, while getting her MBA."

Nate studied me. "I think you're being a little hard on yourself."

"Maybe. I don't think she sees it that way. Although she did come in the shop a couple of times this summer. She doesn't cook much, but she buys gifts. Remember, we're meeting Laurel for brunch in the morning." I never wanted to be one of those women who gives up on her girlfriends when a guy comes along, but when I met Nate, Laurel had completely understood that our long-standing Sunday tradition needed an update. If I wasn't available, she met other friends. Occasionally, Nate joined us, as we'd planned for this weekend well before the Friday night revelations.

I do have a dining table—a weathered, round cedar picnic table with two benches and a pair of pink wrought iron chairs, refugees from an ice cream parlor. A café table and chairs sit on the veranda, for days when the weather permits. But this felt like a "dinner on the couch with a movie" night. Salads first, then steaming bowls of fish chowder, soaked up with bread and accented with wine.

With a classic movie I'd seen a dozen times on the TV, my tummy full of good, hot food, and a good, hot man beside me, the dog working on his bone at our feet, I'd had enough of murder. Enough of old horrors coming back to haunt good friends. I didn't want to think about special agents and shots fired in peaceful neighborhoods. All I wanted was what I had, a quiet evening in a space I adored with the man who'd set his hook and reeled in my heart.

I picked up the remote and switched off the TV, then leaned close to Nate, holding my face for a kiss. He obliged.

"Please, sir," I said. "Might I have some more?"

Six

Good bread is the most fundamentally satisfying of all foods; and good bread with fresh butter, the greatest of feasts.

—James Beard

"CUTE HOUSE," I SAID. THE THREE OF US STOOD IN FRONT A sage green cottage with cream trim and a front door painted a deep plum. Four of us, counting Arf. We were all dressed for rain, a preemptive strike.

"Surprised to see it up for sale again. They want a hundred grand more than I got for it, three years ago," Laurel replied, pointing at the FOR SALE sign at the edge of the tiny yard. "Though that was more than double what we paid, the year Gabe was born. All they did was paint it and kill Pat's favorite rhodie."

The landscaping did look a little ragged. The flip side of Seattle's mild temperatures and long growing season is that some homeowners lose their enthusiasm for yard work long before the yard work is done. That was one of the attractions, and drawbacks, of the ubiquitous rhododendrons.

"So Pat was the gardener?" Nate asked. I appreciated his tenderness toward Laurel. Though I'd met him on a walk after a Sunday brunch with her, at Fisherman's Terminal, they'd only seen each other a few times. At our age, a new relationship means stepping into a busy life with its own friendships and routines. For me, the biggest adjustment was to Nate's schedule—six months here, six months in Alaska, more or less.

Huddled in her forest green Gore-Tex, hands stuffed in her pockets, Laurel nodded. She'd wanted to see the house again, but I suspected that walking this neighborhood was more bitter than sweet. When I left Tag, he stayed put, and Nate's ex-wife had kept their house. But those marriages had ended by our own hands, through divorce, not sudden violence.

I looped one arm through hers and another through Nate's. "Coffee time."

We strolled up the block, headed for a funky neighborhood joint on Twenty-Fourth, Montlake's main drag. The homes were lovely, most dating back to the 1930s and '40s. I'd never been in Laurel and Pat's house, but it was small, one bedroom up, one down, and the price jump sounded modest to me. Seattle's crazy-hot housing market had cooled lately, but prices had been on the rise for a long time. Laurel hadn't held out for top dollar, eager for a quick sale. The stigma attached to a "murder house" hadn't helped. No wonder the buyers had painted everything.

"I do miss living here," she said. "Good people. Environmentally conscious. Lots of activities. Great parks."

"A lot like the houseboat community," Nate observed.

After my family moved out of Grace House, the co-operative peace-and-justice community headquartered in the big house now home to Kristen's family, my parents bought a little bungalow a few blocks up the hill. I'd been twelve then, back when a pair of teachers could still afford a small house around here. Although I had an idea my grandmother helped. And my dad was handy with home repair, which the place had badly needed.

But it had been years since I'd walked these streets, and I found myself reeling a bit from the memories. Did the prosperous folks we passed, walking their dogs or coming back from coffee in their North Face and Patagonia rain jackets and their Hunter wellies, remember that a well-loved man had been murdered a stone's throw away, in the safety of his own home? Now that a second incident had occurred, were they keeping a closer eye on their kids and double-checking their doors? Though tragedy can strike anywhere, most of us blessedly oblivious.

I don't tell many people this, because I like my life and have no desire to be shuffled off to the funny farm, but sometimes, when emotion hits me hard, I hear things. Grace House ran a free meals program for families and older adults in the basement of St. James Cathedral, and occasionally when I helped out, unloading donations, we could hear the choir practicing. Though my mother loved the community and was devoted to its work, she was never crazy about Mass or the trappings of Catholicism, except for those medieval chants. She'd take my hand and lead me to a back stairway where we'd sit and listen.

I heard those harmonies now. What they told me was to stay alert. To follow my nose and my heart, and take care of the people I love.

We rounded the corner onto Twenty-Fourth, pausing to stare at the old grocery where Maddie had been shot. It was an ugly building even in my childhood, but the owner—an old man we called Emby—had made it inviting, with baskets of flowers and brightly painted wooden benches. He'd carried staples like milk and potato chips, and the things commonly forgotten until dinner prep, like onions and sugar. He knew his community, so his shelves and coolers also held decent wines, tasty cheese, and boxes of good crackers. Racks near the front door held the local paper, and on Sundays, *The New York Times*.

I smiled to myself. Though the Montlake Grocery had mixed the upscale with the utilitarian, Emby had been practical. His candy shelves were filled with kid favorites, but if an adult asked, he'd happily reach behind the counter and slip a copy of *Playboy* into a brown paper bag.

Now, though, the glass door was smeared with dirt, the windows covered with newspaper. A swath of yellow tape screaming CRIME SCENE AREA—DO NOT ENTER stretched across the front of the building, between two orange barricades stenciled SEATTLE POLICE DEPARTMENT.

I shuddered and squeezed my friends' arms.

The other buildings in the block dated back as far as the homes, a mix of classic styles and materials. Similar blocks dot the city, each once the commercial center of a neighborhood. Some thrive, while others struggle.

We reached the coffeehouse, a row of brightly painted Adirondack chairs lining the sidewalk. Empty now, splashed with rain. I looped Arf's leash around the dog rail, both coffeehouse and rail the modern version of the frontier-day saloon and hitching post, and made sure the water bowl was full. "Don't you worry, little guy. I'll keep an eye on you."

Busy as the place was, we found a table in the window in dog's eye view, though Arf didn't seem concerned. It wasn't the full-on breakfast joint Laurel and I usually choose, where we sip coffee, savor the latest Northwest flavor experiment, and linger for hours. But the coffee was good and my quiche yummy, the crust crusty and the eggs creamy. Laurel picked at a scone, and I resisted the urge to go all anxious mother on her, as I had yesterday. She was a grown woman with a kid of her own.

"Have you talked to Gabe?" I asked.

She pressed her lips together. "He called this morning, so happy. They won Friday and he got to play a few minutes. Then the football team won yesterday. I couldn't burst his bubble when I don't have any real news."

"You'll know when to tell him."

"I can't wait long," she said. "If he finds out from someone else, he'll never forgive me."

Especially if he knew how much his father abhorred secrets, and why.

"I just wonder," Nate said, "what the connection between Patrick's death and Maddie's shooting could possibly be."

For a long moment, Laurel said nothing. Then, "Refills?" She rose and gathered up our mugs. Nate and I exchanged a wordless glance. She returned a moment later and we gratefully accepted the creamy white mugs. She cradled hers, staring into the black liquid.

"I know there is a connection. Because of the dreams," she finally said. "And the gun. But beyond that, I have no idea."

"What do you think happened? Back then, I mean." We'd been casual acquaintances before the murder, but as our friendship grew closer, I had never wanted to ask. Too intrusive. But now was different. Both she and Detective Tracy had pulled me in. I needed to know.

"None of the theories made any sense. A neighbor Pat had a dispute with, over the compost pile, of all stupid things. Pat got pretty heated, which was so not like him. But the cops couldn't pin anything on him. The neighbor, I mean. Everybody worried about a random burglar who didn't expect Pat to be home, but nothing was taken."

"You always said the police were convinced it was related to his work," I said. "That the killer wanted revenge, or to destroy evidence."

"Right. They combed through his case files, and his home computer. Pat worked on white collar stuff—embezzlement, money laundering, corporate crimes. Not that those kinds of cases can't turn violent."

"You never know what people will do to protect their money and keep it flowing," Nate said.

Conversation stopped while an employee scooped up our plates, and I wondered what crazy schemes Nate had encountered in the wilds of Alaska.

"We should probably get going," I said, conscious of my dog outside and the caffeine-starved humans clustered by the door.

"They even interviewed friends and relatives in Chicago," Laurel said. She reached down for her bag. "He left there ages ago."

I started to push back my chair when she grabbed my hand. "Go with me. To the hospital."

"They won't let us see her. I told you Kristen talked to Tim. He said maybe in a few days."

"You know him. I don't. I at least want to tell him how sorry I am."

I wanted to see Tim, too, to offer my sympathy. To find out what I could and reassure myself that Maddie would recover. There was no reason I couldn't go—the shop was in good hands today with Matt and Reed.

I glanced at Nate. If I said yes, if I went with her, I was all in, committed to finding out everything we could about Maddie's involvement with the property, her shooting, and its link to Patrick Halloran. And he knew it.

"Laurel?" a man said.

Laurel jolted upright, her head snapping toward a man a few feet away. He took a step closer, momentarily hesitant, then a woman swept in.

"Laurel, how good to see you!" She was on the short side, trim with short, dark hair, in black pants and a cashmere sweater.

Early fifties, like her husband. Laurel rose instinctively, the way you do when someone is intent on an embrace. In normal circumstances, Laurel is a hugger, but her stiff posture told me this wasn't a normal circumstance. The other woman knew it, too, and the hug turned into one of those awkward things where you touch each other's upper arms and lean in, but avoid actual body contact.

"How *are* you?" the woman said, stepping back and letting her hands fall away, her nails a pinky-beige, her diamonds bright. "We've missed you and Gabe. At Notre Dame, I heard. You must be so proud. What brings you to the old neighborhood?" Her gaze swept over Nate and me, then returned to Laurel.

"Coffee with friends," Laurel replied, then to us, "next door neighbors." She made no introductions.

"You heard about the shooting down the block," the woman said, her voice low, as if speaking quietly would lessen the tragedy.

I scooped up my jacket and stood. "We're just leaving. Take our table."

"Thank you," the man said. He unsnapped his dark rain jacket and reached for the back of my chair, then held it for his wife.

She extended a hand. "Seriously, Laurel, you know we wish you nothing but the best."

"I appreciate that." Laurel gave a tight-lipped nod and we headed out, wriggling into our coats as we wove our way to the door.

On the sidewalk, I untied Arf and glanced in the window. The woman leaned across the table and spoke to her husband, her eyes flicking toward us, then back to him. "They seemed nice enough."

"They only wanted our table."

There was a prickliness to her voice, beyond the smart-aleck remark, that surprised me. "Is that the guy? The neighbor who was pissed at Pat, the one they suspected?"

"Yes," she said. "He's also the man who found Pat. Spotted him from his office upstairs. It looks down on our old backyard."

"Ohhhh." I forced myself not to turn for another look.

"Bruce and Deanna Ellingson," she continued. "She's a real estate agent. Condos. He's—retired."

"Young for that, isn't he? I should have guessed about her. Real estate ladies have a distinctive personality." We headed for our cars, in the next block. "So what about this argument between him and Pat?"

"Bruce is super anal about their yard. We had a compost pile in the alley next to the fence. Yard waste, no food scraps, perfectly legal. Bruce thought it was a blot on the block and wanted it moved. They got loud over it, but that's hardly a motive for murder."

Maybe so, but cops and prosecutors and very special agents had crawled over every inch of the neighborhood. They'd strip-searched his life. And from the wary look he'd given Laurel, I was certain: He still resented it.

At the car, Nate reached for the leash. Kissed my cheek. "Text me later."

I nodded and watched him drive away with my car, my dog, and a piece of my heart.

"Let's swing by Tim and Maddie's house," I said when we were tucked inside Laurel's SUV, bought when she was hauling half the soccer team and their gear around town. "On the other side of Boyer, overlooking Interlaken Park."

She headed toward the Montlake Bridge, its Gothic sandstone tower a defining landmark. In last summer's heat, the drawbridge had gotten stuck open for more than an hour when the steel swelled, so road crews had started giving the century-old bridges cold water baths during hot spells. Some residents find the drawbridges a nuisance, and I admit, when you're running late and the span opens to let a cruiser packed with tourists sipping wine drift by, it's easy to get a little steamed. But the wait is never more than a few minutes, and the bridges are quite charming, especially this one.

Then I realized it wasn't the bridge that had prompted Laurel's detour but the wetlands alongside the cut, as locals call it.

One of the city's founders had the bright idea to cut a channel connecting Puget Sound to Lake Union, and another linking Lake Union to the much larger Lake Washington. A set of locks keeps the saltwater from the fresh. Both crazy and brilliant, the channels created enormous possibilities for commerce and later, for recreation. They also necessitated those pesky drawbridges.

In the distance, the bridge clanked open.

Laurel pulled over, her hands white-knuckled on the wheel. Gray skies dampened the view, but the place was still stunning, an urban refuge for wildlife and human life alike.

"He loved coming down here," she said. "Bringing Gabe and the kayak and binoculars. He worked with Neighbors United to curb the damage to the wetlands from the highway expansion. They didn't stop the project completely, but they did limit its impact on the neighborhood."

"Then when the corner grocery project came along, they turned their attention to stopping it," I said.

"They didn't want to stop it, not completely. They wanted developers to consider the community, not just their own profits. They wanted to be part of the conversation." Her voice caught and she poked at the corner of her eye with a fingertip. "And boy, could Pat talk."

What had he not been telling her?

Before I could say a word, before I could reach over and touch her arm, she shoved the car into drive. Pulled away from the curb and gunned up the hill.

Sometimes the only response to a painful memory is to keep moving.

Seven

An amateur detective's approach "must rest mainly on the observation of character, which is of far more interest than forensic detail."

—Ellis Peters, author of the Brother Cadfael mysteries

MADDIE PETROSIAN AND TIM PETERSON LIVED IN AN angular, glass-and-metal, three-story contemporary on the north end of Capitol Hill that should have been everything my vintage-loving heart hated in a house, but the one time I'd been inside, I'd been smitten.

It was both warm and light-filled, Frank Lloyd Wright meets Bilbo Baggins. A major redo of a 1950s split level, the house was set back from the road, hidden by a hedge-like swath of dense shrubs and lacy trees. The terraced backyard led to Interlaken Park, a hilly stretch of urban forest that even some locals don't know about. At their house rewarming party a year ago, Maddie had taken me into the master suite, cantilevered over the ravine, to show off the expansive views that remained virtually private. You could stand in the bedroom window in your birthday suit and no one but a raven or intrepid chipmunk would ever see you.

At the moment, though, the house emitted a dark, mournful air, a soccer ball on the front step the only sign that children lived here.

I took a deep breath, then exhaled slowly, remembering my

yoga teacher's exhortation to inhale calm, exhale stress. Then I opened Laurel's car door, straightened my spine, and marched to the front door.

No answer. I'm ashamed to say I was almost relieved. It's easy to poke your nose into other people's business when you barely know them. With old friends, it's easy on the one hand, but hard on the other—you never know what you'll find.

Besides, I liked thinking Maddie Petrosian had the perfect life. She didn't, of course; I knew that. No one does. But of all the people I knew, she come closest. Seeing her as the flawless Golden Girl—though brunette, and probably salon-assisted—let me imagine perfection possible.

Not fair, was it? Hence my embarrassment, over my own foolishness, and my distance. She couldn't possibly live up to my fantasies of her unassailable life.

Okay, so maybe I was jealous. Just a little.

I followed the perfectly hewn slate pavers around the corner of the house, pausing to admire an elegant Japanese maple—no scraggly rhodies with spent blossoms waiting in vain to be decapitated here. Picked my way down the slate steps set into the slope and peeked into the living room, where leather furniture and glorious Persian rugs sat on gleaming wood floors.

No lights, no cameras, no action.

Well, considering the neighborhood, there probably were cameras, live-streaming my every move to Tim or Maddie's phone. Neither of them would be watching, at the moment.

When I hiked back to the car, Laurel had the window down, listening to a woman holding the leash of a handsome German shepherd.

I held out my hand to let the dog sniff it. "Good boy," I said, my tone low and steady.

"You're Maddie's friend?" the woman said, giving me a once-over. "How do you know her?" Clearly, she could not imagine someone like me knowing someone like Maddie, despite my shiny plaid rain boots.

"We went to school together, up the hill." At the Catholic girls high school. Maddie's family was Armenian Orthodox, and I'd always assumed her parents chose a Catholic education for her as the next closest thing. "I'm Pepper Reece. You've met Laurel." The hand I extended was not the one I'd just let her dog lick, but she ignored it anyway.

"Well, you can't be too careful," the woman replied. "After everything that's happened. I'm in the next block."

The houses in the next block weren't in the same stratosphere as Maddie's, but nothing to sneeze at, either. Or sneeze in—our inquisitor looked like the kind of woman who followed her guests around with a broom and a dust cloth. How did she put up with a dog?

"We keep an eye out for each other around here," she continued. "My next door neighbor has a bad cold, so I'm walking Duke for her."

Ah. That explained it.

"They won't tell us what's going on." By "they," I assumed she meant the police.

Duke pushed at my hand with his muzzle. "Duke, sit," I said, and he sat. I ran my palm over his head, scratching behind one black-and-tan ear. "Good dog."

"We have a right to know," the neighbor said. "We pay their salaries."

"I'm sure they'll tell you what they can, when they can," I replied.

"For all we know," she said, as if I hadn't spoken, "we could be next."

"Didn't it happen down in the old grocery?" I said. "Not up here."

"Well, no," she said. "Not up here. But if we don't know what happened, we can't say we're not in danger, too, can we?"

Paranoia or a good point? I believed Maddie's shooting had not been random; the gun tied it to the murder three years ago. But this woman didn't know that and I wasn't going to tell her.

Besides, I could be wrong.

"Have there been other incidents in the area?" I asked. "Anything out of the ordinary?"

"No. But they better have some answers for us at the public meeting Wednesday night." She tightened her grip on the dog's leash and he stood. "Give Maddie our best. Come on, Duke. Eight thousand steps to go."

I'd have laughed if the situation hadn't been so horrible. The woman's fear made some sense, as did holding a public meeting. Still, I couldn't help feeling a bit sorry for the SPD's community relations officer.

We zipped over to Madison and down to what some people call Pill Hill. Harborview Medical Center is a hulking gray edifice that lurks above I-5. It did once have a harbor view, but the downtown office towers have all but blocked sight of Elliott Bay. I imagine that from the higher floors, you can still glimpse the industrial end of the bay, where the giant cranes and ships create a Lego-like charm. I'd last been here after Louis Adams, Cayenne's grandfather, was jumped by a desperate vet hired to silence him. Thank garlic it hadn't worked. Harborview's trauma center is top-notch, its burn unit serving the entire Northwest. But it's also crazy and chaotic—ambulances coming and going, down-and-outers seeking shelter, the walls echoing with pain and anguish and relief.

Laurel managed to squeeze into a spot in the block behind St. James Cathedral. No chance an hour earlier, but morning Masses had ended.

The instant the hospital's electric doors swooshed open, an antiseptic odor attacked my nostrils, trailed by a whiff of something I could only label "fear." Inside, we were directed up several floors and down a maze of hallways, some crowded, some empty. Finally, we reached a waiting area outside a set of wide swinging doors labeled ICU—AUTHORIZED PERSONNEL ONLY. The security station, a boxy faux-wood desk, was vacant. A row of once-comfortable chairs stood against the wall, empty.

No sign of Tim. No signs of life anywhere.

"Kinda creepy," Laurel said.

Had the guard stepped inside? Could I peek in and get some help? I took a step forward, ready to push open a door.

"Hey! What are you doing? You can't go in there!"

I turned to see a uniformed security guard hustling toward us. "Can't you read? No unauthorized access."

"We're here to see Maddie Petrosian," Laurel told him.

"Name?" The burly man sank onto the chair behind the desk, and it groaned in protest. Laurel identified us. He clicked a few buttons on the keyboard and stared at the top of the desk. The screen must have been hidden beneath a glass insert.

"Sorry, ma'am." he said, not sounding sorry. "Access is limited to immediate family. You two aren't on the list."

"Oh. I don't suppose you can tell us her condition?"

"No, ma'am. That information is strictly confidential. My apologies, but we gotta be careful. People are always trying to get in—old friends, distant cousins."

"But—but I was hoping—I thought we might—"

One side of the double doors opened. The person standing in the doorway was not the hospital staffer I expected. It was a Seattle police officer, an athletic-looking woman around thirty with a brown pony tail, wearing a navy blue uniform and sturdy black shoes.

"Something going on, Ramon?" the officer asked. "Need a hand?"

"No, Officer Clark," the guard replied. "Under control."

Holy shitake, was my first thought. My second? I had to get out of there before she recognized me.

Because I recognized her in an instant. Even though the last time I'd seen her, she'd been wearing a slinky red dress with spaghetti straps, at a table for two in the dimly lit corner of a downtown restaurant, running her bare foot up my husband's leg.

Eight

Directions in Seattle are skewed and street grids collide because the founders argued over whether streets should follow the cardinal directions or the shoreline; when they couldn't agree, each platted his land grant to his own whims.

OH, MY GOD. I HAD NO IDEA. TAG HAD NEVER SAID. NO ONE had ever said.

Why had no one ever said?

"Pepper, wait!" Laurel called, her footsteps rushing down the hall after me.

She caught up with me at the elevators. I'd have taken the stairs if I could have found them. Hospitals must have been designed by the same mad scientists who build mazes for lab rats.

"Pepper!" Laurel grabbed my arm. The elevator door opened and I stepped in. She followed. I punched L for Lobby. The door closed and I lifted my eyes to the display, watching the numbers tick by.

"What is going on?" she said through clenched teeth. "You just blew any chance we had of getting in to see Maddie or Tim."

"Didn't you see her?"

"Who?"

"Lovely Rita, meter maid. Looks like she went from screwing cops to being one. Not that the two are mutually exclusive."

"Oh," was all she said. We reached the lobby. The door opened and an elderly woman with a walker pushed her way in before we could get off, so we wriggled around her. As a rule, you should let people off before you get on. But there's a rule against knocking down little old ladies, too.

Not to mention a rule against sleeping with other women's husbands.

We made it outside without me bowling anyone over and stood on the sidewalk a few feet from the entrance. After we'd caught our breath, Laurel spoke. "What is she doing here? Lovely Rita, I mean. That isn't really her name, is it?"

"Worse," I said. "It's Kimberly Clark."

Laurel snorted. "Who would a name a kid after toilet paper?"

"Don't ask me." Needless to say, Pepper is not the name on my birth certificate.

I leaned against the building, the bumpy gray stone poking my back. "I had no idea she'd joined the police force. She had to attend the state law enforcement academy, go through all the training." She'd had plenty of time. It had been three years—three and a half, if I were counting. As I apparently was. Not to mention overreacting.

"Did she see me?" I said. "She'll think I'm an idiot."

"Why do you care what she thinks?" Laurel zipped up her coat and shoved her hands in her pockets. It was chilly, but at least it wasn't raining. "They aren't still seeing each other, are they?"

"No. He broke it off—to save our marriage, he said, but I was done with the secrets and lies. If they got back together, I haven't heard."

We'd come here to find out who was keeping secrets about Patrick Halloran's murder, and then I'd gone and let Lovely Rita punch my ticket.

"Hey, I'm sorry. Let's go back up. I'll tell the guard I'm super upset about Maddie, known her since kindergarten, yada yada. Ask him if Tim's there. ICU must have its own waiting room—maybe the guard will let me in to talk with someone."

"Are you kidding? You pull a stunt like that, Lovely Rita will be on the phone to Detective Tracy faster than the speed of light. He'll never trust you again."

Oh, gad. I'd not only overreacted to old news, I'd seriously mucked up my chances in this investigation. The apology was forming in my rattled brain when I spotted a man studiously avoiding us.

"Don't look now, but there's a man on the other side of the doorway who was upstairs when we were. Not that that's suspicious, necessarily, but . . ."

"But you are suspicious." Laurel's voice was tight, her eyes twitchy.

"Let's take a walk. Just act normal." Of course, the moment someone tells you to act normal, that becomes nearly impossible, but we tried. We strolled past him, me jabbering about a problem customer made up on the spot. When we got within a few feet, he leaned down to stub out his cigarette. Ah, the irony of a smoking area outside a hospital entrance. A trick, to avoid letting us see his face?

The rain and fallen leaves had made for slick spots on the sidewalks so we walked with extra care. At the next intersection, I glanced behind us.

"Can you see him?" Laurel asked.

"No." FBI? I hadn't noticed him in Montlake. Was he watching over Maddie, or watching out for us? I did see Ramon, the security guard, crossing the street a block back. He was wearing a rain coat. Security staff shift change?

"I—I'm pretty sure I've seen him before. The guy you spotted at the door, I mean."

"What?" I stopped midstride and nearly tripped over my own feet. Better than my tongue, which happens with some regularity.

"Friday afternoon, at Ripe. You know that open passage between the main tower and the café?"

I nodded. I'd worked in the tower for years.

"I stayed late to help prep for a catering gig. When I left, about four thirty, I crossed the passage, then headed to the garage elevator. He—I'm sure it was him—was sitting on a bench inside the lobby."

"Alone? Doing anything?" Friday afternoon. After Maddie was shot, but before we knew about it. By then, the cops must have had the ballistics linking the bullets recovered from Maddie's shooting to Pat.

"On his phone, I think, though he did glance up when I walked by. I could be wrong, but I'm pretty sure it's the same guy."

The phone. The perfect surveillance cover.

And the guy. A guy you wouldn't notice, unless you did. Average height and build. A ball cap and a dark rain jacket, the kind of jackets half the men in Seattle wear. Some even wear them with suits. I closed my eyes briefly to picture it. Navy. Like that narrowed things down.

"People wait outside hospitals all the time. And sit in building lobbies, too. Had you seen him before? Does he work there?"

"I don't think so. Seen him, I mean—I have no idea whether he works there. Thousands of people work there. They don't all come into Ripe."

"Fools. They have no taste. He must be FBI." I told her about seeing Special Agent Greer in the Market, even though I'd convinced myself she wasn't watching me. "Do they smoke? I always think of them as super-healthy, clean-living types. Runners."

"A secret vice."

Or the cigarette had been another bit of innocuous cover, like pretending to be on his phone while he kept an eye on Laurel Halloran.

A familiar figure caught my attention and I called out. "Tim!"

Tim Peterson stopped and looked around. I called out again and hurried toward him.

"Pepper," he said. We hugged.

"We were hoping to run into you," I said. "How is she?"

"Still in a coma, but her vital signs are good. Thank God they got to her quickly, so there wasn't a lot of blood loss." His voice mingled exhaustion with relief, and he pushed back the hood of his rain jacket and ran a hand over his thinning light brown hair. Maddie hadn't changed her name when they married, saying that since Petrosian and Peterson both meant "son of Peter," why bother? Tim used his middle name; his real first name, like his father's, was Peter. I'd roll my eyes if I hadn't been the victim of parental naming weirdness myself, though I'd lucked out when my grandfather bestowed the perfect nickname on me as a toddler.

I introduced Laurel. At the sound of her last name, Tim's eyes widened. "Patrick Halloran's wife?" he said.

"I am so sorry," she said, holding his hand in both of hers. I felt my eyes swell and my jaw tighten. Why did tragedy strike good people? It's an age-old question, and there is no answer.

"Thank you for coming. I'll let Maddie know—I like to think she can hear me."

"Tim, a quick question. Do you know why she was there? In the old grocery? I know you don't get involved in the company, but . . ." Tim was on the management team for the Sounders, though doing what, I couldn't say. Soccer isn't my game.

"All I know is she was meeting her builder there. He was late—got caught on the other side of the drawbridge." Tim shook his head. "Thank God he got there when he did."

"Was someone else meeting them? Or did someone follow her?" I asked.

"Not that we know. The police have her phone and they're checking, but they haven't found anything yet. I've gotta run and pick up the kids. Maddie's mom's coming in on the red-eye." We air-kissed and he hurried down the block, aiming his clicker at his car as he went, the lights flashing in response.

When Laurel and I reached the back side of the Cathedral, we sat on the steps. I could almost hear the medieval chants, though I was pretty sure they were only in my head.

"So what do we know?" I stuck out my thumb. "Maddie was shot last week in the building she was about to tear down. After years and a fight with the neighbors."

"Who knew she would be there besides her builder?" Laurel asked. "And presumably, her secretary. I mean, she owns the place, but she's not tearing down the walls herself, is she?"

"I wouldn't put it past her, but no, probably not. So that's the first question: Who knew Maddie would be in the old grocery?"

"Second question: Did she take a burglar by surprise? Who would break in to a building about to be renovated? To steal the old refrigerator? That doesn't make any sense."

"Don't thieves break in to old buildings to steal copper wiring or plumbing? But the police would know if anything like that had been taken."

"And they wouldn't break in in broad daylight, with a gun," Laurel said. "The same gun that killed my husband."

I sighed. "Maybe everybody's wrong about the gun. Maybe Pat's killer tossed it, or sold it, and it's coincidence that it was used in another crime in the same neighborhood."

Laurel gave me a sidelong glance that dismissed the idea as

ridiculous. Was it? Detective Tracy says he doesn't believe in coincidence, but when odd things happen involving the same person or place, check it out. My mother, with her woo-woo ways, says the Universe has reasons beyond human understanding, and uses coincidence to direct our attention to signs we might otherwise ignore. They were saying the same thing. Not that either would ever admit it.

Why would a halfway intelligent killer use the same gun twice? Didn't everybody know forensics examiners could match bullets? It wasn't easy; they had to get lucky and find bullets that were intact enough for the marks from the gun barrel to be compared. But it wasn't just NCIS TV magic.

"Okay, so let's talk about Maddie. We don't know why Rita—Officer Clark"—it was going to take me a while to change my mental image of her—"was in the ICU. Yes, Maddie's a crime victim in a coma, but they don't have the manpower to guard every crime victim. Her presence might not have anything to do with Maddie."

"She could have been checking on another patient," Laurel said. "When she heard the guard shout, she responded. Or she stopped in after her shift to visit her grandmother, and swung by to get an update on Maddie. That's a reasonable request of a young officer."

"She's not that young," I said, aware that I sounded like a petulant teenager instead of a grown woman. I couldn't help it; that's how Rita made me feel. *Kimberly.* "Tell me about Pat's role in the protests against the grocery project."

"He went to the public meetings, and the Neighbors United board met at our house a couple of times. That could have been earlier, though. I'm not sure. He didn't get as involved with the grocery project as he did on the wetlands issue. It was soccer season—he still coached little kids, plus following Gabe's team, and work was crazy busy."

"He tangle with Maddie?"

"No. You know, I remember her being at the first big public informational meeting, but I didn't think she was part of the grocery project."

"Why was she there then? As a neighbor?"

"I guess. I never knew. It was years ago, right before he was killed, and a lot's happened since then. Some builder-guy did the talking—I don't remember his name—and Deanna. We did feel a little uncomfortable around her, but no big deal. We were never close."

"Deanna, you mean? The woman we met in the coffee shop, who lived next door to you?" The stone steps were cold and damp.

"Right. The original plan was to tear the building down and build condos. She would get all the listings. But the group contended that the project was out of character with the neighborhood, and they thought eventually some of the other buildings would get torn down, too. Like dominoes. I haven't kept up, but at some point, the whole project was redesigned, with a gourmet market on the ground floor and a few midprice rentals upstairs. That's when I started hearing that Maddie was involved."

"No condo sales and no commissions," I said, musing. As Nate had noted this morning, people can get antsy about protecting their income stream. Maddie had plenty of other irons in the fire, I was sure. But what about Deanna? The builder-guy who'd done the talking in the early phases? Who else had lost a bundle to the change in plans?

Laurel peered over the stone balustrade. "No sign of Mr. FBI. Though I feel better, knowing they're keeping an eye on us."

FBI agents are trained to blend in, to not be noticed. He had the right clothes. But we had noticed him. Maybe he wanted us to know he was there, like Greer yesterday in the Market. She hadn't been trying to hide from me.

Was their presence meant to be reassuring, or a warning?

I like to think I'm a pretty decent observer, and that I can watch out for myself just fine, thank you. But this was a tangled web, and I was getting a very unsettled feeling.

LAUREL dropped me off near my building. I put a hand on her arm. "If you see anyone you feel hinky about, promise you'll call the police. Don't try to tough this out on your own."

Her throat tightened. "You know, I've never had a friend who would do what you did for me today."

"Meet for breakfast, drink coffee, and go for a drive in the rain?"

A smile tugged at one corner of her full lips. "You know what I mean."

"I do. And I appreciate you not telling me what an idiot I was for freaking out over Lovely Rita."

"We'll let that be our little secret."

I was half a block away when the drizzle turned to downpour and I broke into a sprint, not stopping until I reached the front door of my building.

No sign of a tail, in the car or now that I was on foot. Though if he were any good, we wouldn't notice. And he, whoever he was, probably knew where each of us lived and worked.

You're giving yourself the willies for no good reason, Pep, I told myself as I reached for the door, key in hand.

My loft is in a 1920s warehouse. During build-out, in developer-speak, the builder created a new entrance with a modern lock and intercom system. The door is one of those pneumatic thingies that close firmly on their own, the lock making a satisfying snick when it catches.

So why was it already open?

Nine

In October I'll be host
To witches, goblins and a ghost
I'll serve them chicken soup on toast
Whoopy once, whoopy twice
Whoopy chicken soup with rice

—Carole King and Maurice Sendak,
"Chicken Soup with Rice"

I'D TOLD LAUREL TO CALL THE POLICE IF ANYTHING SEEMED amiss.

Would I follow my own advice?

No damp footprints dotted the slate entry way. None led up the wide plank stairs to my floor, or down to the lower level. But the rain had only just turned serious. An intruder could easily have had dry feet.

How could someone have broken in? The doors were state-of-the-art. The developer had assured me of that, and when Tag helped me move in, he'd confirmed that the locks were all but unpickable. If that's a word.

"Don't be an idiot twice in one day," I muttered and reached into my bag for my phone.

"How" turned to "who." Who would break into a downtown residential building on a rainy Sunday afternoon? Surely a burglar would pick a more opportune time.

Someone who wasn't after jewels or fancy electronics. Someone with more personal harm in mind. Under the circumstances, it was not necessarily narcissistic to imagine that someone was after me. My thumb hovered over the keypad. Was I really going to call 911 for a balky door latch? I could practically hear Tag saying "better safe than sorry—it's what we do." But calling felt like a waste of precious police officer time. It felt foolish.

From a lower level came the sound of—what? A door, closing softly. Deliberately.

Then, footfalls.

I pressed the nine and moved my thumb across the keys to the one. A loud burst of laughter rose up the stairs. Female, followed by male tones, low and indecipherable. She laughed again and so did he, the sounds growing closer.

I hit pause on my panic. Burglars might work in pairs and close doors quietly, but they don't climb stairs laughing and joking.

A young couple came into view, she in a bright yellow slicker, the hood back, her blond hair in a French braid, he wearing the same kind of navy outdoor jacket as the man at the hospital, though the coat was the only resemblance.

They caught sight of me and stopped. She found her tongue first. "Were we disturbing you? Sorry."

I opened my mouth but nothing came out. I had never seen them before. I jerked my thumb over my shoulder toward the entrance. "The door—" I said.

"Oh, geez. Did we leave it open again?" She turned to him. "I told you I didn't hear it shut."

"Sorry," the man said. He looked about thirty, clean-shaven, his dark hair in a short fade. "We'll be more careful, I promise."

"Oh-kay. Thanks." I glanced between them, aware that my heart was beating too fast. "But who are you? What are you doing here?"

Turned out that the owner of the unit below mine, a man who used it a few weeks a year when business brought him to Seattle, had decided to rent the place on Airbnb. I think I'd seen him twice, maybe three times. This couple had taken the train up from Portland for a few days. They were quite sweet, actually, and felt terrible about having scared me. Sadly, that made me feel like an old lady in need of coddling.

But whatever our age, we all need a little coddling now and then, I thought as I headed up the stairs after they left, the door firmly shut behind them.

Inside my loft, I double-checked my own door. It was a silly incident with an innocent explanation. Short-term rentals were hot downtown. I didn't know if our building rules allowed them, but at the moment, the idea of strangers coming in and out was unnerving.

I stripped off my damp clothes and pulled on fleecy pajama bottoms and a sweatshirt. Wool socks. In Seattle, in October. If you'd told me last August, when the mercury rose past ninety for so long we all thought it was stuck, that October would feel like an ice bath, I'd have said "bring it on." But now that the rainy season was here, I was less impressed.

In the kitchen, I brewed a cup of Earl Grey. Normally, I'm a coffee drinker, and I'd recently become quite fond of chai. But when you need to warm up in a hurry, nothing works quite like hot tea.

Nate had taken Arf and gone to visit a fishing buddy. He wouldn't be home until evening. When we started seeing each other and I'd fretted to my mother about his here again–gone again work schedule, she'd pointed out that time apart is good for a couple. Now that Nate planned to stay in Seattle until spring, we were working out our own schedule. At the moment, half of me wished he were here to wrap his strong arms around me, and half was relieved that he couldn't see how I'd overreacted. Twice.

I was starving. Breakfast had long worn off. I put together a small antipasto platter, with chunks of cantaloupe, sliced prosciutto, marinated asparagus, and fresh mozzarella, all from the Market. Found some crackers and perched on a bar stool to eat my Italian snack and sip my English tea. Perfect.

The unlatched door had me rethinking my assumptions about other things as well. What if the man outside the hospital was just a man sneaking a cigarette outside a hospital? The FBI hardly needed a man at the door—and hospitals have many doors—if the SPD had an officer outside a patient's room. If they did—I didn't know that, either. Even if he was the same man Laurel had seen downtown, so what? Despite my misgivings about coincidence, Seattle's not so big that you can't run into the same person in more than one place.

My blood had begun to warm and my blood sugar to rise,

clearing my head. I clicked on my iPad. I knew Pat only through Laurel's stories and the yearly updates the news media ran. For the next hour, I followed the trail Patrick Halloran had left behind. We all leave one, I suppose, but the trails a federal prosecutor and community activist leaves can wend, wind, criss, cross, jump off, meander, and dead-end. As Laurel had said, the investigation was multi-pronged, probing his cases, the neighbors, known burglars, and more. At one point, I grabbed the notebook where I jot ideas for the shop and recipes—the closest paper—and began scribbling. Names, arrows, question marks—the result looked like a map drawn by a blind woman.

In other words, it led me nowhere. Except to the conclusion that for a guy everyone seemed to love and admire, Patrick Halloran sure had a lot of potential enemies.

Time to shake off my murderous musings and get busy. The Flick Chicks were meeting Tuesday at Kristen's. This week's movie was *Tampopo*, a noodle Western, the menu a soup exchange. It's a ritual I relish. Once or twice during the cooler seasons, each of us brings enough soup to share. After dinner, we divvy up the leftovers. For one stint in the kitchen, you end up with four varieties to freeze for a day when you're in the mood to eat soup but not in the mood to make it. Only once have two of us brought the same dish—tomato, if I recall correctly, and you can almost never have too much tomato soup.

Tomato soup would hit the spot right now—a cup and a grilled cheese sandwich are my definition of comfort food. Instead, I'd planned a carrot soup redolent with toasted pecans and spices. It's a Spice Shop fave, in part for the spices—duh—but also because it's easy, quick, and doesn't require much shopping. The only thing you might not have in your pantry—and why not; it's so flexible—is a can of coconut milk. I've learned to keep a couple cans on hand and stash what I don't use in the freezer.

First, though, music to chop, stir, and simmer by. I cued up a jazzy playlist, heavy on local musicians—Quincy Jones, Ernestine Anderson, Bill Frisell, and of course, Diane Schuur, since we'd missed her performance Friday night. Jazz has a long history in Seattle, dating back to the clubs on Jackson Street where Jelly Roll Morton played in 1919 and where Ray Charles hit the scene thirty years later.

I danced my way back to the kitchen, swaying to the warm notes and phrases of Frisell's jazz guitar. Strange, though, not to have my canine companion underfoot.

I took a bag of focaccia dough out of the fridge and turned on the oven, then started the soup. If I'm making soup for one or two, I don't bother with a recipe, but I've learned the hard way that when making a double batch, it pays to pay attention. I brought up a copy, then lined out the ingredients on the counter. The habit amuses my mother, Lena, who cooks by instinct, but I'd adopted it after grabbing the garlic instead of the ginger while baking cookies. The dangers of alphabetizing the spices—and yes, she laughs at that, too.

I melted butter in a large stock pot and threw in chopped onion and garlic. Scrubbed the carrots I'd nabbed from a farm stall, then sliced them with the food processor. Thought about Laurel and Patrick and Maddie.

Was there some connection other than the tenuous link of the proposed development? If Laurel knew, she'd have told me.

I tossed the pecans into a hot pan, eyes and sniffer on alert. Maybe—and here I swung back to the theory of Smoking Man as FBI agent—the cops were watching both Maddie and Laurel for exactly that reason. Hoping a connection they had never suspected would emerge.

What was the character on that old show, *The X-Files*? Cigarette Smoking Man, the mysterious government agent who sometimes helped Fox Mulder and sometimes frustrated him.

Great. An alien conspiracy. That's all we needed.

I did wonder if the FBI was watching me, as a woman connected to both victims. Although I'd never met Pat—I only knew his wife. Widow. What about Kristen, who was helping Tim with the kids?

No need to worry. Kristen is far more sensible than I. If she saw anyone lurking around her home and family, she'd call the cops in a nanosecond.

I shook the pan. A fragrant aroma was beginning to perfume the air.

The cops and agents would do everything they could to trace the gun, but that was an iffy proposition. I slid the pecans onto the butcher block counter to cool and added the spices to the hot pan.

Tag had been right about one thing: I could trust Mike Tracy to do his job. What about Meg Greer, with her new perspective? If a new perspective was needed, I'd give them mine. Tracy had as much as invited it.

Let them rehash the old investigations—they had the resources and the badges. I turned off the heat and poured the toasted spices into an electric grinder, one that never touches a coffee bean. Pulsed a few times, lifted the lid, and savored the earthy combo of toasted cumin, red pepper flakes, black pepper, and celery seed. Threw them into the soup, then gave the mixture a quick puree with the whizzy-uppy thing, a.k.a. the immersion blender.

Naturally, the whirring and grinding brought my brain to Lovely Rita. Officer Clark. I had to admit, it was a shock to discover she'd joined the police department. Had she and Tag gotten back together? I didn't know, and I shouldn't care. It had been three years. I'd left him. He was free to move on, though as far as I knew, he'd had no serious relationships since our divorce. He'd tried hard to win me back, and I had briefly wavered last winter. Instead, we'd settled on being friends.

And I loved the turns my life had taken since then.

When the soup was ready, I poured a couple of servings into a glass bowl, found the lid, and cut a wedge of focaccia. Carried my offering out to the landing and rapped on Glenn's door. The Grateful Dead was playing in the background. With him, you never know what the soundtrack will be—Pink Floyd or Wagner, Jimi or Emmy Lou.

"A thank you for keeping Arf Friday night," I said when he opened the door.

"Oh, you're welcome. Anytime. You know that." He took the dish and stepped back. "Come in. We got the final plans for the remodel—come see."

Glenn's loft is the same size as mine and we'd both kept the industrial feel, but the layouts were completely different. And while my design sense is generously described as rustic eclectic, Glenn's is midcentury modern. Eames chairs, white leather chaises, walls the colors of a Rubik's cube.

"How's your Nate?" I asked. "And his mother?" A year ago, Glenn married a lovely man named Nate Webster who'd left his journalism job to marry a city councilman and start the long-dreamed of novel. Then Nate's mother's health took a turn and he went back East to help her. When I started seeing Nate Seward, Glenn's and my conversations had become a tangle of references to "your Nate" and "my Nate."

Glenn sighed. "It won't be long, I'm afraid. Though we've been saying that for months."

"I'm sorry."

He pressed his lips together and nodded, then turned to the roll of blueprints on the sleek teak dining table. "Floor plans, detail drawings, materials lists. We're actually going to do this."

"So exciting," I said. The unit below Glenn's had been sold a couple of times since the century-old warehouse was converted to housing a few years ago, but it had never been finished. He and his Nate bought it to combine with their existing one-bedroom and make a two-story haven.

Now he unrolled the prints and pointed out the main features. The steps would be located near the entry. His office would move from a corner of the living room into the current bedroom. Downstairs, they planned a luxurious master suite, including a bath any spa aficionado would envy. Writing space for his Nate and a relaxing family slash media room would fill the remaining square footage.

"No guest room?" I asked.

"Nope. When I'm home, I want to be home, not running a makeshift B&B." Though serving on the city council was demanding, and occasionally frustrating, Glenn planned to run for another term. He had my vote.

"That reminds me." I told him about the young couple I'd met earlier—I admit, I called them "kids." "Are short-term rentals allowed? Is this one legal? Not that I want to create a problem, but . . ."

"If it's put you on edge, it already is a problem. I've never had any trouble with that door. You?"

I shook my head. I hadn't heard any complaints, either, but while my neighbors and I exchange greetings, take in the mail when someone is away, and occasionally walk a dog or feed a cat, we weren't close. When my mother announced last summer that she and my father wanted to return to Seattle for part of the year, she'd enlisted me as her house-hunting partner. We'd toured half a dozen cohousing collectives and condo complexes, and even a tiny-house village up north. What she wanted above all was community. Though I have great personal friends and tons of friends in the Market, a city within the city, Glenn was my only real friend in the building. And that might have been because our doors were four feet apart and our verandas were conjoined twins.

But now, I wondered. With only eight units, one never occupied, shouldn't we all be better friends? Shouldn't we have known what our downstairs neighbor was planning?

"I don't mean to put you in a tough spot. City councilman pointing a finger at a neighbor . . ."

"No, no." He held up a hand. "I've got the covenants handy, so I'll check. If it looks like there's a violation, you can invite everyone in the building over for wine and a chat."

That, I could do. Convene an informal meeting of the HOA. The original docs set one up, but we'd only met twice in my time here, once to make sure everyone knew the city's plans for removing the viaduct outside our windows, and a few weeks ago, to review and approve Glenn's proposal to consolidate the two units. It would be a good excuse to socialize with my neighbors.

Back in my own cozy space, I sat at my picnic table with a bowl of soup, a plate of bread and butter, and a glass of a classic, unoaked Chardonnay. This building started life as a warehouse for nearby canneries, and later for other goods—some legal, some not. It stood empty for years. Now, with the demolition of the viaduct that ran along Alaskan Way and the relocation of the elevated highway to a tunnel under downtown, the area was transforming again, from the city's back alley to its front yard.

And it was the perfect home for me.

All I needed at the moment was a good book. A year ago, I'd found a box of historical mysteries my parents had stashed in my storage locker and gotten hooked. I'd read my way through the Brother Cadfael series by Ellis Peters, and a former law firm staffer now working at the Mystery Bookshop had fed my growing addiction with the Sister Fidelma and Dame Frevisse mysteries. I'd stumbled across the Crispin Guest Medieval Mysteries by Jeri Westerson on my own, and was nearing the end of the first, *Veil of Lies*, when I heard a clicking noise and sat bolt upright, heart racing.

And rolled my eyes at myself. The moody mystery, dicey lock, and gloomy weather had me spooked at the sound of my Nate unlocking the door.

I greeted the canine with a pat on the head and the human with a long, deep kiss.

"Mmm," Nate said, and came back for seconds.

"What time is it?" I asked a little while later. "Dog walk?"

"No need. I think he sniffed every tree in Discovery Park, then he chased Aaron's kids around their back yard. He peed before we came up."

Over wine, I gave Nate the short version of our failed attempt to see Maddie. I told him about the man we'd seen at the door, the one who might or might not be FBI. I downplayed that speculation. My suspicions could easily have been my imagination. Fear and anxiety can mess with the mind.

Lordy, can they.

But I kept my mouth shut about my encounter with Officer Kimberly Clark. You have to be judicious, talking about past relationships. Besides, I'd had enough embarrassment for the day.

He filled me in on the visit with Aaron, a former crew member on the Seward brothers' Alaska boat, whom I hadn't met yet. "He's liking life off the water," Nate summed up, "and it's liking him. Though I talked him into making the trip up to the San Juans with me this week."

Was there a message in his tone? Nate was forty-four, a year older than I. Hardly an ancient mariner. He'd spent his adult life fishing. If he was thinking of giving it up, he hadn't said, or hinted at what he might do instead. But life had changed for both of us since Arf and I took a stroll along Fisherman's Terminal last June, and I had a hunch the changes were just beginning.

"Sounds like you had a great time. Clearly Arf approved." I sank to the floor to rub my dog's belly, and his happy sounds gave way to a soft snore. "I'm glad you'll have an extra pair of hands on board."

"Their house is a few blocks from my old place. Aaron said it's back on the market." Nate's ex, a nurse, had kept the house for a while, until she remarried and moved. We hadn't met, though I'd met her sister last summer when Nate called her for info that helped identify the weapon in a murder case. I could only imagine the mix of emotions I'd feel if Tag sold our former home.

"Do you want to own a house again?" Arf would love a yard. I stood.

"Maybe. Someday." He wrapped his arms around me. "Every phase of life has its own places. Right now"—he gave the side of my neck a tickling kiss and I suppressed an involuntary giggle—"this is the place."

"Can't beat this view," I said, and gazed out the windows at the lights along the waterfront. I'd never have been able to afford this view had it been here when I bought the loft.

He nudged me toward the bedroom. "I had a slightly different view in mind."

I definitely approved.

Ten

In northern India, a floating wholesale market operates every morning on Dal Lake in Srinigar, where men paddling low wooden boats buy and sell produce for small shops, restaurants, and hotels.

MONDAY DAWNED, DRY FOR THE MOMENT. NATE HEADED out on a parts run, so the boat would be ready for his trip in search of the wily coho. I was glad Aaron had agreed to join him. No job is perfectly safe, a lesson I'd learned as a police officer's wife. But commercial fishing involves dangers that would reduce most of us land-lubbers to puddles of salty tears.

I tried not to dwell on that as Arf and I climbed the Market steps. No gym membership needed when you live and work downtown. The rain and Maddie's shooting had combined to create a mental murk that called for strong medicine, so I bypassed my usual morning stop and headed for Three Girls Bakery, whose sign proclaims it a "luncheonette." The oldest continuously operating business in the Market, it was also the first business in the city licensed to a woman, back in 1912. No fancy cappuccino or decaf caramel macchiato here—drip coffee reigns. The mere scent of the stuff fired up my appetite, so I ordered a breakfast sandwich and perched on a stool at the back counter to sip my cuppa joe while I waited.

"Speak of the devil," Misty, the head baker, called. Her long braid swayed as she reached into a glass jar for a house-baked dog treat. I broke the treat in two and gave Arf half. "We were just talking about you. Over the weekend, a customer asked about you—did we know you, where did you work?"

My eyes narrowed and my spine tensed. Special Agent Greer, or her mysterious partner? "Male or female?"

"Lemme check." She returned with a woman who handed me my breakfast in a white paper bag. I repeated my questions.

"Well, yes," she said. "I don't mean to be a smart-ass, but I couldn't tell, which is why I remember. Slender, about your height, streaked blond hair. Female, I assumed. But when she spoke, her voice sounded male."

Who that could be, I had no idea.

"She headed for the craft stalls," the woman continued. "A new artist, maybe? You'll know her when you see her. And hear her."

Right now, the daily tenants were busy unloading, not the best time to interrupt. Later.

Besides, the last time I'd gone hunting an artist new to the Market, I'd inadvertently kicked over a hornet's nest of secrets that rocked several families, including Kristen's and mine. I'd learned my lesson: Inquire with care.

A young man in a white T-shirt and olive cargo pants came in through the back, toting an empty plastic crate. Misty greeted him, then turned to me.

"Hey, you still thinking of hiring someone to help with deliveries? Cody here is looking for extra hours after he finishes the morning bread run for us."

"Not sure. Maybe," I said. "Yes. Come down and talk to me. Tomorrow afternoon?" He agreed and the dog and I headed out.

The shop was dark but for the lamp with the red silk shade glowing in the far corner, sitting on an antique Chinese armoire an elderly neighbor had left me years ago. We use it to display our signature tea and tea accessories. A glass-fronted cabinet below the front counter holds my collection of antique nutmeg grinders, rusty metal spice tins, and canning jars cloudy with age, the handwriting on their red-and-white labels faded and spidery.

The place had history. And, I hoped, a long and successful future.

I turned on the lights and started the morning routine, pausing now and then to sip my coffee. Delish as a double mocha is, and as much as I enjoy a cup of cold brew or a pour-over made with the swankiest new equipment, a good old-fashioned cup of strong black drip does wonders when brain fog rolls in.

Kristen swept in a few minutes before ten, unwrapping the layers of scarves that made her look a mummy dressed for a fashion show. She disappeared into the back room and reappeared moments later, tugging her apron over her blond head.

"We had Tim and Maddie's kids most of the weekend. Her mom should be at their house by the time they get home from school."

"How are they doing? Any update on Maddie?"

"Still unconscious. The doctors say that's not bad—it's the best way for the brain to heal." She finished tying her apron strings. "The kids—well, kids are resilient, but it's hard to tell. Especially with Max—I am no good at reading teenage boys."

"Is sending them back to school so soon a good idea?"

"They wanted to go," she replied.

"My mom was killed on a Thursday," Matt said, "and I went back to school on Monday. It was the best thing I could have done. A few people knew and they said sorry and all that, but then it was time for class and I could act like everything was normal."

Kristen and I stared at him. Finally, I spoke. "Matt, we had no idea. I'm so sorry. How old were you?"

"Fourteen. It was a car wreck. My dad was driving. He kinda never got over it—his injuries or the guilt. He died when I was twenty-one. Reed and I got the delivery crates loaded and the route mapped out yesterday during a lull." He pointed at the hand truck, parked by the front counter.

I took his change of subject as a cue and got back to the business of business. I couldn't blame myself for not knowing Matt's family history. In his five months at the shop, he had proven himself very private.

And even those of us who have been spared the obvious tragedies carry burdens others can't see. Every family has its trials and tribulations—a volatile marriage, financial struggles, health problems. Every adult has her failures and regrets.

Though apparently I had assumed that rule didn't apply to Maddie Petrosian.

After opening, Matt and I headed out, me leading the way, he pulling the cart. The Market is home to a year-round farmers' market, bakeries, meat and fish markets, produce stands, and specialty food stores. Not to mention more than two hundred craftspeople renting daystalls, an equal number of owner-operated shops and services, and four hundred-plus residents—all in nine acres.

And nearly a hundred sit-down restaurants, from the creperie and the chowder joint to bistros with white tablecloths. So it made good business sense to nurture commercial accounts close to home. I'd worked hard, learning individual chefs' tastes and needs, devising custom blends, and offering free samples, good prices, and good terms, including reliable delivery. The butcher in the Sanitary Market unexpectedly runs out of fennel for his custom sausage blend or a prep cook drops an open jar of oregano—call me. The spicy shrimp special proves too popular and you're desperate for red pepper? Leave me a late-night voice mail and I'll have a fresh supply on your doorstep before you've finished your first cup of coffee.

But we were having trouble keeping up with our own success.

"What would you think about a part-timer to help with deliveries?" I asked as we boosted the hand truck over the threshold of the Soames-Dunn Building and across the tile floor to the oyster bar.

"Great idea. I'm proof that you don't need to be a spice wiz to bring back orders." He flashed me a grin.

The Persian café, two Greek spots, the Falafel King, the chowder joint, and three restaurants with an Italian flair—we hit them all and everything in between. We were welcomed and thanked in half a dozen languages. The Market is a polyglot world.

"Matt." I laid my hand on his arm after we left our last stop. "I had no idea you'd lost your parents so young."

"No reason you'd know," he said. "It's just one of those things."

Before I could tell him he was a fine young man and they'd be proud of him, or utter some other embarrassing platitude, he'd turned and headed for the shop, the hand truck clattering behind him.

My search for the artist who'd been searching for me didn't take long. "Jamie Ackerman—Coloring the World" read the banner above a stall in the North Arcade bursting with vibrant acrylics. The artist was equally colorful—long hair streaked with shades of pink and orange, eyelids striped in pink, orange, and lime green. A puffy purple jacket hung open, revealing a bright floral T-shirt and narrow black pants.

"Pepper Reece," I said, extending my hand across the table.

"Pepper!" As the woman at the bakery had said, the voice was at odds with the appearance. In my years in HR, I'd worked with a handful of transgender people and while those incongruities are initially jarring, they're simply based on expectations. And expectations can get us into all kinds of trouble. Despite the baritone, Jamie Ackerman's manner was the bounce and bubble of a Valley Girl. If that phrase isn't dating me.

"I live in the same building as Tory Finch, and when I got accepted in the Market, she said I had to meet you. She said you know everyone and everything going on down here. But it's been cra-a-azy getting set up and figuring everything out, so I asked about you at the bakery. A spice shop! You're a real-life spice girl!"

"I am." I get called "spice girl" half a dozen times a day, or more, and it never gets old. I surveyed the paintings, a kaleidoscope of color and playful images. The most eye-catching was a portrait of a woman—the artist?—with boldly colored hair piled in spirals on top of her head, swirls of color on her cheeks. A tiny bird perched on the woman's shoulder, whispering into her ear. "Your work is delightful."

Tory had worked at the Spice Shop when I bought the place and inadvertently triggered my first murder investigation. When it wrapped up, she left to pursue her true passion, painting. A few months ago, I'd helped her find space in a terrific old building on Beacon Hill with apartments upstairs and studios below. As a bonus, the owner runs a dynamite bakery and deli on street level, and a mix of thriving retail shops fills the other storefronts.

The kind of space I imagined the block on Twenty-Fourth could be.

"I had no idea Seattle was so beautiful—or so expensive. Finding a space where I can live and work has been heaven. Painter-girls need lots of room." Jamie swept a hand dramatically over the canvases.

Painter-girl. The cue that ended any doubt about whether

Jamie identified as male or female. HR trainers suggest modeling gender-accepting behavior when you meet someone new. "My name is Pepper and I use the pronouns she and her," you say, inviting the other person to do the same, and I get the point, but it doesn't fall trippingly off the tongue. Making space for natural revelation is more my style.

"And now I'm here!" Jamie crowed, the gold ring in her nostril catching the light.

"Pop over and meet my crew when you have a chance." A shopper reached for a painting of a path leading into the woods, a fantasy world of color, light, and happiness. It drew me, too. You just knew you would like the person who created it. Jamie Ackerman had found the perfect palette and subject matter for her personality.

By the time I got back to the shop, my tummy was rumbling as loud as the delivery trucks on the cobblestones. Between customers, I finally managed to finish my breakfast. Then I checked the stock to see if we could fill the orders Matt and I had received on our rounds.

I was crossing the shop floor, a jar of marjoram in my arms, when I glanced out the front door and saw two wheels spin by. Moments later, a second bike sped in and out of view. Bike patrol on a mission. Though I hoped Tag could tell me more about the investigation, I didn't mind putting it off. Had he talked to Officer Clark since Sunday? Did he know I'd embarrassed myself by fleeing at the sight of her in the hospital? Though I didn't honestly know if she'd seen me, or known who I was. Either way, a can of worms better left unopened.

Because worms have a way of crawling into unexpected places and catching you by surprise.

And when it comes to Tag, I am no better at keeping my lips zipped than at keeping my emotions off my face. That's the lingering effect of umpteen years together and thirteen years married. It's not always bad. It's good that we're still friends.

But my curiosity about the meter maid turned cop might not be so good.

Behind the counter, I started on the spice orders. As I spooned out marjoram and weighed bay leaves, I considered what we knew so far about Maddie's shooting and its possible link to Pat Halloran.

Not much more than a tablespoon or two, to use a cooking metaphor.

What would Cadfael do? Keep an eye open and when the time was right, talk to young Sheriff Hugh Beringar.

The shop's landline rang and Matt answered. He cupped a hand over the receiver and held it out to me. "Edgar, from Speziato."

One of our best customers, creator of the very popular baked paprika cheese. I handed Matt the bag and an invoice. "Thanks. Run this up to the chowder shop, please." I took the phone. "Edgar! Great to hear from you. Arf misses you." What Arf missed were the bones the chef saves for him.

"You know I think worlds of you, Pepper," the Salvadoran chef who runs a terrific Italian kitchen said. "But when you made my special spice blend, you said it was mine. Nobody else's."

"And so it is."

"Then how come another chef is using my spices?"

"What? No! Edgar, that's impossible."

Cayenne had come behind the counter to ring up a sale and gave me a worried look, her nearly black eyes wide. If we mix a blend for a commercial customer, whether it's our creation or theirs, we hold that recipe in confidence. We don't sell it in the shop and we certainly don't share it.

It's a promise we make, and I keep my promises.

"Look at his menu. The description, it is the same."

That couldn't be. "Edgar, let me go to my office. Hang on."

I handed the phone to Cayenne and sped to the back room, closed the door, and grabbed the other receiver. The computer was on, thank goodness. "Okay, I'm back. Who is it?"

I heard the click of Cayenne hanging up. Edgar told me the name of the other restaurant. "We have never done business with them," I said, and cradled the receiver between neck and shoulder while typing in the name. "Not in the two years I've owned the shop. I've never even met the chef." I'd heard the name, though, in Madison Park. I'd thought about calling on him but hadn't gotten around to it.

I found the website and started scrolling. "I'm looking at the menu. At the crab cakes. Ohmygosh." The entry was virtually lifted from Edgar's menu, down to the description of the flavors, though no individual spices were listed. "How did you find out?"

"Customer told me she had crab cakes at his place but mine was better. 'Yes,' I say, 'because of my own special spices.' 'No,' she say, 'spice the same. You use better fish.' When she leaves, I look up his menu and see the same as mine. But those are my spices."

You can't copyright a spice blend, like you can't copyright the list of ingredients in a recipe. After all, you need certain things to make brownies or a cake. But it's entirely possible for more than one chef or spice merchant to come up with the same combo, independently. I created my Italian herb blend from scratch, to give my customers a flavor profile that would please nose and tongue, but it isn't much different from others on shelves around the country.

"Edgar, that blend is yours. You came to us with an idea, and we worked to find exactly the right combination until you were satisfied." Trial and error. So. Much. Trial and error. "We have not given the recipe or the finished product to anyone." No need to mention the small jar in my kitchen. No need to muddy roiling waters.

"Then one of your staff . . ."

Impossible. Only Sandra and I have access to the Blend Book, safely stashed in our commercial kitchen. The electronic version is password-protected. I'd planned to bring Cayenne into the mixing and blending side of the business, but put that off until her health stabilized.

But defending my staff would sound like I was blaming his.

"It could be completely innocent, Edgar. Maybe your rival had a bite of Speziato's crab cakes—"

"Never. Never has he been in here."

"Or someone described them to him. Heck, maybe he spotted them on your menu and was inspired to make his own blend."

"No," Edgar barked. "He is not that good."

"I'll figure this out, Edgar, I promise. But you have to under-stand that we can't stop him from using the same ingredients you use. All we can do is talk to him." Would that be true if he had stolen the recipe, not just managed to recreate it? I wasn't sure.

"*My* recipe," he repeated. "*Mine.*"

I suppressed a sigh. I didn't think Edgar would make a big stink, but the best way to protect our reputation and our relation-ship with Speziato was to figure out what had happened. Even if I couldn't prevent the rival from sprinkling the blend on everything from crab cakes to ice cream.

"I'll figure this out," I repeated, and we hung up.

I flopped back in my chair. *For the love of cardamom* . . . Edgar had stopped short of accusing me of impropriety, but I didn't blame him for being upset. So was I. We'd put tons of time into creating that blend—I'd been generous because Edgar works hard, treats his staff well, and is a tremendous cook. He'd learned from one of the best chefs in the city, the disgraced Alex Howard, now traveling the world and blogging about it. I'd wanted to help Edgar create his own place in Seattle's lively restaurant community.

It crossed my mind that maybe he'd learned this bluster from Alex, too.

For shame, Pepper, I told myself. That is beneath you.

I checked the other restaurant's website. Closed Mondays.

Good. I had time to make a plan.

I was going to need one.

Eleven

In Europe in the Middle Ages, designated "market towns" had the right to hold a public open-air market where growers, butchers, and other merchants could offer their wares, fostering trade and a cash economy.

I TEXTED LAUREL TO ASK IF SHE KNEW THE MAN I'D DUBBED RC, for Rival Chef. *No*, came the swift reply. Sent a similar note to Sandra, on her day off. She, too, had never heard of him.

Meanwhile, more deliveries awaited. I hot-footed home to fetch the car, then eased my way down Pine, parking on the steep slope beside the shop, emergency brake and flashers on. Popped in the side door, and Matt helped me load.

Dog nails clacked on the wood planks. I crouched and scratched Arf under his chin. "You sure you want to go, little buddy? Your bed is nice and warm." In answer, he sat and cocked his head, offering his collar. I air-kissed his little black nose and found the leash, and off we went.

Edgar's spice trouble nagged at me as I navigated through downtown and up to Capitol Hill, home to many of my best customers. But all those years working HR had taught me to be a problem-solver. I'd learned by watching some of the city's top lawyers and HR managers that finding the right solution matters way more than salving one's pride.

My last delivery took me to the back side of Capitol Hill, and from there, it was an easy slide into Montlake. I passed the Spite House, a local landmark. The mostly likely origin story for the narrow house, built long before tiny houses were fashionable, is that errors in platting created a sliver of a parcel between two larger lots. When the neighbor made an insultingly low offer, the owner of the parcel responded by building a wedge of a house, four and a half feet wide at one end, fifteen feet at the other, that blocked the neighbor's view and forever kept the dispute in his line of sight. Whatever the true story, it's a charming house, at least from the outside—yellow stucco with a curved white eyebrow arch over the front door.

And it was a reminder that the neighborhood was an old one, with plenty of mystery in its history.

"Let's stretch our legs, boy," I told the dog and parked near the coffee shop. Walk first, snoop later. My little gentleman was drawn to the puddles and I had to tug gently on the leash more than usual.

I paused in front of Laurel and Pat's former house. When they tell you not to make any drastic changes for at least a year after your spouse dies, they aren't talking about a spouse murdered in the back yard. Talk about drastic.

Sweet house, sweet neighborhood, and a great place for a kid to grow up. Murder aside, that is. I admired how the residents valued their community, advocating for safety, the parks and schools, and the wetlands nearby.

What was I doing here? What was I hoping to find? A feeling, I supposed, as much as facts.

I took a flyer out of the plastic box attached to the "For Sale" sign on the sidewalk.

"A little gem. New on the market." At the sound of a male voice, I turned to see a man strolling down the adjacent rose-lined driveway. The man we'd run into at the coffeehouse. "Hey, don't I know you?"

I shuffled flyer and leash to my left hand and held out my right. "Pepper Reece. Laurel's friend. We didn't get a chance to introduce ourselves yesterday."

"I'm Bruce Ellingson. You in the market? Great neighborhood."

Took me a moment to realize he meant the real estate market

and this neighborhood, not Pike Place Market and downtown. Like I would really be interested in buying the house where my good friend's husband was murdered. "I know, I know. I grew up a few blocks from here." I glanced at the flyer. His wife's listing, her picture on the bottom. "I was never in this house, and I hear it has a nice back yard. Can you see it from your place? Though it can't be as nice as yours. What beautiful roses."

"You're a rose lover? Come take a look at the back." He led me around the tall hedge that separated the two driveways to the side door of an olive green two-story with a steeply pitched roof. A common style, a variation of the classic Four-Square known as a Seattle Box. "I just got a delivery of mulch and it's blocking the path on the side of the garage, so we'll have to go into the house to get to the backyard."

He held the screen door for me. Inside, I told Arf to wait and he stretched out on the door mat.

"Bought this place when our youngest started first grade," Ellingson said. "Hard to believe he's a junior in college now. Or would be. Spends all his time in the basement when he bothers to come home. You got kids?"

"Just the four-footer in your mudroom."

We walked through the kitchen, done in the French country style popular about twenty years ago and due for an update. That surprised me. Not that every real estate agent has to live in a show piece, but the ones I knew all lavished time and money on their homes. And Deanna Ellingson seemed like a woman who would want her home to look just so. I'm a nester with a fondness for home decor myself, so I understood that, though our styles could hardly be more different.

Glass doors at the end of the dining room opened on to a deck and we went outside. I had never seen so many roses in such a small space. Tag and I had planted a few, and I knew rose lovers could get carried away, enticed by new cultivars, colors, and scents. Bruce Ellingson seemed to favor teas and grandifloras, and they filled a deep curving bed that lined the yard, but a pale peach climber, still in bloom, covered a wide swath of the cedar fence between his place and the yard next door.

Bruce pointed out half a dozen favorites, calling them by name. My appreciation was genuine, even though barely half were still in bloom, and the recent rains had done them no favors. Despite his complaints about weeds and the challenges of keeping out the blackberries that grew in the alley, it was clear that roses were his passion.

"You take care of all this yourself?" I asked.

"Yes. My wife enjoys the results, but doesn't have much time for digging dirt."

Not to mention what it might do to her manicure.

"I imagine this does take a lot of time," I said. "What kind of work do you do?"

"Bond broker," he said and held the door.

Inside, instead of returning to the kitchen, I walked through the dining room to the front entry. A staircase led to the second floor. "Can I take a peek from upstairs? To get the full effect?" I started up, leaving Bruce no choice but to follow. Pushy, I knew, but I wanted to see into the Hallorans' old yard and couldn't think of any other way.

At the top of the stairs, three doors stood open. I beelined to the corner room. His office—the decor masculine, the mahogany desktop clear except for a green-shaded banker's lamp. Prints of ancient sailing ships hung on the walls, papered in a soft gray with a subtle herringbone pattern.

As I'd hoped, the windows opened to the yard next door. A narrow perennial bed curved around the foundation and the small wooden deck Laurel had mentioned, then stretched along the fence on one side. A yard designed not to show off flashy blooms, but to give a child space to play. I could almost see Pat and Gabe kicking around a soccer ball, Laurel leaning over the railing with a cup of coffee in hand as she watched.

I could almost see Pat Halloran sprawled across the deck, bleeding to death from a gunshot.

It gave me a chill and I turned away. Bruce Ellingson had remained in the doorway, shoulders rigid, skin pale.

Back in the hallway, I spotted a small student desk in the adjacent bedroom, covered with papers and files. Gray sweatpants had been tossed on the pink-and-orange flowered bedspread, a pair of well-worn men's slippers on the floor.

Bruce Ellingson had forsaken an office that appeared to have been designed for him. And while he and Deanna looked the part of the perfect couple when they stopped for coffee on Sunday morning, I suspected they were using separate bedrooms. Not uncommon, for a host of reasons, but combined with the abandoned custom office, it seemed strange.

"Thanks for showing me your roses," I said, my hand on the stair rail. "They must be gorgeous in summer. You have a lot to be proud of." I bounced down the stairs and moments later, Arf and I were back on the sidewalk, making tracks.

I couldn't believe what I'd just done, appealing to the man's vanity about his roses to worm my way into his house. Mystery readers call that TSTL, too stupid to live. Happily, I had lived.

I could understand Ellingson not wanting to work in his office for a while. After all, he had found Pat. You didn't have to be good friends with a neighbor to be haunted by his death. But it had been three years. If his office held too many terrible memories of the sight I'd seen, why not swap rooms, making the girl's room his office and his office a guest room?

And though he'd gone along with my ruse, he'd seemed on edge. Because I'd pushed my way in, and in the process, gotten a disquieting look at his personal life? A second shooting in the neighborhood would upset anyone, as would an attempted burglary. Though Ellingson could have no reason to think the recent shooting might be linked to Patrick's killing.

This was all getting tangled up in my brain.

We turned the corner on to the side street, where the houses and yards were smaller. A few feet ahead, a woman stood on her front steps, flipping through the mail. She glanced up at us and brightened. "Oh, an Airedale. My neighbors had one when I was a kid."

As if he knew she were talking about him, Arf looked at her, then me. I stopped and the woman came down the sidewalk toward us.

"May I?" she asked, one hand extended for the introductory sniff, and I agreed. "How old?"

"Four or five—I don't know for sure."

"He's a doll," she said, and having gotten the sniff of approval, ran her hand over the top of his head and rubbed the magic spot beneath his chin.

A small white car zipped down the street, a little too fast, and I instinctively tugged on Arf's leash to keep him close.

"Where are those police officers now?" the woman said, sounding annoyed. At my puzzled look, she explained. "There was an—incident nearby last week. A pair of detectives came by, asking questions."

"I heard," I said. "The shooting at the old grocery." I kept my friendship with the victim to myself.

"Attempted burglary. It's slated for demo any day now, so what they thought they'd find, I have no idea. Sadly, the owner arrived at the wrong time and was critically injured."

"Oh, my gosh. Is he okay?"

"She," the woman corrected. "And I don't know. The detectives were more interested in gathering information than sharing it."

"You must all be upset," I said. "I grew up a few blocks away. It's always been a safe, quiet neighborhood."

"It still is," she quickly replied. "Well, you might have heard about the prosecutor who was shot and killed at his home a few years ago. Right around the corner, in the next block. They never have solved that crime. But things happen everywhere, right?"

"You mean Pat Halloran," I said. "Laurel is a friend of mine. I'm Pepper Reece. And this is Arf."

"Lindy Harmon. Oh, poor Laurel. This must bring everything back for her." She crouched next to Arf, who raised his chin for the extra attention. "Barry, my husband, worked with him on the NU protests."

"En-you? Oh, oh, um, Neighbors United? Laurel's mentioned it, but I don't really know what it does."

"Whatever we need to do," Lindy replied. "We fundraise for the library and community center. Worked out a compromise when the highway expansion threatened the wetlands. Made our voices heard when the original proposals for the corner grocery were announced."

Maybe she could tell me what no one else had. "Right. So you didn't like her original proposal? The owner's, I mean."

"She had nothing to do with the original proposal," Lindy Harmon said. "She'd had her eye on that property for years and along comes this other developer and buys it out from under her."

"What?" This was news to me.

"But she got it back—I don't know how. She listened to the community. She understood what would work in that location and what wouldn't." From inside the house came the sound of a telephone. Who still has a land line, I wondered, as Lindy straightened, gave Arf a last quick pat, and headed for her open door. "I can't convince my mother to call my cell phone. She always says she doesn't want to interrupt me. Nice to meet you both."

"Well." I glanced down at the dog. "Learn something new every day."

If you didn't, it wouldn't be a very good day.

Twelve

Researchers believe that we choose what we eat and drink partly through sensory cues that draw on experience, such as our memory of enjoying the taste of an expensive wine, which prompts us to choose an expensive vintage the next time we scan a wine list.

WOULD THE NEIGHBORING BUSINESS OWNERS TALK TO ME? They had to be on pins and needles. First, all the rumors and struggles over the development, and now a shooting. No doubt some of them remembered Pat Halloran's murder, as Lindy Harmon did, although I hadn't heard anyone connect the two crimes yet. Whether they thought Maddie's shooting random or targeted, and whether they approved of her plans or not, they had to be worried for their own safety and their businesses.

Though I had learned, to my astonishment, that crime is not necessarily bad for the bottom line.

We circled back to Twenty-Fourth, cars and busses whizzing by. I had no idea what kind of building the corner grocery had replaced, but it was hard to imagine that this had ever been an improvement. Will today's hip new looks become classics, or dated eyesores like the boxy stucco grocery? But despite its appearance, it had been a central meeting spot, a hub that helped define the community.

It's a fact of life and age that the places that hold our memories change without asking our permission.

Of course, the moment you turn out the lights and walk away, a building takes on a shabby air. As if it knows it's been abandoned and plunges into depression, the sidewalk sprouting cracks and weeds overnight. And that breeds crime, if you buy the broken window theory.

Emby must have had a family. What had happened to them?

"Come on, boy." I tightened Arf's leash. "Time to get to work."

The rest of the buildings on the block were a mix of styles, some the redbrick popular in the 1920s, another with a recessed doorway under a stately stone arch. It was the classic commercial district with a floor or two of apartments above the shops that once defined a neighborhood, before we all began hopping in our cars to work elsewhere. These days, it was a struggle to find the right mix that would serve nearby residents and remain viable. To its credit, the city made an effort to balance changing needs and keep the neighborhoods vibrant. But gentrification has its costs, and community can be one of them.

Though I knew, as the tenant of an aged building in the Market, that no amount of character beats reliable wiring.

The name on the first door we came to read FRANK THOMAS INSURANCE Serving Montlake Since 1977. I pushed it open and stepped inside, Arf at heel. An electronic chime announced our arrival, and the sounds of radio news drifted from a back room.

My dad had brought me here to see the agent when I got my drivers' license, to teach me some of the costs of driving.

"Coming," a male voice boomed. The radio clicked off. The front desk sat empty; it was lunch time.

I scanned the walls, hung with a series of black-and-white photos of the neighborhood. One shot, partially hidden by a silk ficus tree, caught my eye and I stepped closer. The corner lot, taken from across the street. Two men in dark suits and hats stood on the sidewalk in front of a two-story redbrick building, still under construction. A slight distance apart stood a third man, in dark pants, a white shirt, and suspenders. Their faces were impossible to see—too far away, the sun too bright in their eyes. The owners and their tenant? Two bankers and the owner? No way to tell. I could only imagine what they might think, knowing that their businesses and buildings were long gone, and about to be replaced again.

"Bygone days," the man I'd heard earlier said. "Lively block, back then."

I turned to see a man of about fifty, wriggling the knot of his tie into place beneath a broad, friendly face. He finished the job and held out his hand. "Frank Thomas. How can I help you?"

The son, not the father I'd met as a teenager. "Pepper Reece. Chuck and Lena's daughter. Hope you don't mind me dropping in, or bringing the dog in out of the drizzle."

"No, no, he's fine. I thought you looked familiar. How are the folks?"

"Good." What few financial matters my parents couldn't handle long-distance they'd entrusted to my brother, Carl, who does, after all, make a living in finance. But I remembered the Thomases, one of the few black families in the neighborhood. "They're still in Costa Rica, loving it, but they're thinking of moving back part of the year. I was passing by and thought I'd drop in, let you know they'll be calling." I'd have to remember to tell my mother I'd promised she'd call.

"My pleasure. They renting or buying?"

"Haven't decided yet. You know my mother—when she sees the right place, she'll snap it up. She was curious about the condos—or are they apartments?—going in next door, but now, with the shooting . . ."

Frank Thomas's heavy eyelids closed briefly, his jaw tight. A woman had been shot on the other side of these walls, and Sheetrock isn't much of an insurance policy. Pun, if it is one, not intended.

"Such a tragedy," he said. "For Maddie and her family. We're all praying for her."

"She and I went to school together. She's a fighter. I'm sure the police will catch whoever did this."

"That's right—you're married to a police officer, aren't you?"

I gave him a half-smile of acknowledgment. No need to set the record straight.

"Her project would have been a huge boost to the neighborhood," Thomas continued. "Heaven knows, we need it. The upkeep on old buildings like this one is a major hassle. I didn't wanta be saddled with it. Not to mention juggling renters and all their complaints."

"Big job."

"First priority is for her to recover. Then I hope we can all get to work alongside her, bringing this block back to what it ought to be."

I liked his spirit.

"When your parents settle on a place, tell them to call me," he said. "I'll get them fixed up."

I assured him I would and plucked his card out of a holder on the reception desk.

But before I did any more sleuthing, I had to pee. I tied the dog up outside the coffee shop and went in. In the corner, two men played a silent game of chess, while a young mother read at another table, her baby asleep in a carrier perched on a chair next to her. It's bad manners to use the restroom without ordering something, and besides, the moment I smelled the coffee, I was suddenly desperate.

"Nonfat double latte, and what scones do you have?"

"We're down to cranberry orange," the barista told me. "Monday mornings are always busy."

"Cranberry orange, then," I replied. While he ground beans and pulled levers, I slipped into the restroom. On my way back, I noticed the rear door was open and peered out. The cobblestone alley had been closed to vehicles and reclaimed into outdoor space. In warm weather, the café tables and chairs would be full, the space made cozy by the brick walls and the box planters filled with shrubs and flowers. From here, I could see the rear door of the old grocery, at the opposite end of the block.

Back inside, a bulletin board in the hallway caught my attention. It held a flyer for the library's used book sale, another for a school event, and a host of business cards, including that of the neighborhood real estate agent.

I carried my afternoon snack to a comfy brown leather chair by the window and waved at my dog. The coffee was terrific but the scone was bland. A simple dash of cinnamon or cloves would brighten the flavors. Though I had no samples with me, I asked the barista if the owners were in. Turned out I'd just missed them.

"Quiet in here," I said. "Peaceful."

"Monday afternoons are always slow," he replied, and began wiping the counter.

"I hope the shooting doesn't scare people away."

His head jerked up, eyes wide, and he tightened his grip on the towel. "She used to come in every Saturday with her husband and kids. They were so nice."

Saying that I knew her, though true, would intrude on his feelings, and I didn't want to do that. "Paper says she's expected to recover fully. I'm sure she'll be sitting in here sipping dark roast and nibbling a scone before you know it." I put an extra dollar in the tip jar and left, keenly aware that the repercussions of tragedy ripple far and wide.

Two buildings stood between the coffeehouse and insurance agency. A pair of street-front businesses occupied one. A note on the acupuncturist's door said the clinic was closed for vacation, and the designer was closed on Mondays. Inside, a limed oak table was set with turquoise Fiestaware; I'd have to come back.

To my surprise, the salon next door was open. SHEAR DESIGN, the sign read.

I stuck my nose in. "Mind if I bring the dog in for a minute? It's about to pour."

The stylist, a leopard-print shop coat over her black leggings, her feet in leopard-print flats, broke off her conversation with the client in her chair. "Oh, come in, come in. Just don't tell the Board of Cosmetology. What's his name?"

"Arf." That was the name he came with and I couldn't change it, even if half the people thought I'd said Art and the other half Barf. Besides, it suits him.

"Cute hair," the stylist said, pointing her scissors at me, not the dog.

I love my short dark spikes, though I have been accused of cutting my hair with kindergarten scissors and sticking my finger in a socket. "Thanks." I sank onto the wicker love seat, the jungle print cushion poofing up around me. The salon was small, two chairs and a nail station, plus a massager pedicure chair, though only the one stylist was working at the moment. Pop music played in the background. I suspected Deanna Ellingson would favor a swankier salon, but dated decor doesn't signal poor service any more than an on-trend look guarantees a good cut.

"Friend of mine's a dog groomer," the stylist said. She fluffed the highlights on the side of her customer's head. "Got one of those mobile grooming vans. She comes to you."

"Handy," I said. Detective Tracy says it's okay to fib in the search of truth. "This must be the salon my friend Maddie told me about. Cute place."

"Maddie," the stylist said, scissors pausing midair inches from her customer's ear. "Maddie Petrosian?"

"Yes. Can you believe what happened?"

"I didn't know anything had happened until the ambulance pulled up out front."

"Her husband says she's holding her own. Knowing her"—I shook my head and blew out a breath—"it will take more than a bullet to slow her down."

The stylist and customer exchanged a glance in the mirror. I had to speak carefully if I wanted to learn anything useful.

"The new building should be good for business, right?" I said, taking a cue from Frank Thomas's upbeat attitude. "People popping in for milk will see your shop, give you a call. The people in the apartments upstairs will be thrilled to have a salon close by."

"Hmmph," the stylist said, squinting at her customer's roots. "We'll touch those up next week when you come in for your manicure."

"With all the plans and rumors over the years, who knows what will actually go in," the customer said. "Now she comes along and promises an old-style neighborhood grocery with a modern wine and cheese shop. Sounds great, but I'm not holding my breath."

She'd unwittingly touched on my own confusion. "So somebody else proposed something else? Before Maddie got involved, I mean."

"I went to a couple of meetings," the customer said. "I didn't trust that Burns or Burke, whatever his name was. He acted like we should be grateful that he was here to save the neighborhood. I mean, we all knew something would happen to the property—the old guy wasn't going to live forever, and that lot has to be worth a bundle. But we could never get the straight scoop. My impression, he meant to tear down the whole block and put up fancy condos. He and that pushy real estate agent."

"His name was Byrd," the stylist said. "With a Y. And he called the project Byrd's Nest. With a Y."

"That's right. He had all these fancy drawings, but they were ugly as sin."

"What meetings?" I asked.

"Oh, Neighbors United. They asked him to make a presentation, up at the community center. So we would know what was going on. Then they claimed his proposal violated city standards, and wasn't in keeping with the neighborhood. They were right, but developers do what they want, no matter what we think." She looked in the mirror and touched the side of her head. "A little shorter, maybe?"

"That went on for ages," the stylist said. "A couple of years. Then all of a sudden this summer, he was out of the picture and your friend had bought the corner grocery. Her proposal looks nice. It looks great." Snip, snip, snip.

"But can we trust her, either?" the customer said. "I mean, she says she just wants to put up a new building on the corner, so why buy the whole block?"

Whoa. This was news to me. It must have cost a pretty penny.

"Right?" the stylist said, nodding at the mirror. "I admit, this place needs work, but the rent's been fair. She promised to upgrade all the wiring and stuff when she remodels upstairs—her electrician's already crawled over every inch—but she also said she had no intention of raising our rent. If you believe that . . . Except the coffee place. I heard they wouldn't sell." She put her scissors down and twisted the lid off a jar of product. A sweet, gooey smell filled the air.

"Well, why would they?" the customer replied. "That building's been in their family for ages. But I will say this. Once Maddie took over, tensions eased. When she held a community meeting, she listened. Made a point of saying she lives here, too, and intended to address our concerns. Even the NU people seemed happier."

"I still don't believe her about not raising the rent," the stylist said.

I understood her skepticism, but from a developer's perspective, it made sense. If Maddie needed to rent out the upper floors to help pay for the building, she'd need to bring them into the twenty-first century, and she couldn't do that without upgrading the entire structure. By holding rents steady, at least for a while, she could mollify the existing tenants and keep the street level space occupied.

"Maddie just bought the corner grocery this summer, right? When did she buy this building?"

"A year ago," the stylist said. "Same time as she bought the one next door. I think she'd already bought the insurance agency and the apartment building, a year or two before."

That was what I wanted to know. When Patrick Halloran was killed, Maddie did not own the corner grocery, the property at the heart of the neighborhood dispute. She'd bought all these buildings after his death, and finally acquired the corner lot.

"If she hasn't raised the rents yet," I pointed out, "sounds like a promise kept."

"True," the stylist admitted.

Time for me to go. I stood. One more question, though I thought I knew the answer. "Who was the real estate agent? The one you thought was so pushy?"

"Oh, what was her name?" the customer said, again looking at the stylist via the mirror. "It's plastered all over the neighborhood."

Deanna Ellingson.

Thirteen

According to a 2018 study, Seattle drivers spend fifty-five hours a year stuck in traffic.

WE DON'T ANY OF US FIT IN THE BOXES PEOPLE BUILD FOR us, do we? Not me, and not Maddie.

Maddie ran her business from a small second-floor office in a commercial block not unlike the one I'd been prowling. But asking questions had taken time I didn't have, so there was no chance of stopping by today. And I wanted to get back to the shop before closing, though that might mean springing for a spot in the Market garage. My plan was to zip over to Madison, then shoot straight down the hill and over the freeway into downtown.

But I'd forgotten to tell the traffic gods.

Cars were backed up on Madison for blocks. My best guess was a wreck at the I-5 on-ramp. I slipped the Saab into park, cracked a window, and turned off the engine—the gas gauge had been stuck for years, and the last thing I wanted was to run out of gas in a traffic jam. I sent the Universe a silent prayer that no one was seriously injured, and reached for my phone. It's technically illegal in Seattle to even look at a mobile device when you're behind the wheel, but I'd challenge any cop who dared ticket me when the motor wasn't running.

Who to cyber-spy on first? My old friend, or the real estate agent whose plans she'd scuttled? Both Bruce and Deanna

Ellingson had seemed perfectly pleasant in our brief exchange at the coffeehouse Sunday morning, but my view of him had already shifted.

Gad. Had that only been yesterday? So much had happened in the last few days. I once complained to an elderly friend that time seemed to go faster as I got older. She'd laid a wrinkled hand on my arm, trained her glacier-blue eyes on me, and said "Oh, honey. It just gets worse."

At the moment, though, time was standing still. More accurately, the cars were. That sometimes seems like the same thing, in our addicted-to-motion society.

Deanna, Google told me, worked out of the Capitol Hill office of a big real estate outfit. Though the legal assistants and secretaries at my old firm had scattered to all variety of work after the firm's dramatic demise, and I managed to keep tabs on most of them, I didn't recall any landing there. I found her page, tilting my phone for a better angle. Recent and true-to-life, the photo showed a lively woman in her mid-50s with a healthy glow and a perfect haircut. I'd seen the same picture on her business card and the flyer for Laurel's old house.

Looking that perky all the time had to be exhausting.

The website touted her decades of experience in commercial and residential property, single and multi-family. Unusual to handle both, I thought, but then a website is supposed to brag a bit. I read on. The bio listed training and certifications that sounded impressive, but what did I know? No mention of the Byrd's Nest or the mysterious Mr. Byrd. With a Y.

Traffic hadn't budged. In my rear view, I saw a vehicle attempting to wriggle out of the backup and turn around, but as tightly packed as the cars were on the narrow street, it would be nearly impossible. Besides, there wasn't anywhere to go—a city of hills, water, and bridges, bisected by an interstate, didn't offer many alternatives.

I turned back to my phone and scrolled through Deanna's listings. Tons of condos. Seattle had gone a little condo crazy, not that I could complain, since my loft is one. A handful of listings for houses, all in her neighborhood.

How much longer? "Hang in there, buddy," I told Arf, then called the shop.

"Don't worry," Cayenne said when I told her I was stuck in traffic. "If you're not here by close, I'll wait."

"If I'm not back by close, I'll die of boredom and a burst bladder. Go ahead and lock up at the usual time. I'll deal with the cash register."

Bladder talk made me shift in my seat. What was a bond broker doing home on a Monday afternoon? Surely he wasn't running his business from the spare bedroom.

A bond broker. I barely knew what that was, but I was on close personal terms with a man who knew the field inside out. I texted my brother and asked him to meet me for lunch tomorrow.

A siren pierced the air, coming toward us. Around me, engines turned on, anxiety and relief spewing from tail pipes. "Take it easy, people. It's gonna be a while."

An ambulance came into view, then turned toward Harborview. Two more crested the hill behind it. Whatever happened, it had indeed been serious.

Meet you at Ripe, Carl replied. *I could kill for a bowl of tomato-basil soup.* One of Laurel's classics.

Deal, I said, then clicked off the phone and tossed it aside.

Finally, cars began to inch forward. Twenty minutes later, at the corner of Third and Madison, I saw the remains of the problem: A black Suburban had crashed into the side of a Metro bus, clad in the purple and gold of the University of Washington. A tow truck was hitching up the SUV, and a giant tow idled on Third, waiting to remove the disabled bus. Police officers directed traffic. The bike patrol, with their ability to respond quickly, were sometimes called upon, but I didn't see Tag. What had caused the SUV to lose control coming down the hill, I could not imagine. Thank God only three ambulances had been needed.

Trouble can hit you when you least expect it.

Arf and I made it back to the shop in time to count the till while Cayenne swept and Matt emptied the samovar. Business had been good for a rainy Monday in October. My concerns aside, we could weather the ebb and flow. No pun intended.

Assuming this glitch with Edgar and his custom blend didn't blow up on me. I crossed my fingers and made for home. The door of my building was firmly latched this time, thank goodness.

Nate had texted to say he had dinner in hand. One of the

advantages of dating a man in his forties is that he's used to planning his own meals, even if it's takeout. One of the advantages of being a woman in my forties is that I consider takeout pizza on the couch with a great guy to be a romantic dinner for two. Plus the World Series was on TV. What could be better?

Seeing the Mariners make the Series. Next year.

Next year. I tried not to think that far ahead in our relationship. But with the talk of houses and condos and apartments swirling around me, not to mention Glenn and his Nate expanding and my parents planning a return, I had living space on the brain. Though this space did seem to work rather well. By the time Nate went back to Alaska in the spring, we'd know.

We'd know if the loft worked for the two of us. But more importantly, we'd know if *we* worked.

Patience, Pep. Patience.

In between bites and at-bats, we talked about our days. I filled him in on Maddie. Kristen had talked to Tim, who said they were beginning to see signs of responsiveness—a twitch of a hand, movement behind the closed eyelids—but they still didn't know when she'd come around.

"The grapevine's buzzing—I've gotten oodles of texts and emails from our old classmates. I keep saying, 'I know Maddie. It will take more than a bullet to the brain to stop her.' But I still can't believe this has happened." My eyes watered, and my jaw tightened, my lips pressing together.

Nate took my hand. "I'm sorry I've never met her. Not that we don't both have friends the other hasn't met yet."

Thinking of Maddie plunged me into a tangle of emotions I didn't want to deal with right now. As if her success made me a failure because she had everything a woman was supposed to have, and I didn't. Which wasn't a fair assessment of my life and I knew it. Cadfael, my patron saint of investigation, would visit the Abbey chapel and contemplate his unworthy thoughts, confess if he needed to, and move on, taking solace in his balms and tinctures and the good his herbs did in the world.

Me, I changed the subject, telling Nate about Edgar and the copycat spice blend.

"Can he do that? The other chef, I mean."

"Sure. You can't copyright a list of ingredients. That's why

McDonald's keeps its secret sauce secret and Kentucky Fried locks its recipe in a vault. Or at least, they say they do. Could be a ruse, to make us think it's something special."

"So you could make your own version of Old Bay and change the name and become a millionaire?"

"Just because it's legal doesn't make it smart."

"Like intentional walks," Nate said, his eyes back on the ball game. "I hate when the pitcher intentionally walks the hitter."

We put our feet on the packing crate that serves as my coffee table and he slipped an arm around my shoulder.

"We're heading out at the crack of dawn," he said when the game broke for the seventh inning stretch, "so I need to go back to the boat tonight. I hate to leave you. But I'll be home Friday or Saturday, depending on the catch."

"It's what you do," I said. "You go out on boats and catch fish. That's part of the deal."

Home. Had he meant the loft, or his slip at Fisherman's Terminal? Or just Seattle?

"Besides, I won't be alone," I continued. "I've got Arf."

"And the FBI might be watching you. Although you didn't sound sure he's FBI."

I hadn't seen Agent Greer or Smoking Man all day. Kristen hadn't mentioned seeing anyone. And Laurel had texted the all clear when she left the deli midafternoon.

"Honestly, I think I was overreacting, because I was upset about Maddie. If the guy we saw at the hospital is the same guy Laurel saw Friday, then he's FBI and we should feel better."

"Wouldn't that Agent Green have given you a heads-up?"

"Greer." I swung my feet up on the couch, cradling my knees, and met his gaze. "Good point. If the two shootings are connected, and they need to guard Maddie, it makes sense to guard Laurel, too. But why not tell her?"

"Unless they suspect her."

"Doubtful. Dozens of people saw her at the soccer tournament in Vancouver the night Patrick was killed. And Thursday when Maddie was shot, Laurel never left the deli. Besides, Maddie didn't own the building back when Pat was protesting the project. Laurel barely knew her—saw her at the public meetings, but that was it."

The commercial break ended and the game resumed. As a

Seattle native, I'm an American League fan. Nate claims to favor the Nationals, but I've caught him urging my guys to throw a strike or make a double play. Either he's been playing opposites to get my goat, or my tastes were rubbing off on him.

This was our last evening together this week, and I tried to squelch all thoughts of crime and investigation. But as the center fielder raced to the wall to rob the lead-off hitter of a home run that would have tied the game, my mind was racing, too.

The women in the salon had been skeptical of Maddie's promises, but I hadn't heard them describe anything Maddie herself had done to warrant their distrust. Still, the salon owner wasn't convinced.

No, it had to be that the previous would-be developer, this Byrd, had poisoned the well.

Lindy Harmon said Maddie had been trying to buy the corner grocery for ages, but she hadn't mentioned the rest of the block. Though Frank Thomas trusted Maddie, the women in the salon had asked a good question: Why buy the other buildings, if all she wanted to do was redevelop the one lot? To protect the block from the kind of development the neighbors despised? An insurance policy, of sorts. A very expensive one.

I might need to talk with Lindy's husband, or track down other Neighbors United stalwarts.

The game ended, the National League team the winner. But the Series is best of seven, so I wasn't worried. About baseball, anyway.

I hooked up the dog's leash and the three of us walked a few blocks before we returned to the parking garage beneath the building, where Nate had stashed the old pickup he bought when he came back from Alaska.

"Stay safe," he said as he took me in his arms.

"Always," I said. "You know I never do anything to put myself in danger. Or anyone else."

"Liar." But he was smiling as he leaned in for a long, sweet kiss.

Fourteen

The best murder weapon would be a Tupperware lid, because no one would ever be able to find it.

—Anonymous, on the web

"IT'S ONLY A FEW DAYS," I TOLD ARF AS WE TRUDGED UP THE stairs from the basement, past the rental unit. "We'll be fine on our own." We'd been fine long before Nate Seward came on the scene. But my furry friend's footsteps lacked their usual bounce, and I suspected mine did, too.

"That you, Pepperoni?" Glenn called out from above. As we neared the landing, I saw him in his doorway, my soup container in hand.

"Just sending my Nate off to the San Juans for a few days. Fish feed when he gets back."

"My Nate is glad that he doesn't need to worry about me wasting away. Not with you two so close."

"Glenn, how do you track the ownership history of a building? Or who applied for permits to do—I don't know. Stuff. To the building."

He swept his arm over the threshold, inviting us in. Tonight's musical selection was Bob Marley. "Red or white?"

"Yes," I replied. The remodel plans still lay on the dining room table. They drew me like a magnet. "This is going to be so great."

"Big mess when we get started." He set a bowl of water on the kitchen floor for Arf, then handed me a glass.

I took a sip. "Mmm. Love Washington cab."

He nodded and pointed at his desk, computer screen glowing. "I've spent so much time visualizing the new space that sometimes I forget we don't have it yet. Sit. What are you after?"

A few minutes later, he'd shown me how to access the city's public records system for parcel data, including details about the property, present use, and current taxpayer, a.k.a. the owner. Additional screens showed the appraised value, and the date and price of the most recent sale. I pulled Frank Thomas's card out of my coat pocket. "Try it with this address."

"You try," Glenn said, and I did. Sure enough, Petrosian Properties, LLC had purchased the building occupied by Frank Thomas Insurance not quite three years ago. "You want to find out who that is, you'll have to go to the state's business entity search page—those aren't our records."

"No, I know the Petrosians. Where would I find applications for building permits?"

"No one-stop shop, I'm afraid. How far back do you want to go?"

I didn't know, but it turned out the process would not be easy. I'd have to search for each building in Maddie's block by address, then track back in time, sale by sale. Records from the last thirty years or so were online, but before that, it was all micro-film. Unless I wanted to pay for a title search, which I did not.

"But Maddie Petrosian would have, wouldn't she, as part of her purchases?"

Glenn faced me. "She's the woman who was shot in Montlake last week, isn't she? What are you up to, Pepper?"

"I've known Maddie practically forever," I said. "I want to know what happened." I did not want Glenn to think I was taking advantage of our friendship to get info on a police investigation, or a proposed development. Nor could I risk dragging him into anything that might create a conflict for him. I stood and clapped my hand against my thigh to signal the dog that it was time to go. "Thanks for the education. And the wine."

"Pooh," I said when the dog and I were home. I'd forgotten to ask Glenn if he'd had a chance to check on the rental downstairs.

But I didn't want to give him an opportunity to lecture me about messing in police business. We'd figure out the rental thing another time.

I gave Arf a chew bone, which reminded me that tomorrow, I needed to solve the mess with Edgar. Checked my phone, and smiled at Nate's sweet "home safe" text. The *Thalassa* was his home. He'd lived aboard it a good chunk of the year for ages. But he was coming to see the loft as home, too. At least, I thought he was.

In the bedroom, I undressed and glanced at the *tansu*. My plans to buy it last summer for Nate to use had been stymied, but then, it had arrived as an unexpected thank you gift. He loved it as much as I did. A stack of books sat on top and I was about to move them when I stopped myself. They were his, and they could stay where he'd put them. Like his shoes on the closet floor next to mine, or his toothbrush and razor in the bathroom. I felt his absence when I saw his things. One more sign, I hoped, that the relationship was right.

But that didn't mean it wouldn't require care and attention.

The book on my nightstand, *The Satapur Moonstone* by Sujata Massey, sent me its siren call. My friend Seetha had given me it and the first in the series, *The Widows of Malabar Hill*, knowing how much I loved historical mysteries and how curious I was about India, particularly Bombay, where her mother had grown up.

Later. I had a different historical mystery to work on now.

Back in the living room, in my jammies, I sent Laurel a "checking on you" text. I didn't expect a reply—she keeps baker's hours. But a minute later came two words: *Doing okay.*

Under the circumstances, "okay" was good enough.

I fired up my iPad to see what the newspaper said about Maddie—Madeleine—Petrosian. Nothing more about the shooting since the weekend update identifying her as the victim. A couple of archived articles referenced the proposed development in Montlake and the community meetings. But none gave any details or mentioned a prior developer or competing plans.

"She's got to have a website," I said out loud. These days, every retail shop and service provider needs a website. Even doctors and lawyers. They're the first thing we check when we want to do business with someone and if we don't find one, we're a tad suspicious.

Petrosian Properties, LLC's website was attractive but basic. The homepage showed the building where she kept her office, a well kept redbrick on Nineteenth Avenue East, with the phone numbers and email addresses for the reception desk and property manager. A second page listed currently available spaces and invited interested persons to contact the property manager. Only a handful of offices and one retail space were listed, no apartments, and nothing in the buildings on Twenty-Fourth. There was no mention of the corner grocery project, not even a "Watch this page for future announcements!"

Google also linked me to the secretary of state's business entity site, where I was assured that all the company's papers were filed and its fees paid. I crossed my arms, thinking. The Spice Shop's website is crucial to our business, allowing customers across the U.S. and Canada to place orders any time of day. It's got tons of pictures and detailed descriptions of every spice and blend we carry, recipes, and the scoop on our boxed sets and Spice of the Month club. Plus hours, location, and contact info, and a map.

But—and this was the distinction—my business depends on the public. Hers didn't. The efficient, no-nonsense site told me that Maddie felt comfortable with her business as it was. She wasn't boasting about growth potential or investment opportunities, trying to make the company sound bigger and better. So why expand now? Why commit so much time and money to the new acquisitions and the corner grocery?

Maddie didn't do anything without a good reason. What was it?

Though Byrd isn't a common name, Google couldn't help me without more information. I paired it with Montlake, construction, and development. Nothing. Byrd's Nest produced only a couple of mentions in a real estate blog, but the links to further information were dead.

I backtracked to the business entity registry where I'd found Petrosian Properties, LLC. No Byrd's Nest, with a Y. I tried the regular spelling.

"What?" I said, so loudly that Arf stopped chewing and raised his head. Bird's Nest, LLC, with an I, had been registered a few months ago. The official representative was Jessica Somers, a name I had never heard, with an address in a Seattle suburb. It was a cute name; no wonder someone else had chosen it.

Next target: Neighbors United. Whoever was responsible for updating the website was behind on the task—the last event listed was a potluck at the community center three months ago. Barry Harmon, husband of the dog lover I'd met today, was board chair; I didn't recognize any other names.

Back to flipping through screens. I looked at each of the available commercial rentals on Maddie's website and half a dozen articles referencing the company. A pattern emerged. Maddie focused on projects much like the current one, rescuing buildings with a past and an uncertain future. Some projects involved a single building; others an entire block of two- and three-story structures, with storefronts on street level and offices above. They were scattered across the city.

Frank Thomas and the stylist had underscored the challenges in keeping buildings like these rented and maintained. But I knew, from my connection to the block in Beacon Hill where my new painter friend, Jamie Ackerman, and my former employee, Tory Finch, now lived, that it could be done. The right mix of tenants, the right attention to the needs of the neighborhood, and the right owner could make these classics profitable.

Figures Maddie would have the right touch.

My eyes blurred and I yawned. Put the iPad to sleep and climbed in bed, reaching for my novel. A chapter or two following the first woman solicitor in India as she trod behind walls where men could not go, asking questions no one else could ask, would be just the ticket to a good night's sleep.

And maybe Perveen Mistry, Esquire, would give me a few ideas for my own investigation.

"I DON'T know anything about Maddie's business," Kristen said as we sat in the nook Tuesday morning sipping double mochas, her treat. "When we get together, we talk kid stuff. Books. Houses, since we both just survived top-to-bottom remodels. Or we gossip about girlfriends."

The heat rose up my throat. She saw it.

"Yes, including you. She brags about your shop to everyone, you know. She thinks what you've done is terrific."

Ha. More likely she was astonished that the classmate who dropped out of college after barely getting a passing grade in basic accounting had bought a business and hadn't gone broke within a week. Although to be fair, she was always complimentary when she came in.

"Any news?" I said, pushing my less charitable thoughts to the back of my brain.

"No. I'm meeting Tim at the ICU this afternoon." Most days, Kristen left at three. "She's graduated to visitors from outside the family, if he puts them on the list."

"Fingers crossed. If I'm right, Maddie bought that entire block in Montlake to keep it out of the hands of this Byrd guy. As if she didn't trust him to handle the project properly."

"Wouldn't the permit process address that? I mean, the city's got tight restrictions on what you can do and how long it takes. At least for residential properties, but commercial rehab can't be any easier."

"It could be. Money talks." I drained the cup. "No, what I'm wondering is why she decided to focus on older buildings like these. Almost every project of hers that I found is one of these neighborhood blocks that conventional wisdom says aren't good business."

"Since when do you buy into conventional wisdom?" Kristen held out her hands, palms up to indicate the shop. No one had thought I should buy it, except her. And my mother.

"No, seriously. Looks to me like she runs a small-but-successful company that has its hands full. Why was she so determined to buy up that block?"

Kristen met my gaze, and I could see the wheels turning. People sometimes dismiss her because she's a pretty blond with a manicure and an upscale wardrobe, but there's a heck of a brain behind those blue eyes. And a heck of a memory.

"Ten o'clock," Sandra called. "Time to get spicy."

I cleared off the nook table and glanced at this week's book delivery before Kristen started shelving the new titles. A cookbook from David Lebovitz, an American living in Paris, and a kitchen memoir we'd thought intriguing. A stack of new foodie mysteries from Cleo Coyle, Laura Childs, and Vicki Delany.

And three new cookie cookbooks, in time for Christmas, which would be here before we knew it.

I retreated to the office to make a few calls and place some orders. When Kristen said Maddie bragged about me and my shop, my immediate reaction had been to doubt it. To think she couldn't possibly mean it.

Why was I so resistant when it came to Maddie? Because she had the perfect husband, the ideal marriage, the beautiful children I didn't have?

So did Kristen, and I never begrudged her a thing.

Although I hadn't told Kristen about seeing Officer Clark at the hospital and making an idiot out of myself. Too embarrassing.

I was acting like a fifth grader, projecting my doubts about myself onto Maddie. That wasn't fair to either one of us.

No one has it as easy as it sometimes looks. As my street-wise buddy Hot Dog had reminded me not long ago, first-world problems like failed marriages and lost jobs may feel like the darkest depths when we're plunging into them, but they won't kill you.

And I did desperately want to find who'd shot Maddie, and how it was tied to Patrick Halloran's murder. To help Laurel, and to repay my debt to Maddie.

"Hey, boss," Sandra said from the doorway. "You wanted to talk. Now a good time?"

"Yes, yes." Always better to talk spice than ruminate about the past. I told her about Edgar's complaint.

She crossed her arms and set her jaw. "No way anyone working for you told anyone what's in Edgar's secret spice. If there's a leak, it's on his end."

"The most likely explanation is that the other chef, or someone who works for him, figured it out by tasting it. Edgar says that's impossible, no one could have figured out all the spices in the blend, and I tend to agree, but we don't know that it actually is identical."

Her eyes flashed. "We could taste it ourselves. They're open for lunch, right, this other joint?"

"That is brilliant. Tomorrow. I've got a lunch date today."

"Something to do with the shooting and the cold case?"

"With any luck." I reached for my shop notebook. "Now, let's talk sugar and spice."

Fifteen

Efforts to fake saffron, the world's most expensive spice, date back to the ancient Greeks. The Unites States Pharmacopeia database lists 109 phony saffron substitutes, including marigold flowers, corn silk, gypsum, chalk, and cotton or plastic thread.

"OKAY, SO WHAT EXACTLY IS A BOND BROKER?" I ASKED CARL after we were seated at a corner table. Laurel had greeted us both warmly, looking wan but clear-eyed. "I mean, I know what *you* do, but not what *they* do. Or what Bruce Ellingson does."

My brother, who is two years younger than I and at six feet, five inches taller, is way smarter. He is also a virtual copy of our dad, from features to gestures to tastes in food.

"So there's municipal bonds, which is what I manage," Carl said. "City needs to raise money for, say, light-rail expansion, or the waterfront project."

That one I knew. Tearing down the viaduct had removed a major earthquake hazard and not incidentally, given me stellar views. But it had also created both a years-long mess and an opportunity to rebuild the seawall along Elliott Bay. In the process, the city decided to upgrade the surface streets and create new waterfront parks and paths. Glenn had been particularly proud of his work bringing together "the stakeholders"—the people affected.

Downtown residents were a core constituency, and at his urging, I'd attended several meetings and voiced my opinions. Not that I actually need urging to voice my opinions.

"When a city faces a large capital expense, it borrows money by selling bonds. Each bond is for a specific amount and matures, or comes due, at a specific time. In effect, each bondholder is making the city a small loan. Combined, they give the city the cash it needs."

"And the loans are repaid over time, out of future revenue," I said and he nodded.

We sat back while the server set my mac 'n cheese and Carl's tomato-basil soup on the table.

"You know you could order something different," I said. "Variety is the spice of life."

"I am a creature of good habits." Both habit and reply came from Dad. "Munies are tax-exempt, so high-income investors love 'em. Corporations issue bonds, too, when they need more money than a bank wants to lend them, say for an expansion or to develop a new product. The interest on those is taxable, so they have to pay a better rate to make up for it."

"Where do brokers come in?"

"They help with the initial offering, or sale. And bonds that have already been issued can be bought and sold, like any other securities."

"Securities meaning stocks," I said. This wasn't my language.

"Mm-hmm," he said, his mouth full.

"So that's what Bruce Ellingson does."

"I'm surprised he still calls himself that," Carl said. "He hasn't worked in the field in years. Two, three?"

"What?" Though that would explain why Ellingson was home on a Monday afternoon.

Carl set his spoon on his plate and steepled his fingers, another Dad echo. Like our dad, he excels at explaining difficult concepts. Even to someone without a degree in finance. Or in anything.

When he was done, I sat back, astonished.

I glanced toward the kitchen. Surely the police knew the history Carl had relayed. Patrick Halloran had been instrumental in pursuing Bruce Ellingson's firm for systematically lying to customers, for years, about the prices at which they could buy or sell bonds, boosting their profit on the trade. A customer had stumbled over the truth and filed a complaint.

Now that I knew the story, I wished Carl had chosen another spot for lunch. But of course, neither of us had known we'd end up discussing all this right under Laurel's nose.

"Their defense," Carl said, "and it would sound crazy except that it kinda worked, was that puffing isn't a crime—it's part of business. They also claimed their lies weren't big enough to influence decisions. That's double crazy, in my opinion, because why else would you bother to lie?"

"Puffing is me telling a customer our lemon thyme is the freshest on the planet. Or that our smoked paprika will change her life," I said. "Which it will. But that's not the same as me telling a chef the ingredients he wants in his custom blend cost two dollars an ounce when I paid a buck and a half."

"I agree, it's not the same." He picked up his spoon. "Good example, though."

"So what was Ellingson's role? Did he lose his license?"

"The case had nothing to do with the city, so I never knew the details. The firm closed shop. No criminal charges were filed, but I heard they reached a consent decree with the feds, which usually means agreeing to give up their licenses and find a different line of work, not involving other people's money."

Laurel makes the best mac 'n cheese—no puffing—and mine was getting cold. I took a bite. If Bruce Ellingson could no longer work in the field, was that why his wife worked so hard? What was he working on at home, in his daughter's old bedroom? Personal stuff?

"What's Nate up to?" Carl asked, and we chatted about family stuff for a few minutes. Carl and Andrea and the kids had gone to Whidbey Island last weekend, combining a getaway with a Mom errand, scouting out the site of a planned senior cohousing community she'd heard about. Ground-breaking was months off, though, so even if our parents bought in, they'd need a place to stay next summer. I immediately thought about the loft for rent in my building and immediately perished the thought. I love my mother dearly, and her living half a continent away is too far, but her living one flight of steps away would be far too near.

Carl started to push his chair back. "Thanks for lunch."

"And another thing," I said, leaning forward, my voice low. "Bruce Ellingson lived next door to the Hallorans. Doesn't it seem like a conflict for Pat to investigate him?"

"I'm not a lawyer, but Pat always had the best reputation."

"But it's got to have been uncomfortable as heck. Even though they weren't friends." Had the dispute over the compost pile been a cover-up? Or a real disagreement that took on greater significance because of the underlying tensions?

"You never know about neighbors. We thought we saw ours a few weeks ago, but it turned out to be the UPS guy."

I laughed. In the six years they'd lived in their house, Carl and Andrea could count the number of times they'd talked with one set of neighbors on one hand with fingers left over. Like me and the guy in the unit below mine. Their near-invisibility had become a family joke.

"Both Bruce and Deanna were pretty friendly when we ran into them at breakfast on Sunday." Too friendly. And Laurel had been tense. I was beginning to think she must have known about Pat's role in Bruce Ellingson's downfall. It was a key piece of evidence, and she'd kept it from me. Still, I supposed Pat hadn't made the ultimate decision whether to pursue the case or let the regulators obtain a compromise. That would have been up to the U.S. Attorney.

We stood and put on our coats. The door opened. Special Agent Greer walked in, followed by Detectives Tracy and Armstrong.

The tall, thin Armstrong had worked with Tracy on last summer's murder in my friend Aimee's shop. He'd told me how much he admired Tracy, but it had been clear from the start that he was more willing than the older man to listen to the citizenry. To me. He was young and scholarly. What my mother would call an old soul.

"Well, Ms. Reece," Tracy said. "You're saving us a trip to your shop. I hope you'll stay and spend a few minutes with us."

"Call me if you need to, sis." Carl kissed my cheek and edged past the new arrivals.

"Mrs. Halloran," Tracy called over my shoulder, and I turned to see Laurel standing behind the counter, her face pale. "I trust you can make time for a word. In your office, if you don't mind. Ms. Reece will be joining us."

My eyes flicked toward him involuntarily. Did I have a choice? Laurel would not have withheld information from me without good reason, and I'd never know what that was if I walked out the door now. In fact, I had a pretty good idea that if I walked out, I'd be torching our friendship. I'd never find out why she'd kept silent about Pat's real relationship with Bruce Ellingson. And I wouldn't be able to help her, or Maddie.

Besides, when a cop invites you to stay, it's hard to say no.

Five minutes later, the five of us were crammed into Laurel's office. She and Tracy took the two seats while Greer leaned against the desk and Armstrong the wall. That left me to squeeze between the file cabinet and door, making me wish I'd had the soup and salad for lunch.

Though all eyes were trained on Detective Tracy, it was Agent Greer who spoke first, drawing a small manila envelope out of her pocket. Her black pantsuit looked straight out of the TV version of an FBI agent, though the TV version would probably wear a lacy, low-cut tank instead of a gray silk tee. She handed Laurel a photograph.

"Recognize him?"

Laurel shook her head, then passed it to me. An Asian man, probably Chinese, about forty. When you work in a busy place like the Market, you see a lot of people. Making deliveries doubles or triples the count. I've got a good memory for faces. But this one—I wasn't sure.

"You know him," Tracy prompted.

"Maybe. Who is he?" I asked Tracy, who turned to Greer. This was her part of the investigation.

"His name is Xian Huang, though he goes by Joe. Chinese national. Ever hear the name?" she asked Laurel.

"No. Where would I have heard it? What's his connection to Pat?"

"We're conducting an investigation into the head of a Chinese import–export firm based in Seattle," Greer said. "Huang works for the company, though we're not yet sure of his relationship to the person of interest or his crony."

Crony. Now there's a word you never want to be called.

"What kind of investigation?" Laurel asked. "Was it Pat's case?"

"I can only say that the investigation had just begun when your husband was killed," Greer said. "Huang left the country shortly after that. He returned a few weeks ago."

A collective shiver chilled the room.

"How's he connected to Maddie?" I said. "She's a small-scale developer and property manager. Her husband's a business guy for a sports team." Move on, folks; nothing to see here.

"We're looking into that," Greer replied. "We don't think Huang is dangerous, and he's not our target. But we are hoping he can give us information that will confirm a few key details."

Was this the Mr. Big operation Tag had mentioned? Had to be. I held the photo out to Greer but instead of taking it, she handed me another.

"He appears to be associated with this woman, whom my partner and I followed to the Market Saturday morning. But in the chaos, frankly, we lost her. We don't know if she is employed in the Market or was shopping." She handed me a second photo, showing a small woman in black pants and a black hooded jacket holding the hand of a child in a purple coat. I thought the woman looked young, the child likely her daughter, but the rain made it hard to see their faces as they crossed the intersection of First and Pike.

Where I'd seen Greer Saturday morning when Nate dropped me off.

I started to hand the photos back, then stopped. "Wait. That's why you said"—I glanced at Tracy—"that my lunch date with my brother saved you a trip. There's an Asian grocery on Pike Place." The little old lady whom I'd always assumed to be part of the family that ran the joint liked to perch on a stool at the entrance and snap at the feet of passers-by with one of those Chinese string toys. Her favorite was a paper alligator or crocodile. Kids were her main target, but she'd taken to nipping at my ankles then cackling when I jumped. I was finally on to her, but played along. Was this her daughter, the younger woman I'd sometimes seen at the cash register? "Does she work there? Or in a restaurant? You might show this around at the PDA, the Public Development Authority—that's the agency that runs the Market. If she's an employee of a tenant business, they won't have a record on her. But someone might know her."

"We tried that. No luck, on her or Huang."

Maybe they were watching Maddie to see if Huang or someone he worked with tried to make contact. To figure out the connection. Smoking Man must be part of their detail.

"Can I keep these? They look so familiar—it may come to me later."

Greer opened her mouth and I was sure she intended to say no, they didn't need an amateur's interference, but Tracy raised a hand and she said nothing.

"Be careful, Pepper. Don't go searching for them. Just let us know if you see them. Or let the bike officers know."

In other words, I was their inside gal in the Market.

I slipped the photos into my tote.

"You must have other suspects," Laurel said, turning to Greer. "From Pat's cases."

The agent nodded. "We're scouring those files. Retracing our footsteps, taking a closer look at everyone we looked at three years ago." She hadn't been part of that "we," but cops and queens like the royal pronoun.

"We're reconsidering the burglary theory," Armstrong added, "and checking into Ms. Petrosian's business interests for any possible overlap. And of course, working on tracing that gun. We're putting everything we have into this."

I believed him. Up until last Friday evening, I'd have likened the chances of finding anything amiss in Maddie Petrosian's business interests to those of the proverbial snowball. But I was seeing some of the people in my life a little differently now.

"Overlap," Laurel said. "You mean the community activists, the people who fought the original development."

"Right," Tracy said. "Your old friends and neighbors."

"Pat was concerned, naturally," Laurel said. "He knew how to talk the right language, about setbacks and quiet zones and all that stuff. His point was that the proposal was not in keeping with the neighborhood. Others were pretty hot, calling it an abomination. Californication. Pat could speak more reasonably."

Eventually the reasonable side had won out. Any possibility that the conflict led to Pat's murder would have been investigated at the time. And it couldn't be connected to Maddie's shooting—she hadn't owned the corner grocery then. Though I did wonder whether his death had prompted her to step up her efforts to buy the property.

At least one neighbor hadn't opposed the plans at all. A neighbor who'd lost a ton of potential business when the project downscaled from high-end condos to low-end retail and rentals. But before I could ask about Deanna Ellingson, Laurel rose.

"I'm sorry, but I have to get back to work. Thank you for the update."

Greer stood but Tracy remained seated, his eyes on me. "Something else on your mind, Ms. Reece?"

Infuriating as it was, I had to admit that the man was awfully perceptive.

I wanted to ask why they had a guard on Maddie. Was she truly in such danger that the hospital security guards, not to mention the maze of hallways and doors, could not protect her? But if they were guarding her, then the answer was yes. And raising the question would only prompt Detective Tracy to make a wise crack about my encounter with Officer Clark on Sunday.

I kept my mouth shut.

Some questions are better left unasked.

Sixteen

*When you are walking, do not throw your arms
and legs about carelessly, but keep your elbows
well in, or you might knock a ghost over.*

—Arnaud Gélis, 14th-century *armarié* or "messenger of
souls" quoted by Robert Moss, *The Dreamer's
Book of the Dead*

AFTER THE QUICKEST OF GOODBYES TO SEATTLE'S FINEST
and a "see you tonight" to Laurel, I zipped out of the deli and
through the lobby of the office tower. No sign of Smoking Man.
Relieved from duty while Special Agent Greer had Laurel in her
sights?

I glanced at my pink Kate Spade watch. *Holy cardamom.*

This part of downtown slopes steeply to the waterfront, and
the larger buildings have entrances at two levels. I rode a trio of
escalators down to Third Avenue and stepped outside. The skies
were gray, the air cool, but no rain. For the moment, anyway.

My head was spinning. The walk would do me good.

If the cops were taking a closer look at everyone connected to
Pat's death, viewing them in a new light after Maddie's shooting, I
had no doubt that included Bruce Ellingson and everyone connected
to the investigation about his firm.

What a tangle. Pat had helped investigate Ellingson, who had
not been charged or sent to prison, but had apparently lost his

business and his professional license. I'd heard enough talk among the lawyers I'd worked with to know that risk struck terror in their hearts. Losing the license meant losing the career they'd trained for, worked for, sacrificed so much for. And with that came a loss of income, reputation, and identity. If you weren't a lawyer anymore, who were you?

No wonder Ellingson continued to call himself a broker.

A twenty-something sped past me on one of those battery-powered skateboards with the fat single wheel in the middle, a white Chihuahua poking out of his backpack. Ah, Seattle. Still quirky after all these years.

Both the Ellingsons had reason to blame Patrick Halloran for their misfortunes. But resentment was one thing, murder another.

Was I judging people unfairly? Making the easy assumptions? There were oodles of instances of unlikely criminals, the killer next door, right here in Seattle. Ted Bundy, the handsome UDub law student with his suits and neatly trimmed hair. The factory worker and religious zealot who turned out to be the Green River Killer.

But Bruce Ellingson?

I knew nothing about Joe Huang, but he and his cronies—it was a fun word—might be the better suspects. Though I could see no link to Maddie.

If I remembered the news coverage of Pat's murder correctly, he was the first Assistant U.S. Attorney believed to have been murdered as a result of his professional activities. Obviously, then, AUSAs were not common targets. But investigators thought at least two of Pat's cases could be linked to his murder. So much for the idea that so-called white-collar crime—financial crimes and fraud cases—isn't violent. Crime gets its hands dirty, no matter what color shirt it wears.

And I thought again of the nature of coincidence. Ellingson next door. Huang's comings and goings.

I tightened my grip on the bag looped over my shoulder, hunching as I picked up the pace. As if that would make me less visible, less vulnerable.

Going after Pat Halloran would not have stopped an investigation—dozens more prosecutors could pick up the case. If they thought one of their own had been targeted to stop them from doing their job, they'd double down.

Organized crime is a fact of life worldwide. Not surprising that it might rear its ugly head in the import–export business.

But clearly Joe Huang's employer had not unleashed a crime wave against American law enforcement. If the crime was personal, then the Ellingsons were good candidates.

At First and Pike, I crossed the all-way intersection, as the woman in the photo had done. I waved at the florist on the corner. Just past Left Bank Books, I took a hard right down one of the Market's many corridors, hoping the back door of the Asian grocery would be open. It wasn't. I slowed in front of the creamery, contemplating a snack. Not that I was hungry; it was a habit. I'd reached the cheese shop with its tempting display cases when I heard a door and turned. The old lady edged into view, propping open the door of the Asian grocery with one shoulder. She wore a print blouse and black pants, and the black cotton shoes with white bottoms that I'd seen on display out front. She spoke in Chinese to someone I couldn't see. Then a girl emerged, maybe four or five, in a purple jacket. The woman let the door clang shut and grabbed the child's hand, tugging her down the hall past me.

It's not unusual to see children in the Market, shopping with their families or taking in the sights. The Market runs a preschool, and I love seeing the line of little ones, holding hands, as their teachers take them on a walk or a field trip. Was this girl the old woman's granddaughter? Was she the child in the photo Agent Greer had given me? And where were they going?

All questions that would have to wait. I made a left past the cheese shop, waved to Misty at Three Girls, and came out on Pike Place. Moments later, I reached my shop. Stashed my tote and grabbed the dog leash. My staff are perfectly willing to tend to Arf when I'm away, but it isn't fair to leave him alone with them too long or too often.

"Good boy, good boy."

On our stroll toward the park, I wondered about Joe Huang and what he might have done. Whether Agent Greer and her partner would return to the Market, watching for him.

A few drops of rain hit my face. In my haste, I'd skipped the dog's raincoat. "Short trip, buddy. I'll make it up to you, promise." As soon as he finished his business, we turned around. Back in the shop, Arf trotted to his cushion. I tied my apron strings and returned to the shop floor in time to hear Matt ask a customer how he could help her.

"Oh, I don't cook," she said.

I paused, wondering how he would handle her response. It was not an uncommon one.

He smiled. Though one arm is covered in tattoos, he has a sweet, boy-next-door smile. "You eat, don't you? We've got some terrific herbed salts. Here—try one." He plucked a tester jar of our lavender-bay salt from a display, twisted off the lid, and handed it to her.

She eyed him warily, as if unsure what to do with it.

"Give it a sniff," he said. "Tell me what you notice. Then sprinkle a few grains in your palm and give it a taste."

I spotted a tea spill on the floor and stepped behind the counter for a rag.

"He's so good," Cayenne said. "People say stupid stuff like that, I want to ask why they bothered to come in. I know, they're with a friend. Or they wanted to get out of the rain."

"But you're learning," I said. My two new hires were teaching each other. Matt didn't cook much when he started. I wasn't sure he cooked much now, though he had talked about watching the famous Jacques Pépin video after hearing Cayenne discuss it with a customer, and teaching himself to make an omelet. "Sometimes, customers say the first thing that pops into their heads, to avoid being pressured into buying something. Laugh it off. Say 'I'll let you browse.' Or offer them tea."

"And sometimes they're poopheads," Sandra said.

Matt's customer may have started as a poophead, but she ended up buying several jars of herbed salt, our best-selling pepper blend, and our spice tea. "Getting an early start on my Christmas shopping," she said.

"If I shopped that early, I wouldn't remember what I bought for who," Sandra said as she took the woman's credit card. "Or where I stashed it in the house."

At three thirty, the front door opened and a young man entered. A few feet in, he stopped, scanning the shop.

I'd completely forgotten that Misty's deliveryman was coming in to interview. What was his name? Cory? No, Cody.

"Cody," I said, holding out my hand. "Good to see you. Been in before?"

He hadn't, though it turned out that he'd met both Matt and Sandra at the bakery. He'd swapped his white T-shirt for a white polo, and added a belt to the green cargo pants. I gave him the nickel tour—the place is so small that that's all it takes. "You'll be working closely with me and Matt. Let's have a chat." I poured us each a cup of spice tea and we sat in the nook.

"This is great," he said. "The shop, I mean. The tea, too." He'd pushed the cup away and now drew it closer.

"The spices are pretty strong," I said. "You don't have to like the tea to work here."

That brought a shaky smile. I hoped conversations with strangers didn't always make him so nervous.

"Misty said you needed a few extra hours," I said.

"I'm working at the bakery from six to ten most days. Then I grab whatever odd jobs I can—help people move, clean out their basements, dig gardens."

Not uncommon for young men, especially a Gen Z-er like Cody. "Are you in school?"

"No. I went to Seattle U for two years." He paused and I kept my tongue. Most people will keep talking, if you let them, and that's when they tell you what you really want to know. It didn't take Cody long, staring at the table as the words spilled out. "I—I played soccer in high school and my parents wanted me to get a scholarship, but I wasn't good enough. Freshman year, I walked on, but didn't make the team. We scraped together enough for sophomore year, but I decided not to go back. I—I don't know what I want to do, and my parents were all stressed and yelling at me and each other. I just—I just want to earn enough to move out. I'll go back to school eventually. I know it's important. But not right now."

He was almost breathless, slowly raising his gaze to mine.

"I can't promise you more than a few hours a day, but it may work into something more." Reed would graduate in the spring, and I didn't know how long Kristen would stay. If we did expand the commercial facility, I'd need at least two employees there.

"It's a start," he said. "Misty says you're great, and she'll give me a good reference."

"She already did." We talked hours, pay, and a start date. "I've got a few forms for you to fill out. It's a formality—you're hired—but I need them for the personnel file."

He relaxed visibly. I slid him the forms and he scribbled while I got back to work. A few minutes later, he handed me the paperwork, then chatted briefly with Matt before leaving. I retreated to my office and began setting up a personnel file.

I stared at the neatly printed name and address. Surely he'd said his full name when he came in. Had I not been listening?

Poor kid. Maybe it was a sign from the Universe, as my mother would say. Maybe I could help Cody Ellingson at the same time as I helped myself.

The shop buzzed the rest of the afternoon. When we closed, the computer balked at running the day's sales. By the time I got the glitch resolved, I was running late. Arf and I sprinted down the Market steps to Western and up to the loft just long enough to grab the carrot soup, then down to the garage for the car. I was happy to see that the front door to the building was firmly latched.

As the dog and I drove to Kristen's Capitol Hill home—the house where my family lived until I was twelve—I wondered how to broach the topic of the Ellingsons with Laurel. We would all talk about the investigation, of course, but annoyed as I was that she'd withheld info from me, I didn't want to confront her in front of our friends. More important to focus on friendship. And I hoped Kristen could give us a good update on Maddie.

Not only was I realizing that Laurel wasn't the open book she always claimed to be, but I was starting to think that Maddie Petrosian, the girl who turned everything she touched into gold, might be a little bit tarnished.

And that murder and friendship might not be the best combination.

Seventeen

The whole of life is just like watching a film. Only it's as though you always get in ten minutes after the big picture has started, and no one will tell you the plot, so you have to work it all out yourself from the clues.

—Terry Pratchett, *Moving Pictures*

ERIC AND MARIAH, THE YOUNGER OF THE TWO GIRLS, WERE walking down the front steps of the stately gray home when Arf and I arrived. Flick Chicks at their house meant a night out with dad.

"Arf!" Mariah cried. She sank to her knees and threw her arms around my boy, who returned her affection by licking her face. "That tickles."

"Hey, Eric." I set the box with my soup pot and containers on the bottom step and we exchanged a quick hug. "Where's Savannah?"

"We decided she could start wearing blush and mascara, so leaving the house takes an extra ten minutes while she triple-checks the mirror."

"Got time for a quick question?" He nodded, and I filled him in on Edgar's complaint about the stolen spice blend. "I told him I didn't think he had a claim for copyright violation, but what about theft? If the facts add up."

"If this other chef simply figured out what was in Edgar's

blend, then he's out of luck," Eric said. "But Edgar isn't publishing the recipe, like when you post recipes on your blog or hand out copies in the store. If the other guy actually got ahold of Edgar's recipe without permission and is using it, then yes, Edgar might have a claim for theft. Hard to show value, though."

"Oh, Edgar will claim plenty of value, you can count on that. But thanks." No sign of Savannah yet, and Mariah was happily distracted by the dog. "Another question. This might sound like blasphemy. Laurel adored Pat, everyone admired him, but I never knew him. Were there rumors? Could he have been involved in something—illicit?" Like what, I didn't know, but ever since the confab in Laurel's back room, I'd been wondering.

"Pat?" Eric shook his head. "No. No, he really was the guy in the white hat. He didn't have any secrets."

That couldn't be true. We all have secrets. The only question is what we'll do to keep them.

The front door flew open and Savannah flew out. She was the image of Kristen at that age. She hugged me and headed for the car while Eric sent Mariah to wash her hands. I took my soup and my dog inside.

"Pepper, good news!" Kristen said. "Maddie's awake. The swelling in her brain has gone way down. Tim says you can see her tomorrow if you have time."

"Oh, thank God," I said, and I meant it. I may have inherited my mother's distrust of the institutional church, but God and I are fine. "I'll make time."

Within a few minutes, we'd all arrived and unpacked our soup kettles and Crock-Pots. Wine and conversation flowed.

"What kind of Seattleites are we?" Kristen asked as she surveyed the bounty on her stove and kitchen island. "All this soup and no clam chowder."

"Who has time to make it?" I said. "And why bother when you can swing by Ivar's or the chowder shop in the Market?"

One rule for soup exchanges is no takeout, Laurel excepted, since she's in the takeout business. And the homemade rule doesn't apply to the dishes the hostess provides, thank goodness. Kristen had sliced up a rustic loaf of bread from Three Girls and scored a dozen truffles from our favorite chocolatier. Add salad for the perfect meal.

"I smell peppers and bay. That Tony's black bean chili, Aimee?" I asked. Our newest addition, Aimee McGillvray, had joined us in August, not long after I'd helped solve a murder in her vintage retail and design shop, the place where I'd found the *tansu* and neon lips. She'd just taken a sip of wine, and wiggled her eyebrows in a "yes." Her brother, who shared her apartment, was the family cook.

"Soup conjures up home," Seetha Sharma said. Laurel had invited the massage therapist to Flick Chicks a year ago, shortly after she moved to Seattle. Though she's over thirty, she avoided learning to cook until this past summer, after resolving tensions with her Indian-born mother. The results were improving. "I always thought I hated Indian food, but it turns out I kinda like it."

"You were probably just trying to differentiate yourself from your parents," Laurel said. She gave her tomato-basil soup a stir. "Like when I was in my vegetarian phase, before I opened the restaurant, and thought that was the only healthy food. Gabe rebelled by demanding McDonalds."

"I bet he wanted the toys," Kristen said.

"Is this your mother's recipe?" I asked as Seetha ladled out small bowls of lentil, potato, and cauliflower curry, rich with spices, and we all snickered. My quest last summer for Seetha's mother's chai recipe had nearly led to disaster, but it had also prompted some great taste-testing. Seetha didn't know the full story, a secret Sandra and I had vowed to keep to ourselves.

After dinner, we migrated to the elegant home theater in the basement, a product of the recent remodel. The wine and truffles came with us. Tonight's offering was *Tampopo*, the Japanese classic that spoofs both Westerns and Samurai movies.

"Why do they call it a noodle western?" Seetha asked as we settled into the comfy chairs.

"You'll know in about two minutes," Kristen said. She picked up the remote and off we went, to the land of truck drivers who wear cowboy hats and single mothers who run noodle parlors. The effort of reading subtitles muted the possibility of conversation, until Kristen hit pause for a potty break.

I refilled wine glasses. "I'm convinced the building is the link between Maddie's shooting and Pat's. But why now? The redevelopment's been under consideration for years. Why try to stop it by stopping her now?"

No one had an answer.

"Why do you suppose," I continued, still on my feet, "the project changed so dramatically? Part of it seems to have been the neighbors—they wanted that wreck on the corner gone, but they wanted the right replacement."

"It isn't unusual for commercial projects to take a long time," Aimee said. "Or change along the way. When I was doing interior design, the final plans rarely looked anything like the initial concept."

"Like your loft," Kristen said. "How many times did we rework the kitchen plans? You were living in my guest room and we laid it out on the floor right here, with colored tape and cardboard."

"And it turned out perfectly, thanks to you," I said. "But who is this Byrd guy who upset everybody? I Googled my eyes out and I couldn't find him. Were he and Maddie partners?"

"Doubt it," Kristen said. "She likes to run the show."

"So she bought up the other buildings, then I guess she bought him out." I'd been too tired last night to try to remember what Glenn had showed me, about looking up purchases and sales. I hadn't thought it mattered. But I was getting more and more curious.

Nobody had any answers. Kristen dimmed the lights and we went back to the movie. Arf lay at my feet. Gun, the trucker determined to rescue the noodle parlor, was taking Tampopo, the owner, to visit other shops. They tasted and compared notes. A master noodle maker came in to teach her. A construction crew arrived to rebuild the kitchen, and a designer to give her shop a new look.

I bit into a ginger truffle and thought about Carl's explanation of how bonds work. How much had financing influenced Maddie's plans? Who would know? Tim had an MBA, too, but he always made it a point of pride to say that Petrosian Properties was Maddie's baby, not his.

But even Maddie wasn't made of money. What if she'd brought in Byrd as a partner to help foot the bill, but then when they couldn't agree, she worked out another plan? She bought up the other buildings in the block, and then what? I'd seen the sales price for the insurance agency's building and it had been substantial though not outrageous, but that was just one building. Borrowing the bond analogy, I wondered if she'd used the buildings and their future income as collateral for a loan, not just to pay for the property, but to buy out the partner, or whatever he was.

Was it underhanded or good business?

I kept coming back to why. If we were talking about other people—faceless, anonymous developers—making money or doing deals might be motive enough. But not Maddie. According to the stylist, she'd promised to update the buildings without raising rents. Just talk—puffing—to mollify the tenants? Stories like that run rampant, new landlords making promises they broke as soon as the ink on the deal was dry.

"Do you remember when Maddie started coming to the meetings about the corner grocery?" I whispered to Laurel.

"No."

"Was she part of Neighbors United?"

"No."

"Quiet," Kristen said. "We're watching a movie here."

The permit files would name the key players, wouldn't they? But I couldn't waste a day digging in city archives and poring over dusty drawings and applications.

I decided to go to the public meeting tomorrow night. Its purpose was to update the community on the criminal investigation and answer questions. Surely people who'd worked with Pat on neighborhood issues would be there. But I didn't live in Montlake. I'd be less like the proverbial sore thumb if Laurel went with me.

After that, I'd ask her about the Ellingsons.

Then, I promised myself, I'd tell Tracy and Greer everything I was thinking. Let them look into this mysterious partner, financing, and other details that took time and computer databases I didn't have.

While I focused on my friends.

IN THE loft, I stashed the soup containers in the freezer and changed my shoes. I was still dressed for work, but no matter. Arf and I headed out to stretch our legs. Clear skies for the first time in days. An orange glow touched the tops of the Olympics, and the air smelled clean.

Some friends and relatives think I'm crazy to walk alone at night downtown. But I wasn't scared, and not just because of the fifty-pound dog beside me. Although he does have good guard dog skills.

If you project a sense of belonging—this was a trick I'd learned from Tag—a sense that this is your turf, people generally leave you alone.

It was easy. Grace House had been a terrific place to be a kid, and our family's Montlake cottage the perfect next step. When Tag and I got married, we bought his great-aunt's run-down bungalow in Greenwood and we'd worked hard to make it into a sweet home.

But living downtown felt right. Too soon to tell what all the changes in the city and in my life would mean. Whether downtown would still feel like home in five years.

As we walked, Arf pausing every so often to sniff something, I ran through the possible links between the two shootings. The same gun, but one shooter or two? The burglary gone wrong theory Detective Armstrong mentioned was one I'd leave to them. Again, they had the manpower. Or person power. The joint task force had kept busy over the years, checking every burglary suspect for a connection to Pat, but found nothing.

No, the link between the victims had to be the building. But what, and why?

Why had Pat, a committed soccer dad, changed his mind and stayed home from Gabe's tournament?

And why was Special Agent Meg Greer following me?

Eighteen

*Two roads diverged in a wood, and I—I took the
one less traveled by. And now I'm lost.*

—T-shirt slogan, after Robert Frost

I STOPPED.

She didn't.

"Pepper. Hello."

I tightened my grip on Arf's leash. She made no move to pet
him, which seemed strange, but he gave none of the usual signals
that something was amiss. "Are you following me, Agent Greer?"

"Actually, I'm not," she replied. "I live up on Elliott. I decided
to take a walk and ran into you."

Elliott Avenue a few blocks north of the Market had become a
haven of urban housing, home to apartment complexes that took
up half a city block or more. I'd been in a couple of the apartments—very modern, very small.

Did I believe her?

Did it matter?

"Why would you think I was following you?" Greer asked.

I gave her a long look. "You better come up."

"Well, don't you have a spectacular view?" she said a few
minutes later, gravitating toward the windows, as first-time visitors always do. "My place overlooks the swimming pool no one
uses."

In the kitchen, I started tea and chai *masala* brewing in the French press. It's an easy shortcut, not as flavorful as brewing the tea and spices in a sauce pan with the milk, but I didn't feel like going all out for Special Agent Meg Greer. I didn't believe for one minute that she just happened to walk by my building, and I wanted answers.

I joined her at the windows and pointed at the lights glowing across the water. "That's Alki, the northern tip of West Seattle. Beyond is Bainbridge Island."

"It all looks so different at night. Love the way the lights shimmer on the water."

Since the viaduct had come down, I'd begun noticing all kinds of lights and shadows that had always been there, even if I'd never seen them.

"Just so you know," she said, her tone a shade darker than girlfriend-confidential. "I am armed." She slipped off her jacket, exposing a small black gun in a small black holster on her hip. Like the other night at the houseboat, she wore black jeans and a turtleneck, and black boots.

"I assumed as much. It doesn't bother me. I was married to a cop."

"So I hear."

It's always disconcerting to discover that other people know more about you than you know about them. Especially when the other person is a cop.

The chai was ready. I set two steamy, fragrant mugs on the dining room table, and we sat.

"If you're keeping an eye on me," I said, "you know I spent the evening with Laurel and other friends at Kristen's house. Is your partner following Laurel? Or is he at the hospital, guarding Maddie?"

She frowned. "We aren't following you. And we aren't guarding Ms. Petrosian."

I wasn't convinced, on either count. "Tell me, how did a nice girl like you end up in a job like this?"

One side of her mouth curled. "The FBI, you mean? I heard a recruiter speak in high school and I was hooked. My parents were baffled—he was an accountant, and she taught kindergarten."

"So did my mother," I said. She nodded ever so slightly and I realized she already knew. Had she had a nice sit-down with Tag, or run me through the databases? I could feel the heat rising in my chest and hoped it didn't show on my face.

"You an accountant, too? Or a lawyer? I gather most FBI agents have some kind of professional training."

"It can be helpful," she said. "Particularly in this case."

"Because Pat Halloran pursued fraud and financial crime. And because of this Joe Huang investigation none of you wants to tell me anything about."

"It's better that you don't know." She picked up her mug. "For your own safety."

"Right. You're all happy to ask me to help you find him, but tell me why? Oh, no, you couldn't possibly. You might endanger an innocent civilian."

"We're not in the tit-for-tat business, Pepper."

"Everybody is," I said. "Whether we want to admit it or not." I wasn't sure I believed that, not a hundred per cent, but law enforcement types are in the information business. The gathering, not the sharing.

Greer gave me a long, hard stare, then set her cup on the table. Expression grave, eyes somber, she picked up her coat and left without another word.

At the sound of the loft door closing, Arf raised his head.

"What? Was it something I said?"

I didn't hear the front door to the building shut, so I went down to check it. Locked.

Back upstairs, I dumped the chai in the sink and poured myself a glass of Sangiovese. The blood of St. Joseph. It fit. My blood was boiling.

IN THE law firm, I'd helped manage more than two hundred staffers—secretaries and receptionists, paralegals and billing clerks. Running a firm that size had taken a team and I'd loved it.

But not half as much, it turned out, as I love working with five people who work hard, laugh often, and report directly to me. Seeing them—Sandra, Reed, Kristen, Matt, and Cayenne—snugged into the nook sipping and nibbling made me smile. If Cody liked baked goods half as much as the rest of us did, he'd fit right in.

The Wednesday morning staff meeting is a chance to chat up new products, puzzle over problems, and stay connected. That's why I bring treats. Sharing good food encourages collaboration. Plus it sets a tasty tone for the day.

We went over the events scheduled for the next few weeks, including the anniversary celebration. The samples we'd offered the food tour—Favorites from the Spice Shop Collection—had been a hit, so I suggested we do a repeat.

"But not the Baked Paprika Cheese," Sandra said. "When people have to spread things themselves, the line slows and the table gets messy."

"The floor, too," Matt said.

"Good point." We debated alternatives, and chose three to price. Kristen had the decorating plans in hand, and Reed had been busy promoting the event on social media.

Then we discussed the mystery of Edgar and the stolen spice. Everyone was aghast, but no one had an explanation. I revealed the new labels Fabiola, our graphic designer, had created for our winter blends. We'd be shipping packages to our Spice Club members in a few weeks.

Earlier, Cayenne had asked me if she could have a few minutes at the meeting, but before I turned things over to her, I had one more item on my list. I passed around Greer's photographs.

"Have you seen either the man or the woman?"

Matt squinted at the photo of the woman and child in the rain. "I see rain. You can barely tell there are people in this picture."

I asked them to keep their eyes open and keep their distance. "If you think you see one of them, let me know right away. And if I'm not around, tell Officer Buhner."

That widened all eyes. They all knew my tug-of-war with Tag.

"Thanks. Now, Cayenne has something she'd like to share."

All eyes turned to Cayenne, who was much loved despite her occasional impatience and smart-aleck remarks. Or because of them.

"You all know I've needed extra time off lately, and that I haven't exactly been myself. Pepper's known the reason for a while now, but it's time to tell the rest of you." She paused. "I'm guessing from the whispers and the looks some of you have been giving me that you think I'm pregnant. I'm not. I have MS. Multiple sclerosis."

Sandra gasped. Kristen pressed her hands into prayer position, fingers on her lips. Even Matt, usually so calm, looked shocked. "I can still do almost everything. But no ladders, and no heavy boxes." She gave me an apologetic smile, no doubt recalling the day a box slipped out of her hands. I'd caught it and wrenched my shoulder.

"We may need to juggle the schedule to accommodate Cayenne's medical appointments or if she has a flare-up," I said. Employee scheduling can be a huge headache. Working HR, I'd found that the more predictable the schedule, the more reliable the employee, particularly those juggling other jobs or child care. But the Spice Shop staff had always been flexible.

"We'll help out every way we can," Kristen said. "You know that."

"Oh, sweetheart." Sandra reached for Cayenne and they embraced, both visibly struggling not to burst into tears. So was I.

"I'm not noble," Cayenne said, her jaw tight, her voice quivering. "I'm not brave. I don't want you to feel sorry for me. I don't want to hear stories about other people with MS. And I don't want your medical advice." She turned to Reed. "Except for you. Last summer, when I started falling and thought my knee was messed up, you said I should see your dad for acupuncture. Your dad." She stopped. No one else spoke. "Your dad knew what it was right away and got me in to see a great neurologist, without scaring me. I will never forget that."

She kissed Reed's cheek, and he blushed.

I exhaled, then glanced up at the clock. "Time to get spicy," I said, and wiped the back of my hand across my eyes.

The mood was subdued as each employee started the morning tasks. Reed slipped out the side door, heading to class.

I stood by the nook as Matt wrestled with the samovar and Sandra straightened a display. Rolled my shoulders and arched my back.

"Told you not to skip yoga last week," Kristen said. "The more you miss, the harder it is to go back."

I stuck out my tongue.

"You knew," she said, her gaze on Cayenne, who was behind the counter, measuring tea for Matt, "and you didn't tell me. You let us think she was pregnant."

"I never said that. I just didn't correct you when you guessed. And you weren't the only one—Matt and Sandra thought the same thing. But it wasn't my secret to share."

She grunted. That reminded me of my grunting friend, Detective Tracy. Surely he'd be at the public meeting tonight. With real news, I hoped. I'd bought a newspaper on my way in and flipped through it quickly before stashing it in my office. The annual update on Pat's murder was on the front page. I'd skimmed it, noting official statements from the police chief and the Agent-in-Charge of the local FBI office. Both said they had nothing to share with the public "at this time," but that there had been developments and the investigation was ongoing. I read that as a reference to Maddie's shooting, which the article did not mention.

"Is the owner in?" I heard a customer ask when I returned to the shop floor. "She's always been so helpful."

"Here she is," Cayenne said, gesturing.

I didn't know the woman, so I introduced myself. "Pepper Reece, Mistress of Spice."

"I was remembering a shorter, older woman with white hair." She ran her fingers across her temples, evoking the coronet of braids the former owner always wore.

"Ah, Jane Rasmussen. She sold me the shop two years ago this month and retired to the San Juans."

"Well, that tells you how long it's been since I've stopped in."

"You only come to the Market when I come to town," her companion said. She said it "mah-ket," her New England accent strong.

"Then, may I suggest that your spice cabinet might need a refresh?" They laughed and agreed, and we got to work filling their shopping baskets.

Nineteen

*Pottery shards found in northern Germany estab-
lish that hunter-gatherers six thousand years ago
spiced their food with crushed garlic mustard
seeds they foraged, giving roasted fish and
venison a peppery flavor, in what researchers call
the earliest known use of spice.*

"WE'RE FIRST-TIMERS," SANDRA TOLD THE SERVER WHEN WE
were seated and had ordered iced tea. "What do you do better
than any other kitchen?"

"Oh, easy," he replied. He wore black, like all the front-of-
house staff, including a knee-length black apron, and a man bun.
I'd thought—hoped—man buns had gone out of style. "Crab
cakes. The chef makes his own spice blend. There's nothing else
like it."

We'd see about that.

"They're served with our house slaw—red cabbage with green
beans, white beans, and cherry tomatoes—and toasted Seattle
sourdough. A little retro and a lot of fun."

"Sold," I said. "In fact, that spice blend sounds intriguing. Is it
in any other dishes?"

The server pointed to two other items and we ordered one of
each to share. Fingers crossed that we weren't being too obvious.

The place was about half full, decent for midweek. The three tables nearest us were taken by pairs of women. A spot for ladies who lunch. Like us.

Sandra leaned forward, her red-and-white zebra striped glasses low on her nose. "Love being a spice spy," she whispered.

The atmosphere was hip, but like the slaw, slightly retro. Not self-consciously so, like those places where you're sure the designer spent days hopping from one thrift shop to another and was determined to cram in every 1950s cast-off she'd found. Instrumental versions of American standards and tunes from the 1960s played. Leather chairs sat at square wooden tables. The flatware had a decent heft. Okay, canning jars as water glasses are a trend better left to picnics and sandwich joints, but I quibble.

"Nice menu," Sandra said. "Modern American with a Northwest accent. Not too precious."

"Meaning they aren't sprinkling hazelnuts and wild hop berries on everything?"

"Exactly." She reached for her water. The twist of her lips said she shared my opinion of the canning jars. "Will Cayenne really be able to keep working? I'm not sure I know how to work with a disabled employee."

"Don't think of her that way. She's still Cayenne, but there's some things she can't do." The server delivered our iced tea and I took a sip. Nicely flavored, with a hint of lemon grass. "Like you can't figure out Instagram."

"Ha, ha."

We talked about the shop and the changes we'd made in the last two years. We talked about Matt's revelation about his parents, which had been news to her, too, and how to be compassionate without being overbearing. We talked about Maddie and the shooting, and how hard it is to know what to do when a friend is in pain, physical or otherwise. Then our plates came.

And they were beautiful.

"Hmm," she said of the crab cakes. "Good uniformity and color—nice browning. Maybe a little scant on the crab meat. But you can't judge the insides by the outsides."

Her tone told me she was talking about more than fish.

I cut a bite and dipped it in the sauce. "Nice." I followed with a fork full of slaw. "Sturdy. The flavors don't compete with the crab cakes, but they don't stand out, either. Wouldn't be hard to spark it up, though. Use a citrus champagne vinegar instead of the basic white wine vinaigrette."

She moved on to the next dish and gave a similar assessment.

"What do you think about the spice blend?" I kept my voice low.

"If it's not the same as Edgar's, it's close." She gestured to the dishes on the table. "All of it is close, but not quite."

"I give the place six months."

"You're too optimistic."

I didn't notice our server approach until he spoke. "How are the crab cakes?"

"Very nice," Sandra replied. "Tell us about the spices. Sweet paprika, marjoram, and . . ."

I recognized her technique. Laurel uses it, too. Show that you've detected some of the flavors and a knowledgeable server will fill in the rest. Alas, our server either didn't know or had been trained not to play along.

"The chef's special blend," he said. "That's all I know."

"Special it is," I replied. He bowed slightly and left.

"The hard part," I said, "will be talking to Edgar."

"That," Sandra said, "is why you are the boss and I a mere servant."

On my way back from the restroom, I passed the kitchen, partially open for show. I paused to watch the blades and flames. Was that Tariq?

As if he felt me staring at him or heard me saying his name to myself, the slender young man raised his head. Recognition struck, but he quickly closed it off and returned to his work.

Was Tariq Rose the answer to our questions? Was he the problem? How could I find out?

Back at the table, I paid the bill—in cash, so I didn't give myself away—and ignored the "what's up, boss?" look on Sandra's face. Normally, I leave my business card. Unlike food critics, I *want* chefs to know I've been there. I want to introduce myself and open the door for future spice talk.

Not this time.

"Thanks—lunch was great!" I called out as we passed the kitchen. "My compliments to the cooks!"

Outside, Sandra headed for the car. "Give me two minutes," I said, then circled around the side of the building. The parallel did not escape me—I had often chatted with Edgar in the alley outside Alex Howard's First Avenue Café, and here I was in another back alley, hoping to catch a word with one of Edgar's old coworkers.

The alley was empty. Had Tariq not caught my signal? Had he not been able to sneak away?

Then the gray steel door opened and Tariq stepped out, unsnapping the collar of his coat. His white cotton T-shirt contrasted starkly with his dark skin.

"Posh," he called, using Alex Howard's nickname for me, Posh Spice. "What are you doing here? Scouting? Want me to introduce you to Chef?"

"No, no, that's fine. We were in the mood for crab cakes and heard they were good here."

"You like 'em?"

"Very nice," I said.

His narrow face broke into a grin. "I made those."

"Good job. Have you eaten Edgar's crab cakes? At Speziato. Similar spicing."

The grin disappeared, the brows furrowed. Tariq's reputation as a hothead, along with some unfortunate timing, had made him a target of suspicion in a murder last winter. I'd never been sure, though, whether he was a genuine firebrand or put on a show of bad temper in imitation of Alex, his one-time boss, who was admirable in the kitchen and other small spaces, but not a model of decorum.

I explained. "You can see why Edgar and I are worried. No one else has access to that recipe."

"You don't think I stole it? How could I?" He threw up his hands, his voice rising. "Why is everybody so quick to point the finger at me?"

"No one's accusing you of anything, Tariq. I know you haven't been in Edgar's kitchen. I'm just hoping you can help me." If he knew I'd briefly suspected him of murder, I hoped he also knew that I'd helped clear him. "Who knows, Edgar might need another cook as good as you some day."

"You trying to bribe me into spying for you?"

"No. Just asking you to keep your eyes and ears open." I reached in my tote for my card case. "If you see any reason to think somebody here might have acted inappropriately—"

"If somebody here is a thief?"

"—then call me. Edgar and I will both be grateful."

He gave me a long look, as though trying to decide whether to trust me. I held out a card. He took it.

Then we both got back to other things.

KRISTEN texted that I was cleared for a visit, so I dropped Sandra off at the bus stop on Madison. Midday, midweek, no point searching for a spot on the street. I pulled into the hospital's parking garage. I turned off the engine and sat a moment.

You can't barge into the hospital room of someone you see a few times a year without a plan. Even if you do have a free pass to get you by the dragons at the gate.

But I did genuinely care about Maddie. The distance between us the last couple of years wasn't her fault; it was mine. Nothing had happened. It was just part of life.

Except that, in a way, something had happened.

The night of their housewarming party, I'd overheard Maddie and another old classmate talking about a large contribution Maddie had just made to the foundation the other woman ran.

"We couldn't do this without your financial assistance," our mutual friend had said.

"I'd rather be doing the work," Maddie had replied. "Helping kids and families directly. Maybe working on affordable housing or to strengthen communities. Not just giving money."

"What's stopping you?"

"Oh, that ship sailed a long time ago. Back in college." Then they'd come around the corner, and run smack into me. Maddie had been so shocked she'd dropped her lipstick and the tube had rolled down the stairs as the three of us watched, oddly mesmerized.

That ship had sailed because of me. I'd taken the opportunity Maddie had desperately wanted, and I'd wasted it. Part of me knew that was old news—we'd been in college then—but part of me still felt like a schmuck.

This wasn't the time to bring up old tensions. That wouldn't help her, and it wouldn't help Laurel.

And it sure as heck wouldn't help me.

Tell the truth. Even if Maddie wasn't fully communicative

yet, Tim might be able to fill in a few blanks. I'd be up front, tell them straight off the bat that I was asking questions to help both Maddie and Laurel. That's what Cadfael would do. And take a gift, as Perveen Mistry had in the latest Massey mystery. Gifts open doors. Of course, the gift Perveen took the dowager maharani had created complications of its own. I rummaged in the box of books in my trunk, mysteries I'd packed up to take to Flick Chicks last night then forgotten. Maddie wouldn't be up for reading yet, not after a shot to the head, so a book might be pointless. But it was a gift of hope, wasn't it, a sign that I believed she would recover.

And I did. Anybody else, I might have my doubts. But I never doubted Maddie Petrosian.

This called for something absorbing, but not demanding. *In Farleigh Field* by Rhys Bowen went into my tote. A World War II mystery, though not bloody or violent. For the lighter touch, I added the latest Dandy Gilver by Catriona McPherson. I might not know how to pronounce the woman's name, but I sure liked the books.

The elevator door opened and I took a deep breath, then headed for the ominous double doors of the ICU. The same burly guard sat at the desk—Ramon, if I remembered right. And beside him stood Officer Kimberly Clark.

Don't call her Lovely Rita, I told myself. Don't whistle the tune. Remember you're on a mission.

Another round of calming breaths. "I'm here to see Madeleine Petrosian," I said, ignoring the uniformed officer and her gun.

"Name?"

One of the doors opened just as I opened my mouth, and Tim Peterson stepped halfway out.

"Pepper, you're here," he said. "Friend of the family," he told Ramon.

I couldn't help glancing at Officer Clark. Pepper is an unusual name, though not as unusual as my legal name. I felt her eyes following me until the door closed.

"How is she?" The hospital smells hit me.

"She's back," he said, relief mingled with exhaustion. "Groggy. Not completely with it. Long road ahead, but for the first time since it happened, I finally feel like I can breathe again."

I'd always found Tim to be one of those innately calm people, much like my Nate. A good counterpoint to Maddie's intensity. Maybe she and I were more alike than I realized.

"The kids got to see her yesterday. Her mom's home now and she brought them in after school. Such a relief." He led the way past several rooms, each with a plate glass window and an open door, so staff could keep an eye on their charges. "But this morning when the police came, she wasn't very communicative. They kept asking who shot her. I don't know whether she can't identify the person, or just can't get the words out."

"I won't stay long, I promise. I brought her a couple of books—something to look forward to. The police told you, didn't they, that Maddie was shot with the same gun that killed Pat Halloran? You met Laurel, his wife—widow—Sunday. I promised her an update."

Tim stopped outside Maddie's door. "Pepper, I know you've helped the police in the past. I'll call Maddie's office manager and tell her she can talk freely with you, show you any records you want to see, same as the police. I want the guy caught, but what I want most is for my wife to make a full recovery."

"It's what we all want, Tim."

If I'd ever seen more flowers and cards in a hospital room, I couldn't remember. One of the two chairs was occupied by a stuffed animal version of Sammy the Sounder, the soccer team's mascot. Rumor said he was an orca, but it was hard to tell.

"That's going to the pediatric floor," Tim said, nodding at Sammy. "And Maddie's already told us to give most of the flowers to patients in need."

Maddie's olive skin was pale, streaks of gray visible in the dark hair that had been shaved around a thick white bandage. I hadn't seen her without lipstick since the eighth grade. Tubes ran out of one arm and a machine hummed beside the bed. She looked so small.

"Maddie, it's Pepper." I leaned in to kiss her cheek and she raised her hand to my face.

"You came." The voice was soft, a little shaky, but undeniably Maddie.

"I came." I sat on the edge of the empty chair. "Of course I came."

"Maddie, honey." Tim stood at the foot of the bed. "I'm going down to the cafeteria to grab some lunch and let you two visit. Thanks for coming in," he said to me. He gave my shoulder a squeeze and left.

"Laurel Halloran sends you her best wishes." Would she remember who Laurel was?

Maddie wriggled back and forth until she was sitting up a little straighter. I raised my hands, not sure how to help. She leaned toward me. "Tell her—not Pat's fault."

Now why would she say that? Had she forgotten that Patrick Halloran had been dead three years this week? "Of course not."

"I went there—I only went there because . . ." Her eyelids drifted shut and her breath changed. Had she fallen asleep? Then she opened her eyes and directed her gaze at me.

"Seventh grade? Sister made us—memorize poems."

"The three of us chose Robert Frost," I said, remembering. "Yours was 'Mending Wall' and Kristen chose 'Stopping by Woods on a Snowy Evening.' Me, I had to go all obscure. 'I have been acquainted with the night. I have walked out in rain,'" I recited in a fake-dramatic voice. "You know, you're lucky you've been in here the last few days—the weather's been terrible."

Her hand scrabbled in the air, grabbing for mine. "You—you always—the other road." She stopped, her voice raspy, and with my free hand, I reached for the plastic water container on the rolling tray. She took a long sip through the flexible straw and set the container on the bed beside her, turning her intensely dark eyes back to me.

The other road. The one less traveled. That was me.

"I wish"—she paused for a deep breath. "I wish I had—your courage."

"Shhh." That was a twist, seeing my tendency to go off-road as an admirable trait. Must have been the pain meds. "You're the strong one, Maddie. You're the one who always knew what she wanted and didn't let anyone stand in her way. I'm the drifter, the one who could never figure out what to do. You will come back from this stronger than ever."

"No," she said. "You. You never—let anyone—push you. You—made your own path."

A pair of aides walked in, their rubber-soled shoes making soft squeak-and-suck sounds on the vinyl floor. "Time for the restroom," one said, a little too cheerily. She started moving the equipment aside. Maddie protested, her focus still on me.

"You're getting her up already?" I asked. "She just came out of a coma a day or two ago."

"Can't let those muscles stiffen," the aide replied. "Movement speeds healing."

Maybe so, but it still surprised me. I stood. I needed to get back to my shop.

"Stay, stay," Maddie said, bobbing her hand at me as the aides shuffled her toward the bathroom. "I know you think—but I never wanted—"

"I'll stay," I said. I'd rescued the water container from the sheets as the staff were getting Maddie up and I set it on the tray next to an old photo album, covered in black leather and trimmed in gold. "What's this?"

"Her mother brought it in this morning," the aide said over her shoulder. "To jog her memory now that she's awake. Along with all those." She nodded to a stack of albums and memory books on the nightstand.

"Good idea." I sat back in the chair, flipping pages. A black-and-white slideshow.

Then I stopped. Flipped back. I'd seen some of these photos in Frank Thomas's insurance office, including one of the long-gone redbrick grocery that had stood where Maddie planned her modern version. In this one, the building was complete. A panel truck was parked on the street, and next to it stood a man and a boy of ten or twelve, sharing nearly identical smiles. On the sidewalk, bushel baskets brimmed with produce. I pegged the picture for the early 1930s.

But what struck me was the name painted above the front door, and again on the redbrick wall of the taller building next door: "GREGORIAN and SON—GROCERS."

Twenty

When it rains, it pours.

—motto of Morton Salt, adopted in 1914, after the
company added an absorbing agent to keep its salt flowing
freely, even in wet weather

WATER, WATER EVERYWHERE AS I DASHED BACK TO THE CAR.
Inside, I blasted the vent to clear the windshield. If only clearing
my head were so easy.

Maddie Petrosian had just upended my entire view of her, and
of our friendship. What was it she'd wanted to say, about never
having wanted—what?

And why did her family album include a photo of the original
building on the redevelopment site?

Tim had not returned by the time the aides brought Maddie
back to bed. Even that simple effort had exhausted her, and she'd
said nothing more than "I love you, Pepper."

I'd kissed her cheek, told her I loved her, too, and left. Ramon
the security guard hunched over his duty post as I walked out.
Officer Clark was not in sight.

Now I let out a deep sigh and put the car in gear. Traffic was no
worse than usual, thank goodness. I parked in the Market garage
for the second time this week and dashed down Upper Post Alley,
past the Pink Door and Vinny's wine shop.

What was I going to do about Maddie, the building, and the

photo? What was I going to do about Edgar? Had I made the right call in trusting Tariq? And if I went straight from work to the Montlake community meeting, what would I do with Arf? Sometimes it feels like life is one big question. I opened the door to my shop and drank in the scents: lavender and clove, cinnamon and oregano. For the time being, at least, spice was the answer.

"THANKS for letting me leave Arf with you for a couple of hours," I told Kristen that evening.

"Are you kidding? The girls can't get enough of him," she replied. "And Maddie's kids will love him. Tell Laurel I'd be there, if I hadn't agreed to take them tonight."

The Montlake Community Center looks like an oversized version of Hansel and Gretel's house. Beyond, in an expansive urban green space, are a playground, tennis courts, and soccer fields. The rain had stopped and the last rays of sunlight lit up the marshes where they dropped into deep shadow beneath the bridge.

Laurel met me in the parking lot. After a quick hug, she surveyed the place. "All the hours I spent here watching Gabe learn to kick a soccer ball, watching him practice, waiting for him . . ."

"Have you talked to him?" I asked. "About the possible break in the case, I mean?" Although it wasn't much of a break, not yet.

"I wasn't sure what to say," Laurel said. "He told me he'd had another dream. He was running across a big field, like this one, and a shadow passed overhead. Everything got cold and he was terrified. But then it moved off and left behind a shimmery golden light."

My mother says dreams are teachers, precursors, guides, as real as waking life, and sometimes more.

"Then, he said that earlier in the day, he'd been crossing campus between classes and the Goodyear Blimp drifted by. They're using it to film overhead shots for the football game this weekend."

And sometimes dreams are jokes.

"But yes, I told him," she said, and slipped an arm through mine. "Pat would have wanted Gabe to know what's going on with the investigation, even if it's still inconclusive. Besides, it's part of growing up, to learn how to live with ambiguity and unsettled things."

Do we ever fully learn? Or is that another of the life lessons that never end?

"Next week is the anniversary. You saw the annual update in the paper," she said. "I want Gabe to be prepared, for when the link to Maddie's shooting comes out."

I nodded. Parenting seemed like a constant balancing act. The large meeting room was already half full when we walked in, passing a pair of uniformed officers. Two more officers stood near the other door, deliberately casual despite their uniforms and gear. My jaw tightened at the sight of Officer Kimberly Clark. Several people greeted Laurel, exchanging hugs and words of encouragement.

On a table near the entrance, stacks of Crime Stoppers brochures lay next to flyers on Block Watch, the Community Police Academy for citizens, and other programs. A reader board on an easel listed upcoming meetings scheduled for this space, including the next Neighbors United meeting.

At the front of the room, a slide on the big screen displayed the city's logo—a line drawing, white on blue, of Chief Seattle in profile—along with a collage of photos of Seattleites at various gatherings. At the bottom was the motto I remembered well from Tag's uniform patch: Service, Pride, Dedication.

Then the slide changed to a picture of Maddie, her dark hair and eyes shining, her lips bright, side by side with a photo of the grocery where she'd been shot, a gray stucco dinosaur.

I spotted Detective Armstrong—at roughly six-five, he stands out in a crowd. He acknowledged me with a nod.

Detective Tracy caught up with us as I was edging into a row of seats. His camel hair jacket appeared tighter than usual. A stress eater, responding to the strains of a complicated investigation?

I could relate.

"Pepper, Mrs. Halloran," he said. "I shouldn't be surprised to see you two here."

"My old stomping grounds," I said. "Pottery classes in the art studio, tennis lessons on the playfield. And you know why Laurel is here."

"People will ask you," he said to her, "if there's a connection between the present incident and your husband's shooting."

"You've admitted that there is," she replied. "The gun."

"We're keeping that detail to ourselves for now, as I'm sure you understand, and we're counting on you to do the same." Point made, he walked away.

"Good thing he's a good cop," Laurel muttered, "because he's an annoying little bee."

I suppressed a snort and we found seats. The Ellingsons sat on the other side of the room. Cody was not with them. In the next row sat Lindy Harmon, who'd petted Arf, beside a tall man I assumed was her husband. Further down were Frank Thomas and his wife, and the hair stylist. Tim sat in the front row with Maddie's mother.

Where, I wondered, were Agent Greer and the agent who'd been watching us?

A black woman in a dark blue pantsuit strode to the podium, and the chatter died down.

"I'm April Stafford, community outreach officer for the Seattle Police Department," she said. "Thank you for coming. I know you're here tonight for an update on the investigation into last week's shooting, so we'll get right to that, then talk more generally about community safety and how the residents and the department can work together. Detective Tracy?"

Stafford stepped back and Tracy took center stage.

"First, let me assure you that we do not believe there is an ongoing danger to the community," he said. He would say that, wouldn't he, whether it was a targeted incident or a random crime. He wanted people to feel safe. "Despite that, we have been increasing our patrols throughout Montlake, primarily along Twenty-Fourth and near the schools, library, and community center. Not, let me repeat, because we think those areas are connected to the shooting, but because we know you are particularly concerned about the safety of areas where children gather."

He paused to consult a 3x5 card he'd pulled out of his pocket. "I am authorized to tell you that the victim of the shooting, Madeleine Petrosian, has regained consciousness and is expected to make a full recovery."

Relief rippled audibly through the room.

"She has not been able to tell us much yet, though we hope that will change soon. In the meantime, we're counting on you to share with us any information you have—anything unusual you've seen or heard. Anything at all. Talk to me or my partner, Detective Shawn Armstrong"—he gestured toward Armstrong, who raised a hand—"or any of the officers here tonight. Our cards are on the table by the doorway. Feel free to call us any time."

"Is there a reward for information?" a man called out. The question irritated me, and judging from the audible responses around me, others too. Had society deteriorated to the point where we only provided critical crime-solving info if we were paid for it? Besides, this was an affluent community.

"Tips called in to the Crime Stoppers hotline that lead to an arrest and conviction may be eligible for a reward up to one thousand dollars. We do hope you'll share any information you have with us, the sooner the better."

For the next twenty minutes, he answered questions. No, they had no useful fingerprints or DNA; trace evidence was still under analysis. "You know, folks, real police work isn't like what you see on TV. We don't have all that whiz-bang stuff that gets the case wrapped up before the ten o'clock news."

A woman behind us asked if the shooting might be related to a string of burglaries in the University District, just over the bridge.

"No connection at this point," he replied, "but we're looking into all crimes in the region that share similar elements."

Then I saw the man sitting with Lindy Harmon start to rise. She put her hand on his arm, said something, and he lowered himself back into his seat. I leaned forward for a better look. His profile was stony, his shoulders stiff as he trained his gaze on Detective Tracy. Some history there, but what was it?

"What about the construction project?" a woman asked. "Will it go forward?"

"On hold for now. We have not released the crime scene. As for when that will happen, or what will be done with the building, I'm told that the family will make a decision when the time is right."

Tracy turned the microphone back to Stafford, who began a presentation on crime statistics and block watch programs.

"Let's get out of here," Laurel whispered. I wasn't ready to leave—I'd hoped to ask Maddie's mother about the photo album. Later.

On our way headed out, I saw Agent Greer in the back row,

in her nondescript, dressed-to-fit-in sweater and jeans. No sign of her partner.

A uniformed officer opened the door for us. "Thank you," I said, looking straight into Kimberly Clark's eyes.

At least she had the grace to blush.

"Well, that was about as helpful as a heart attack," Laurel said once we reached the courtyard.

"What did you expect?" I asked. "He couldn't say much, even if he has a good working theory."

"I expect," she said, coming to an abrupt halt. "I expect that nearly a week after a woman is shot on her own property and left clinging to life that the police would have a clue what happened. I expect that after three years, they'd know what happened to my husband. Not some theory, or vague speculation. And I expect you to be on my side."

Though there was a fine tremor in her voice and her eyes filled with tears that did not fall, her anger and her sense of bitter betrayal came through loud and clear.

Not what I had expected at all.

Twenty-One

Augustus Caesar reportedly wore a garland of bay and bryony leaves to protect himself from lightning.

LAUREL MARCHED ACROSS THE LAWN TO THE PLAYGROUND where she sat on a bench, arms folded, jaw set. In the dusk and the shade of the big trees, I couldn't see the steam coming out of her ears. But I had no doubt.

On the other side of the big windows, Stafford was taking questions. I crossed the courtyard and leaned against the side of the pool building.

To me, the key question was why Maddie had gone to the old grocery Thursday morning. The assumption had been that she was clearing it out, getting it ready for demolition, or whatever came next. Maddie was hands-on, yes, but not like that—she and Kristen met weekly for a manicure.

What if she was meeting someone? Someone who hadn't expected her builder, who'd shown up late and found her. A subcontractor? A potential future tenant?

Someone who brought a gun. Who would take a gun to a discussion about a construction project?

Movement caught my eye. The meeting had ended and people stood, clustering in twos or threes, or heading for the doors.

Lindy Harmon emerged, with the tall man I assumed was her husband.

"Oh, yes, I saw you come in with Laurel," Lindy said when I reminded her that we'd met, and introduced her husband. "Barry and Pat worked together closely in Neighbors United. First on reducing the impact of the highway bridge expansion on the wetlands, then on voicing our concerns about the redevelopment proposal."

Barry Harmon shook my hand. "A neighborhood belongs to the residents as much as to the city or the commercial property owners. Our goal is simply to have a voice in how it changes. If there's no place for the kids to buy a Coke or to stop for milk on the way home, it's hardly a neighborhood."

"I live next door to Glenn Abbott, the city councilman, and he would agree wholeheartedly," I said.

"Pat was a fierce champion for the cause. When he was—" Barry stopped, swallowed hard, then continued. "When Pat was killed, the cops interviewed everyone in the group. There had been some disagreements, but nothing significant. Now they're going down the list, talking to each of us again."

"About Maddie's shooting?" I asked.

He nodded. "I was out of town last week. Soon as I showed them the boarding passes on my phone, they were done with me. I just wish they'd tell us more about what they're thinking."

"Me, too. Is that what you wanted to ask Detective Tracy?"

"I can be a bit blunt at times. My wife wisely stopped me." One side of his mouth curved, and he gave her a quick, appreciative glance. "But the group fully supports Maddie's proposal. It's just what the neighborhood needs."

"That doesn't surprise me. I've known Maddie since kindergarten. I haven't known Detective Tracy nearly as long, but I trust him. They'll do everything they can to find the shooter"—I barely managed to stop myself from saying "the killer" and confirm Barry Harmon's hunch that the police had evidence connecting the two crimes.

We said our goodnights and nice-to-meet-yous, and the Harmons angled across the lawn, hand in hand, toward home.

I turned back to the meeting room and saw Tim and Mrs. Petrosian talking with the detectives, then make their way toward the exit. Several people stopped them for a word, a quick hug, a handshake.

By the time they got outside, only a few people remained, chatting on the sidewalk or drifting toward the parking lot.

"Tim," I called and stepped forward, my hand out. "Mrs. Petrosian. It's Pepper Reece. I'm so sorry. Thank God she's going to be okay."

Mrs. Petrosian took my hand in both of hers. Maddie's parents were older than mine, and age showed on her widowed mother's face. "Pepper, of course. And it's Miriam. Tim said you stopped by the hospital today. Thank you."

"She'll come back stronger than ever," I said. "You know she will. She's a fighter."

"Always has been," Miriam agreed.

"I flipped through one of the photo albums you brought in. Such great old pictures. There was one of a brick building and a cool old panel truck, from the early '30's, maybe? The sign said Gregorian and Son, or something like that. Grocers. Your family?"

"No," Miriam said. "The Gregorians were my late husband's grandparents, on his mother's side. The first generation in this country. So many Armenians immigrated at about that time, after the genocide. My family came here then, too."

In high school, when we studied World War I, Maddie and another girl with Armenian ancestry had brought up the topic of the genocide, although I'm not sure we called it that back then. After centuries of turmoil, the Turks had gone on a last-ditch effort to preserve the Ottoman Empire and rid themselves of the Christian Armenians. Armenians were driven from their homes, and one of Maddie's great-grandmothers, at only fifteen, had led a group of children through the desert to safety. Hundreds of thousands were killed. The Turks continue to dispute the term "genocide," with its implications of a systematic campaign, and the tensions still affect regional and international politics. Maddie had told her family story and I'd been so intrigued that I'd read the nonfiction account of the period she brought in, *Passage to Ararat*. The horrors, and the bravery, were permanently stuck in my mind.

"So that was your husband's maternal grandfather. Maddie's great-grandfather," I said, puzzling out the names and genealogy. "With his son, your husband's uncle?"

"Yes, Haig," Miriam replied. "I never knew either of them—they both died when David was a boy, long before we met. So good to see you, Pepper."

I had more questions, but I also had sense enough to tell when a woman who'd traveled halfway around the world to get to her daughter's bedside was running out of steam.

"Good to see you," I said, "despite the circumstances. Tim, I'll try to get in to see Maddie again later in the week."

"Your visit did her a world of good," he said as we brushed cheeks. Given her frustration at all she'd wanted to say but couldn't, I was not so sure.

I watched them leave, the worried husband, the anxious mother. I'd been wondering why Maddie was so intent on pursuing her vision for the property, sure that it meant more to her than another notch in her tool belt or more rental income in her family's bank accounts. Why, though, I'd had no idea until I spotted the picture in the album, and the brief conversation with her mother gave my theory some credence: What if that property had belonged to her family, and she'd been trying to get it back?

It was kind of a delicious thought, Maddie Petrosian going around someone, undermining their plans, to get what she wanted. Who'd have thunk she had it in her?

But had it gotten her shot?

And how was it tied to Patrick Halloran's murder?

I let out a long, slow breath and headed for my friend on the park bench.

"Forgive me," Laurel said as I sat beside her. "I'm being an idiot."

"Kinda nice to hear somebody else saying that. It's usually me."

Her lips curved in a humorless smile. "One of the few things I know for sure in all this is that you are on my side."

I squeezed her hand, then fished a water bottle out of my tote and passed it to her. She popped it open and took a long drink.

"Have you ever discovered something," she asked, "that changed your entire view of someone?"

Just today, I thought, about Maddie, though I didn't yet know how that would play out. And three years ago, when I tripped over Tag's infidelity.

"But you knew it would change everyone else's view, too," she went on, "and you weren't sure you could stand that, so you kept your mouth shut?"

"Are we talking about Patrick?"

She nodded. I waited.

"Patrick was supposed to go on the soccer trip with Gabe. He always went. By high school, the kids had professional coaches, so he was a parent chaperone, and he loved it." One hand gripped the top of the bottle while the other hand twisted the bottom. "Two days before the trip, he said he couldn't go, he had to work. That left the team short a chaperone, so I rearranged my schedule and I went."

"But you've never thought his murder was connected to his work, because he hadn't brought home any files. Or his office laptop."

"Right." She hesitated, then went on. "It was a small house. One bath on the main floor, between the living room and our bedroom. Another in the basement, off the family room, next to Gabe's room. Not like a modern house with a powder room for guests and a full master bath."

My loft only had one bath, too, accessible from the bedroom or the living room. I wouldn't mind a powder room for guests.

"He was killed in the mudroom, but the police searched the entire house for evidence of an intruder or an altercation. No fingerprints, no nothing that shouldn't have been there. They walked me through the house and one of the officers pointed out a tube of lipstick on the floor in the bathroom, behind the toilet. It must have rolled there."

I had a terrible feeling I knew where this was going. "I'm not sure I've ever seen you wear lipstick."

She tightened her lips and gave a tiny shake of the head. "The police assumed it was mine. I said yes. But I had cleaned that bathroom the day before we left."

"Whose do you think it was?"

The look she gave me cut deep. "No, Laurel," I said. "Not Maddie."

"She wears a very distinctive shade. And they knew each other."

"But she didn't even own the corner grocery yet. Although she did go to some of the NU meetings." If her family had once owned the property, and she wanted it back, of course she was interested.

Laurel took another drink of water. "I kept it. It could still be tested for fingerprints or DNA or whatever, couldn't it, after all this time?"

"Depends how and where you kept it, but probably, yeah. Laurel." I turned to her, the blue-white glow of the lamplight casting an eerie shadow on her face. "It's one thing to suspect they were having an affair, another to think . . . You withheld evidence. Physical evidence, and information that might have been critical."

"I know." Her voice was pained, breathy. "But it wasn't evidence of murder. I am not accusing Maddie Petrosian of murder. I never have, and definitely not now."

"But if the same gun shot them both," I said, "and Maddie was there that night, she might know something. It could be important." If the only connection was the gun, that would be like lightning striking twice.

"If Maddie knew something important, she'd have spoken up," Laurel said. "She didn't, and that was enough for me. I didn't want to destroy my dead husband's reputation, not without any proof. I had Gabe to think about. And I didn't want to cause trouble for her. If—if they were involved, then she was grieving, too."

"You're a far more generous woman than I. I wouldn't have cared about protecting her feelings one bit."

"Never in a million years did I think Patrick would cheat on me. I have turned myself inside out, trying to come up with an innocent explanation. But sometimes I wonder if I ever really knew him."

That was a gut-puncher. The risk of relationship. "You've held this in, all this time."

"I suppose," she said, "I thought if I never told anyone, then I didn't have to admit it might be true."

"We might be able to catch Tracy and Armstrong, if we hurry." I started to stand but she pulled me down.

"Did you know?" she asked. "About Tag, I mean?"

For half a second, I'd thought she was asking if I'd known about Pat and Maddie. Thank heavens I hadn't; I'd have hated to bear that bad news. "I suspected. Little clues—last-minute changes in his work schedule. His phone buzzing with a text at strange times." It had been all I could do not to check his phone when he was asleep. I exhaled, glad she couldn't see my face clearly. "I even followed him one night to a bar near Green Lake, certain he was meeting 'her,' whoever 'she' was. Turned out to be a couple of guys he'd known since high school, like he'd said."

After that, I'd been mortified. How low could I stoop?

"But you were right. Everyone thought you were being hasty when you left him, but you were prepared," she said. Meaning she hadn't been.

It was getting late and I needed to pick up my dog. But I had to ask her about something else she hadn't mentioned.

"Did you know that Pat was part of the team that investigated Bruce Ellingson for fraud?"

"Yes. And before you ask why I didn't tell you, the case was closed with a confidential settlement." She angled toward me. "I wasn't supposed to know, not until it came up in the murder investigation. Even then, I wasn't supposed to talk about it."

"They looked at all his cases, they and the FBI, like they're doing now. And there's a guy with major motive, right next door."

"Pat wanted to prosecute, but his boss decided the case was too weak, and they should let the regulators handle it. Bruce must have known Pat was on to him."

"The real tension behind the spat over the compost pile," I said. "But they never seriously suspected him of murder?"

"No. I think because he found Pat, or said he did—he called 911. If he was the shooter, what did he do with the gun? Anyway, I couldn't keep living next door to them, not under the circumstances."

My head was spinning. No wonder she'd moved. All this time, she'd never said a bad word about Pat; how she managed, I had no idea.

"Speaking of the Ellingsons. Their son works in the Market and he applied for a job with me. Any reason I shouldn't hire him? To help with deliveries?"

"No," she said. "Cody's a good kid. He just had trouble living up to his dad's expectations. Gabe always looked up to him."

The police may have eliminated Bruce Ellingson from their inquiries, but I hadn't.

When we reached the parking lot, Detective Armstrong was

loading boxes into the trunk of April Stafford's car. The extra brochures and pamphlets, I assumed. A few feet away, Officer Clark was listening to Detective Tracy and typing into her phone. Instructions? What was her role, anyway? I still hadn't heard why the police were guarding Maddie, though Greer had insisted they weren't.

"Don't tell me the two of you have been down at the water's edge, feeding the ducks," Detective Tracy said.

"Just catching up," I replied. I held out my hand to Officer Clark. "I don't think we've ever met. Not formally. I'm Pepper Reece."

She took my hand and this time she didn't blush, for which I gave her great credit. "Kim Clark."

A flicker of—what? Amusement? Curiosity?—crossed Tracy's face. He had to know about Tag's affair with the woman. Blessedly, he said nothing.

Stafford drove off and Detective Armstrong joined us.

"Detectives, Officer," I said, "Mrs. Halloran has a piece of information that didn't seem important three years ago, but that she thinks might be helpful now."

All eyes turned to Laurel, who explained about the lipstick tube and her suspicions. I expected Detective Tracy to explode, and his eyes did simmer, but he managed, against all odds, to keep a civil tone when he replied.

"Have you told this to anyone else?" When she shook her head, he continued. "Officer Clark will follow you home and take custody of the lipstick. You will be in my office at eight-thirty tomorrow morning, and you will tell me everything you know or think you know about your husband's murder and about Maddie Petrosian, whether you think it matters or not. Understood?"

She nodded.

"Good," he said. "You might want to bring a lawyer. I'm sure Mr. Gardiner can suggest someone, but keep in mind that he himself is a witness, and what you've just told us puts our entire understanding of the timeline the night of your husband's murder in doubt."

Oh, cardamom. I'd completely forgotten. Eric and Kristen had been with Tim and Maddie at their island place that evening. How could Maddie have been with Pat? Unless she'd been there some other time.

Silence. Then Clark spoke to Laurel. "My patrol car's parked on Calhoun. I'll follow you. Take Boyer to Roanoke, cross the freeway, and drop down to Fairview. Wait for me at the entrance to the docks."

Laurel nodded.

Tracy aimed an irritated look at me and I raised my hands. "I just found out, not five minutes ago."

He grunted. "We'll talk soon." Then he and Armstrong headed for the parking lot and Clark for the street.

"They won't charge me, will they?" Laurel asked. "I mean, I withheld evidence, but I didn't think it was relevant. Eight thirty. That's right in the middle of morning rush."

"Take cookies," I said. "When dealing with Detective Tracy, it's always a good idea to take cookies."

Twenty-Two

*Foods often spark our memories. When I taste
what my aunts used to cook, I am tasting time.*

—Mary Pipher, *Women Rowing North: Navigating Life's
Currents and Flourishing as We Age*

I WOKE UP THURSDAY MISSING NATE. AND NOT JUST BECAUSE
he's the one who usually takes Arf out for a morning pee. I missed
him because my life is better with him. Because I'm better with
him.

Because while you might not ever truly know someone, the
effort of trying is part of what makes life so exquisitely beautiful.

Try putting all that in a text.

"Pepper! Hi!"

I turned, delighted to see Jamie Ackerman behind me in the
coffee line. I introduced her to Arf, who was instantly smitten.

"I'm trying a different spot every day," she told me in a conspir-
atorial tone. "How can you stand all this fabulous food? Greek,
Italian, Thai."

It was our turn to order and I reached into my tote for my
wallet. The photos Greer had given me came out, too, falling onto
the Arcade floor.

"I'll get them," Jamie said, and bent down while I paid for the
coffee. I tucked my wallet away and she stood, pictures in hand.
"Thanks. You didn't have to buy. I've seen them."

"Seen who? Oh, them?" I took the pictures. "She might work in the Market."

Jamie's brow creased. "Yeah, maybe. But somewhere else . . . where?"

"If you think of it, let me know."

Before she could ask why, the barista called my name and handed us our lattes. We headed up the Arcade, Jamie waving and calling hellos to a dozen vendors.

"So, you're liking it here," I said when we reached the spot where our ways parted. She'd been assigned a stall on the Joe DeSimone Bridge today.

"Pepper," she said, her voice dropping. "I have never felt more at home anywhere than I do in Seattle. In the Market."

What could I do, but throw my arms around her.

As I unlocked the shop door, I pictured Laurel trekking down to SPD, as she'd promised Detective Tracy. I'd filled Eric in when I stopped to pick up Arf, and he'd arranged for a criminal lawyer he knew to sit in on the interview. He doubted they'd charge a murder victim's wife with obstruction unless they had good reason. Only if filing charges would help them shake loose info critical to an arrest and conviction. But they would use the lipstick case to pressure Maddie as well—she hadn't mentioned being in the Halloran house that day. Though if she had been, Eric assured me, it was earlier. Maddie had been tied up on business, and met the rest of them at the ferry terminal for the six o'clock boat.

This new evidence would mean every alibi would be checked and rechecked. But not by me. The cops had the resources for detailed investigations like that—comparing witness statements, checking ferry schedules and drive times. Minutiae were them. People were me.

The shop welcomed me with its usual cascade of sights and smells, and I had to agree with Jamie about the Market.

Midmorning, the sun was shining brightly, and I stepped outside to listen to a busker fiddling old-timey tunes on the other side of Pine. Bicycle tires whizzed by, then stopped. Bike cleats clattered on the sidewalk as Tag approached.

"Got a moment?" he said.

"What's up?"

He cleared his throat. "I hear you've met Kim."

"I'll admit, I almost didn't recognize her with all her clothes on."

"Pepper," he said, half chiding, half pleading.

"I know, it's been three years. Past time to give it a rest. Truth is . . ." I glanced at the pavement, unsure whether to say what I'd been thinking, but it had been nagging at me ever since my conversation with Laurel in the playground last night. I met his gaze. "Your affair was not my fault. It was a stupid thing to do, and it was only a matter of time before I caught on. But"—I raised a hand to forestall his interruption—"it was your response to a bad situation. We'd stopped being open and honest with each other a long time before that night. And no, I'm not just now figuring that out, but I am just now realizing it's important to acknowledge to you that I'm as much to blame for our marriage failing as you."

It was an odd conversation for a street corner, I admit, but even odder was Tag's reaction. Was Mr. Tough Guy Bike Cop crying?

Or had a stray raindrop dripped off the dark green overhang of my building and smacked him in the face?

He wiped his cheek with a gloved hand. Then his radio barked. He clicked it on, barked back, and was gone.

Just another day in the Market.

Inside, I placed a few orders, then called a chef who'd fallen behind on his account. Got a text from Nate saying the salmon were running well and they'd probably hit their quota in time to return Saturday. Laurel texted, too, saying: *I survived. Thanks for suggesting cookies.*

Ha. Like Mike Tracy could be bought off that easily. Buttered up, maybe, but bought off, no.

Then Edgar called, and I told him where Sandra and I had lunch yesterday. "The food is nice enough"—that prompted a sound I couldn't decipher, in Spanish, and probably not one I'd repeat, even if I did understand it. "But you're right. The spicing on the crab cakes is very similar to yours."

"What you are going to do?"

"I'm still thinking."

"You think too long, I lose business."

"Edgar, give me time, okay?" He agreed, though not happily, and I changed the subject. "Heard from your old boss Alex lately?"

"An email. He's in New Zealand. Wanted to know if I could

put him in touch with that waitress from the old place who came from there and went back."

Ah, same old Alex. Still chasing the good-looking women.

"His crew's scattered to the winds, hasn't it?"

"When I was a sous, I work four years for one chef. Now I'm lucky they stay four months. Everybody got itchy feet. Bartenders is the worst. They move around like flies on a hot wall."

I asked him about a couple of other ex-coworkers, then about Tariq. If he had any suspicions, he'd voice them now. Loudly. But no.

"I lost track. Great cook, bad attitude."

Maybe the talented young cook could redeem himself, by serving up some reliable spice intel.

IN THE afternoon, I headed up to Capitol Hill to call on a young pastry chef, a friend of Cayenne's from culinary school, who was opening her own bakery and dessert catering company in a space near the old Harvard Exit theater. Talk about a great example of both historic renovation and the city's evolution. Once a women's club, when such spaces were influential, it had been converted into a popular movie theater showing foreign films in the days before streaming was a glint in a tech wizard's eye. My mother swears they used to serve free samples of Seattle Spice tea, back in the day. Now, it houses the Mexican Consulate. I encouraged the baker to include a few south-of-the-border treats on her daily menu.

An order in hand that ran from allspice to za'atar, I wound my way over to Maddie's office. Her building was classic, but without any particular historic significance that would keep it from the wrecking ball, like, say, the Harvard Exit. The door was on the side. A small brass sign read "Petrosian Properties, LLC." I pushed the intercom button and announced myself, then headed up the narrow stairs.

The reception area could have been a backdrop for a magazine shoot. Original redbrick walls, richly colored Persian rugs on gleaming plank floors. The furniture looked inviting but not so inviting that an unwanted visitor would linger. A bouquet of creamy white roses and spiky purple flowers graced the front desk. The scent of orange oil and beeswax polish, tinged with coffee, hung in the air.

"I know you," the receptionist said. "Well, we've never met, but I'm Jess, Jen's sister."

"Jen at the mystery bookshop?" Had she ever mentioned a sister? We'd met at my old law firm. We mostly talked work back then, and mostly talked books now.

"Yes. You run the spice shop. Maddie raves about you. I can't believe what's happened." Her dark eyeliner was smudged, the skin under her eyes puffy. "Why would someone shoot her?"

That, I couldn't answer. "It's terrible, isn't it? Can you help me piece together the history of the Montlake project? Oh, I brought cookies. Samples from a new bakery opening in a few weeks, down on Tenth." I pulled a bag out of my tote. It isn't just major crimes detectives who speak more freely with a sweet treat in hand.

"Those look fabulous. Back in a sec." She bounced up and stepped into a small kitchenette. A moment later, I heard the faint gurgling of a coffee maker. I glanced around. The door to the corner office stood open. Maddie's inner sanctum. From the reception area, I could see an antique wood desk, brass planters filled with rolls of what I assumed were building plans and blueprints, and an oak library table. Another Persian rug lay on the floor, deep purple with golden yellow flowers and twining greenery.

Next to Maddie's office was a formal conference room, the table bare. Several smaller offices ran along the interior wall, all empty. Last came a file room. We appeared to be alone.

Jess returned with two forest green mugs and a plate of cookies. She led me to a pair of wing chairs, upholstered in deep red, at a low oval table.

"It's just me here today," she said. "The property manager and maintenance crew are out on site. The builder, too, though he isn't an employee. He's the one who found her. Got there late, and there she was."

"How awful."

"They all came in last week when the police interviewed us. That short detective is kind of a bear, but the tall one is nice. Cute, too," she said, with a lift of her eyebrows.

"Married." I took a mug and we sat.

"The good ones always are. Tim said I should tell you everything. They mostly wanted to know about the other developer and

Neighbors United. I kept telling them it was his plans that caused the problems, not Maddie's, but I'm not sure I was very clear."

"So who was he? And what was it about his plans that the neighbors didn't like?" I took a sip. The same rich, dark roast I'd had in the coffee house on Twenty-Fourth.

"You know, mostly you know the other people in the business, right? You're looking at the same jobs, hiring the same subs. But this guy was new on the scene. His name was Jake Byrd, with a Y, doing business as Byrd's Nest, LLC. With a Y."

"Cute," I said. Finally, a first name for the man.

"I thought it was dumb." She bit into a lemon coriander crescent. "Oh, wow."

Wait until the baker started using my spices.

"Isn't that common, though?" I asked. "When I bought my loft, I dealt with an LLC named for the location, Western and Union. All it did was that project—the construction work, the legal stuff, sales. I assume the owners form a new entity for every project, so if one fails or gets into trouble, it won't take everything else they're working on down with it."

"You're right, that is common, especially if you work on a lot of projects at a time. Maddie never did it that way, though. She says the Petrosian name is her selling point, and she wants it front and center. Except this one time." Her hand shook as she picked up her mug. "They shot her. How messed up is that?"

"What do you mean, except this one time?"

She exhaled and set her mug back on the stone coaster without having taken a sip. "Okay, so his project was called Byrd's Nest. Giving you this cozy sense, right, except that his designs weren't cozy at all." She reached for another cookie. "When is this bakery opening?"

"Halloween. That's the goal, anyway." I had my doubts. This was the baker's first business venture and her ducks were all over the pond. "You were saying, Byrd's Nest. With a Y."

"Yeah, so Maddie decided to try to buy the rest of the buildings—you know she owns most of the block, right? Except the coffeehouse, which she might as well own, she goes there so often."

Jess might not look like her sister, but they shared one trait. They took their sweet time getting to the point.

"Let me get the file. You'll see." A minute later, she returned with two manila folders, one thick, one thin. She handed me the fat file and sat.

I opened the folder. An entity called Bird's Nest, LLC, with an I, had signed a buy-sell for the corner property. The transaction had closed a few weeks ago.

I felt my brain tilt. No doubt it showed. "I saw Bird's Nest, with an I, listed on the state website. But—ohhh. You're Jessica Somers, the registered agent." I hadn't made the connection; her sister uses a married name.

Jess cocked her head toward Maddie's office. "But the company owns everything."

"Didn't Byrd already own the place?"

"No. Maddie discovered that he only had an option. He was working on financing, putting his plans together. He had a real estate agent on board—you've gotta think about marketing right from the start. Although she acted like she was in charge, from what I heard. I guess this was his first big project."

"Was the agent Deanna Ellingson?"

"Yeah. Lining stuff up in advance was smart. That way, when the owner was finally ready to sell, they'd be ready to go."

I leaned forward. "Then Maddie came in with a more attractive offer and outbid him. But why form an LLC with a similar name? She bought the other buildings as Petrosian Properties. Or at least, that's how she bought the insurance agency building—I saw the name when I looked up the sale. Why the subterfuge?"

Jess gave me a patient look, and the pieces began to fall into place.

Why, though, had Maddie needed to hide her identity from the seller?

"The neighbors hated Byrd's project because it was so out of scale," Jess said. "Not neighborhood-y at all, if you know what I mean."

"Too big? Modern architecture instead of the traditional style?"

"Which is okay in a built-up area. You put a building like that on a major commercial street, it fits right in. There's more going on, more variety. But in a single block where everything evokes a certain era . . ."

I knew what she meant. Last summer, my mother and I visited

a cohousing community a few blocks off Broadway. It was the modern, boxy, mixed-material style, but all super-groovy, eco-friendly, with communal dining and a rooftop garden. We'd both loved it. It didn't seem out of place, because the area around it had become so delightfully mixed. But put that same four-story building on the corner where Gregorian and Son once stood, the only commercial block for miles, and you might as well put a Taco Bell on the moon.

Jess opened the slender file and shuffled through a short stack of color renderings. All appeared to show similar images, though some had more text and others included photos of faces I couldn't see well. She handed me a page labeled "The Byrd's Nest, Contemporary Mixed-use in a Traditional Setting." Tradition, shmission. The sketch looked like a Taco Bell with too much hot sauce, minus the good taste. Five stories, gray and orange, with red-railed balconies so narrow my veranda was a ballroom in comparison. It filled the corner—zero lot line, if I remembered the builder-speak. As Jess had said, in the right location, you wouldn't give it a second glance. Here, you'd be so distracted, you'd run off the road.

She picked up a raspberry macaron. "Maddie called it his bargaining chip. No matter what he proposed, the neighbors and the city were going to insist he scale back, so by starting outrageous, he could bargain down to what he really wanted."

"Ask for the whole loaf so when they offer you half, you can say you'll take three-quarters and claim you compromised for the sake of the community. Even if you tick everyone off in the process."

"Exactly. But these neighbors were smart, organized, and suspicious. They figured the block would never be the same. The businesses would fail, and he would buy them up and bulldoze everything. No more salon or coffeehouse. No more affordable rentals."

Hard to imagine the changes going that far. But when a guy uses fear to get what he wants, you never know how far he'll go.

I turned back to the file, flipping pages as I talked. "Who was the seller? And why did Maddie need to hide behind an LLC? Oh, so the seller died and the property went into his estate." I'd thought the man who ran the grocery ancient when I was a kid, but he'd died quite recently. The lawyer handling both the estate and the sale was Amanda Wagner, a young woman from the old law firm.

I hadn't seen her since its collapse, though I knew she and her husband, whom she'd met at the firm, had set up shop in an old house near Broadway, doing landlord-tenant and real estate work. And apparently, probate. "That would explain the delay. Did you tell all this to the police? Why didn't they take your files?"

"They took some files but let me keep copies, so we can run the business. They copied our hard drives and took Maddie's phone and her laptop. I told them everything, but I'm such a space right now, worried about Maddie. Have you seen her? They won't let me see her yet."

"I have seen her. She should fully recover, but it will take time. One more thing and then I'll let you get back to work. Can you give me a list of her purchases on the block, by date?"

Jess sat at her computer and clicked away, pausing once to consult a paper file. I was surprised at the extent of the paper filing system—I've managed to limit my paper files to personnel, some catalogs, and a few tax and banking records—but chalked it up to the nature of the business.

While she worked, I wandered into Maddie's office. If there had been a course in business school on staying organized and keeping a clean desk, Maddie had obviously aced it. A yellow legal pad lay on her desk, a few notes on the top page. Hard to decipher, but the few words I could make out seemed to relate to a school fundraiser.

In the corner of the room, a poster on an easel showed a water-color-style rendering of Maddie's vision for the new building. Almost brick for brick a copy of the original I'd seen in her family album.

A striking landscape of the San Juan Islands hung above a trio of waist-high bookcases. A few objects and family photos were interspersed with books. I picked up a photo of Tim and the kids, taken a few years back. The boy, Max, was the same age as Kristen's youngest, thirteen now, and the girl, Mia, two years younger. Although kids you don't know well are always older than you think. They were beautiful, and I felt a stab of envy, or maybe it was grief for what I had never had.

Although if Laurel was right about the affair—and I still hadn't wrapped my head around that possibility—maybe Maddie didn't have it all, after all.

Next to it sat a shot of Maddie and her parents. I didn't remember a lot about her father, David Petrosian, one of those dads who seemed more focused on business than family. I'd almost envied that, since I could never escape my dad, our high school history teacher.

I'd made quite a practice of envying Maddie. But not right now. Not right now.

Then came a recent shot of both kids, in soccer uniforms, with Tim and a man in a Sounders uniform. A small wooden stand held a tiny Armenian flag, three equal bands of red, blue, and orange.

On the last bookcase stood a photo of the corner grocery back in the day. If I'd guessed right, the building had once belonged to Maddie's great-grandfather, Mr. Gregorian. How it had left the family, I had no idea. Maddie had been determined to get it back. But what a price she'd paid.

And on the shelf below that, next to a cluster of painted rocks I assumed had been a kid's art project, was a snapshot of Maddie, Kristen, and me at our high school graduation, in our caps and gowns.

I put the photo back. Better get out of here before I lost it completely.

Out front, Jess handed me the list of Maddie's purchases in the neighborhood. As I'd suspected, the first came two and half years ago, when she bought the insurance agency property from Frank Thomas's widowed mother. Then she'd acquired the building that housed the salon, followed by the gray stone apartment building and the other office building. Last came the corner grocery. That gave her five of the six properties on one side of the street. She appeared to have no interest in the buildings on the west side.

"What about the coffeehouse?" I asked.

"They didn't want to sell. The building's been in the family for ages, and they want to keep it for their kids. Maddie respected that."

"Thanks," I said. "You've been a huge help."

"Anything for Maddie," Jess replied. "I can't believe this."

Her eyes filled with tears.

I left the cookies.

Twenty-Three

Let the rain kiss you. Let the rain beat upon your head with silver liquid drops. Let the rain sing you a lullaby.

—Langston Hughes, "April Rain Song"

I SAT IN THE SAAB OUTSIDE MADDIE'S OFFICE. MY BACK WAS stiff from the wingback chair, which as I'd predicted, had not been as comfy as it looked. Jess hadn't thought the police terribly interested in Maddie's real estate dealings, but I suspected her fear and anxiety were skewing her perceptions. Surely they'd trained their radar on Jake Byrd.

He wouldn't have been the first person to leap from losing out on a business deal to murder. He had to have spent a small fortune putting together a proposal, preparing the drawings, and all the other doodah, even if it was preliminary. A hundred thou? More? I had no idea how much his gamble might have cost him.

If this was Byrd's first big project, as Jess thought, what had prompted it? A career change, a step up in the world, a move into the big time? Hopes dashed, money lost, pride wounded.

It would sting; of course it would. And I understood the urge for revenge, the urge to scream and yell and throw things. I had fallen prey to those urges myself, in days better forgotten.

But attempted murder? Why would it have made sense to take a shot at the woman who'd outmaneuvered him? Or to have killed

Pat, with the same gun. If he had—that didn't seem smart. Had a second shooter set him up?

In the law firm days, I had heard trial lawyers say that people get more riled up about disputes over real property than over personal injury claims. It defied logic, but they swore it's true. Losing the safety and security of one's home, a place you had saved for and gone into debt for, evoked more tears and sleepless nights than whiplash from a rear-ender.

But this hadn't been Byrd's home. And why would he have gone after Patrick Halloran? Yes, Pat had been active in the community group, but so had many others who were now alive and well. And Byrd likely would have acquired both the property and the necessary permits, had Maddie not intervened.

I picked up my phone and called Detective Tracy. Voice mail. I didn't leave a message; what would I say?

My back was still talking. That's what I got for skipping yoga. I put the car in gear and turned onto Nineteenth. A new deli had taken over the space on the opposite end of the block from Maddie's office. Ages ago, as the Surrogate Hostess, it had been the heart of the community, serving strong coffee and warm cinnamon rolls. In the seventh and eighth grade, after my family moved out of Grace House, Kristen and I had often stopped in after school. I couldn't picture Maddie in the group of girls at the long pine tables, but she must have been there. It was great to see the place buzzing.

I turned the corner and slowed in front of St. Joseph's, a graceful white stucco church with a tower that pierced the pale gray sky. Very 1930s Art Deco. The anchor of the neighborhood in my childhood, though I wondered how many of my old friends and classmates could afford to live around here now.

Seeing our graduation photograph on Maddie's shelves had shaken me. If I had a copy, it was slapped in an album now buried in a box in my basement storage unit. Clearly I had not remembered Maddie as central to our lives—Kristen's and mine—the way she'd thought about us.

And that made me feel terrible.

BOXES filled the entry of the shabby two-story converted clapboard, a house turned law office. Paint cans and drop cloths were stacked in one corner.

"We found the perfect space. Modern, clean. Parking," Amanda Wagner told me, a copy of the Washington Court Rules in her hand.

"Is Justin moving with you?" Justin Chapman, whose actions had helped destroy the law firm where Amanda and her husband had been young lawyers and where I'd learned the HR trade. He and I had met again this past August, after his wife's murder. I hadn't liked him any better then than I had years ago.

"No. He found an office share—not sure where. Figures, we give notice and the landlord decides to upgrade this place. New paint, carpet. Oh, well." She stashed the book in an open box. "Sit, while I still have an extra chair."

I told her about my long friendship with Maddie Petrosian and that I understood she'd worked on the deal for Maddie's purchase of the corner grocery.

"Horrible news about the shooting," Amanda said. "Sounds like she's recovering, though. I can talk about the deal, but nothing privileged, you understand."

I did.

"Mehmet—Mehmet Barut—was a crusty old guy, but I liked him," she said. "He owned that grocery practically forever. Since 1970, I think. He ran the place himself until two or three years ago. When he hit eighty-five, his kids got after him to sell, but it was hard for him to let go. It gave him financial stability after he and his family immigrated."

Mehmet Barut. M.B. Or, to the neighborhood kids, Emby. "From Turkey?"

Amanda nodded and went on. "He agreed to give Jake Byrd an option, but he was reluctant to actually sell. Then we got another offer. By then, Mehmet was quite ill and had moved down to Portland to live with his daughter. Byrd couldn't match the second offer, so the kids convinced him to take the higher one. He agreed, but died before signing the contract. The kids—they're in their fifties—debated whether to sign or not, so the probate took some time. Got it wrapped up a few weeks ago."

"What was their concern?"

"By then, we'd discovered that Maddie Petrosian was behind the entity making the second offer. The daughter knew Mehmet had refused previous offers from the Petrosians, so she hesitated."

Amanda reached for a stainless steel water bottle. "Sure I can't get you anything? We're packing the coffee maker last so we can unpack it first."

"Smart, but no, thanks."

"Maddie's father had pestered Mehmet to sell, and he didn't like that. Called him a pushy Armenian, out to pull one over on a Turk. But the son lives in Seattle. He'd been to the community meetings, and he knew the neighborhood didn't like Byrd's plan."

"That's for sure," I said.

"The son thought Maddie had the experience to do things right. The neighbors liked her plan and it met city requirements, with a façade consistent with the rest of the block and a grocery on street level." Amanda took a long drink, then continued. "Nothing like packing to kick up dust. Seeing her plans tipped the scales. They knew Mehmet cared deeply about the neighborhood. He'd been part of it for decades. They trusted Maddie to follow through and not go all high-end condo, even if her grocery sells more fancy wine than Twinkies."

Maddie did love fine wine, but I suspected she was not above selling Twinkies.

"And they figured he'd have enjoyed scoring a small fortune off the Petrosians, way more than Byrd could put on the table," Amanda continued.

"Might ease their minds to know the Petrosians weren't after the property because they wanted to outplay a Turk. I believe it once belonged to their family, decades before Barut bought it from someone else." My guess was Barut knew the history, and let the old nationalist animosity get in the way of helping a family regain its legacy. Nothing else explained Maddie's willingness to trick him.

"If it was so important, why'd they ever sell?"

"Dunno." I stood. "Thanks a million. Good luck with the move."

I pointed my creaky old Saab toward downtown. Maddie's scheme hadn't been so underhanded at all. Smart. Shrewd. She'd found a way to get what she wanted. Family trait, though in this instance, she'd succeeded where her father had not.

But Amanda had asked a good question. I intended to get the answer.

BACK in the Market, on foot, I slowed when I got to the Asian grocery, wondering if the woman in the photo with Joe Huang might be working. I had no good excuse to talk to her. But thinking about the shop and its possible connection to Huang, and his possible connection to Patrick Halloran, over the last few days had made me crave cold sesame noodles with a hot stir-fry. That's just how my mind works.

But every plan—and a recipe is a plan—needs a few essential ingredients.

The old lady was not on front door duty, so my ankles were saved their ritual nipping. I found the egg noodles and chili-garlic paste, but wasn't sure I had enough sesame oil on hand. I was staring at the shelf, pondering toasted or regular, organic or inorganic, cute bottle or ho-hum, when a woman spoke to me.

"May I help you? Sesame oil is very good."

No mistaking her. She was the woman in the photo—small, dark-haired, maybe thirty. "Can't make up my mind—too many options. For sesame noodles and a stir-fry."

"This is my favorite." She was several inches shorter than I, about five-two, and the top shelf was a stretch, but she reached for a shapely brown bottle with a white label, the name written vertically in Asian characters. "Plain is good. Toasted is better."

Toasted would have more flavor, ideal for drizzling on top. Plain would tolerate the heat of cooking better, without picking up a scorched taste or setting off my smoke alarm. "I'll take them both."

"What else do you need?" she asked as I followed her to the counter. "Sesame seeds? Soy sauce? Tamari?" Though her grammar was correct, her inflection was off, suggesting she was born abroad and had learned English as an adult.

"Mama!" a small voice interjected. The woman and I turned to see a small girl, who bowed her head, then raised it and spoke. Her purple jacket hung open, the pink backpack dangling from one hand. "I'm sorry. I didn't mean to interrupt."

"Hello, there," I said. The child in the photo, the child I had seen in the back hall with the old lady. Then I heard shuffling feet and glanced toward the back of the shop in time to see the old lady peeling off a coat as she disappeared into the office. "Do you go to the Market preschool? Does your grandmother meet you after school?"

The girl nodded, turning shy.

"I run the spice shop down the street," I told her.

"Oh, where Arf stays," she said. "The dog who used to live with Sam."

"That's right," I replied, surprised, though I shouldn't have been. Sam had been a fixture in the Market, and Arf his faithful companion. The dog had more friends here than I did.

The woman rang up my purchases. I handed her a twenty and as she fished in the drawer for change, my eyes drifted to the photographs on the wall behind her. Family pictures, as in Maddie's office. But the one that stood out was a group of two dozen men and women, all ages and ethnicities, united by their dress-up clothes and beaming smiles. In the middle stood a former lawyer from my old firm who'd been appointed a federal judge ten years ago, in her black robe. She was beaming, too.

The woman followed my gaze and pointed to her younger self, standing beside an older couple. I recognized the old lady right away. "The day we became citizens," she said, and grinned. "The whole family."

I grinned back, then glanced at the photo again. No Joe Huang. "Your husband, too?"

Her smile wavered, and she did not answer my question. "Lily is a citizen times two. She was born later, here." She reached for my tote, but I dug inside for a collapsible bag to hold my shopping. By "times two," I assumed she meant that Lily was a citizen both because she'd been born here and because her mother had been naturalized. Did that also imply that her father was not a citizen?

Is this what we've come to, I wondered, that immigrants feel obliged to explain their status to a virtual stranger?

"She's a delight," I told her mother. "Bring her down for spice tea and to pet the dog. You're both welcome, anytime."

Outside, I stopped at the produce stall, then found a nice flank steak at the butcher. Back in my shop, I greeted my dog and staff, and dealt with a few office matters before closing. The giant sunflowers I'd bought last weekend were looking bedraggled, and I tossed them in the compost bin, reminding myself to pick up a fresh bouquet in the morning. We wouldn't have too many more chances.

Then I took my dog and my full shopping bag home. I sliced

the beef and marinated it with soy sauce and chili-garlic paste, adding a good glug of sesame oil from each bottle. Made the noodles. Popped the cork on an Oregon pinot noir, and let the first sip roll down the back of my throat, fruity and earthy, the perfect taste for the season.

I turned on the pregame show, volume low, so I wouldn't miss the first pitch. My grandfather Reece had nicknamed me for his favorite ballplayer, the fiery St. Louis Cardinal Pepper Martin. He'd given me the love of baseball, too, and though he'd been gone many years, I enjoy thinking of him when I watch a game.

Much the way soccer united Gabe and Pat Halloran, despite Pat's death. I suspected the corner grocery had the same effect for Maddie's father, David Petrosian, reminding him of the grandfather who'd stood so proudly with his produce and his delivery truck. Maddie's determination to honor the family legacy made sense, when I thought of it that way.

I plopped on the couch, the dog at my feet, and texted Nate about the day. *Home Saturday,* he answered. *Can't wait!* I replied.

I was still smiling at the phone when it rang. No name or number, but I had a feeling.

"You didn't leave me a message," Detective Tracy said.

"You're a detective. I knew you'd figure out who called."

"But the question is why."

I told him what I'd learned at Maddie's office, and my theory about her buying up the other properties in order to finance the purchase of the corner property. I could hear him making notes. So much for getting my dinner ready before the first pitch—the lineups were being announced.

"We copied the hard drive of their computer system," he said. "Going over it bit by bit. You learned a lot more from that receptionist than we did."

Take cookies. "She's upset, but she wants to help. And you didn't have the album. I presume you're looking at Jake Byrd."

Tracy grunted. "Again. He and the alibi I can't prove or disprove, despite half the force crawling all over it."

Which crime was he talking about? Didn't matter, I supposed. Not my circus.

"Even so, I don't know what Byrd would have to do with Patrick Halloran's death," I said. "Maddie had tried to buy the property, but lost out to Byrd, so no reason for Pat or Neighbors United to be worried about her. She didn't start buying up the block until after Pat died. That's the only link between them. That, and a love of soccer."

"What?" Tracy said sharply. The home team was taking the field. I talked fast.

"Her husband, Tim Peterson, works for the Sounders. Gabe Halloran played soccer in high school and now plays for Notre Dame. Pat played as a kid and coached Gabe until high school."

But it was too faint a connection to mean a thing.

We hung up just as the pitcher went into his windup.

Strike one.

Broccoli beef cooks fast, and by the time we got to the second inning, scoreless, I had a plate of the fragrant combo paired with a healthy dose of deliciously seasoned noodles. Baseball, good food and wine, and a soft rain falling outside. My sweetie on his way home, my dog happy with a bone.

All should have been well with the world, but it was not. Maddie had a long road to recovery. A neighborhood was anxious. A killer was on the loose. And Laurel was bearing a burden I could hardly fathom.

No, all was not right. But I was going to do everything I could to change that.

Tomorrow.

Twenty-Four

Gather ye rosebuds while ye may,
Old Time is still a-flying.
And this same flower that smiles to-day
To-morrow will be dying.

—Robert Herrick, "To the Virgins, to Make Much of Time"

THE RAIN HAD STOPPED BY THE TIME ARF AND I LEFT THE loft Friday morning. We took the Market elevator from Western to the main level and headed for the flower stalls. The season was changing—had changed—and while I could not hold on to the past, I could enjoy a few more days of bright scented color. The opening bell hadn't rung yet, and the Hmong flower ladies were still filling buckets with water and counting out stems.

"Sunflowers," I said, thinking of the front counter. "And dahlias. Oh, gosh. That one." I pointed to a bouquet of pinks and yellows, whites and apricots, and a deep red stunner.

"I wanted that one," a baritone broke in. Jamie, a bakery bag in hand. "I swear, between the lattes and the pastries, I'm going to be fat as that pig by spring." She gestured toward Rachel, the bronze Market mascot and piggy bank, standing guard near the entrance.

"There are no calories in the Market," I said. If only that were true.

She laughed, a joyful, rumbling sound. "I want flowers for the stall, then I'll take them home to paint. These are my colors."

We found her a bouquet as pretty as the one I'd chosen, and wound our way down the North Arcade.

"I wanted to tell you," she said, lowering her voice. "I saw the people in the picture you dropped."

"Watch where you're going, you idiot!" a man yelled, and we both stopped, unsure what we'd done. But the man wasn't yelling at us. His target was another man, struggling with a balky hand truck.

"Dude, cool it," Jamie said, and we stepped out of the Arcade on to the cobbles, where it wasn't quieter, but was easier to talk.

"This morning, on the bus. I knew I'd seen them somewhere else. They all got on together, the man in the photo, along with the woman and the little girl from the other photo, and an old lady. It was crowded, but somebody in back offered the old woman his seat, so she took it and the younger woman stood in the aisle next to her. The man in the picture stayed up front with the girl, right next to me. She's so cute, in her purple jacket and the pink unicorn backpack."

"That's her."

"I was wearing my purple coat, so I smiled and she smiled back, and we started talking about our favorite colors. I told her I liked her braids. She said her dad did her hair, and looked up at him and he looked back at her, and I—I'd have given anything to have a father who adored me like that." She broke off and I had to wonder what family trauma she'd gone through. "They got off on First and Pike, same as me. She held his hand the whole time. But I got slowed down, lugging a portfolio of new paintings, and I lost track of them. Anyway, I don't know if that's helpful, but it was definitely him."

"That," I said, "is more helpful than you can imagine. And when you paint those dahlias, let me know. My walls would love a fresh bouquet."

First thing I did inside the shop was call Detective Tracy and tell him what Jamie Ackerman had seen. "From what you said, sounds like Joe Huang works with people who had a beef with Patrick Halloran, but you can't tie him, or them, to Maddie Petrosian, despite Special Agent Greer's very special efforts."

Tracy grunted. I took that for yes and went on. "I know you won't rule him out because I said so. I don't know his immigration status, though I assume he's not an American citizen."

"You assume correctly."

"But no man that devoted to his daughter is going to do anything to risk deportation. I'm just saying, keep that in mind."

Another grunt. "You may be right. I'll pass that on. By the way, good thinking last night on Ms. Petrosian. We'll be flying a little closer to Mr. Byrd."

"Tell me about that alibi of his. Maybe I can help."

"Don't press your luck," Tracy said. "Although with your love of movies, maybe I should. 'Course if you broke his alibi, I'd have to give you an honorary badge." Before I could ask what he meant by that, he clicked off.

Then it was time to put my nose to the grindstone, metaphorically speaking. I could not leave work today. The weather was clearing and the weekend was upon us. And I still had to solve the Edgar problem. Kristen was off today, helping chaperone a school field trip, so my questions about our own school days would have to wait.

But the customers could not wait. "Good heavens, did you see what they want for a vanilla bean?" I heard one woman say to another. "Raising the prices right before people start their holiday baking."

"The culprit is weather," I said. "Vanilla is native to Mexico, but these days, the bulk of it is grown in Madagascar, off the east coast of Africa. A cyclone hit the island a couple of years ago and destroyed most of the vines. They've been replanted, but it takes three or four years for a plant to produce a crop. Plus it's very labor intensive. It's basically an orchid."

"Oh," the woman said, her irritation at being overheard turning to mild interest.

"Our vanilla may be pricy, but it's the real thing. You will not find any artificial flavors or substitutes on our shelves." Thanks to the solid relationships the shop's founder had established with farmers and suppliers worldwide. But watching for fakes is a constant challenge.

"You know," the friend said, "I've got an extra bottle, from when we cleaned out my mother's kitchen. It's nearly full. You can take it."

The complainer agreed. They sampled our tea and left empty-handed. You can't win them all.

Cody Ellingson arrived right on time. His black polo was a little big, and I wondered if he'd borrowed it from his dad. We found him a spare apron. Turned out he'd had a psych class with Reed, who flashed me a thumb's up. Matt showed him the new delivery system he and Reed had devised, moving from a clipboard with a list of the day's stops and a stack of paper invoices to an electronic version we could run on our phones.

"So, you played soccer with Gabe Halloran?" I asked as we guided the loaded hand truck out the door and onto the cobbles, away from foot traffic.

"Same team," Cody replied, "but I was never in his league. He was two years younger, but always better."

"That must have been hard. Here's our first stop."

"No. Gabe loves the game. I played for fun. Though my dad could never understand that. He and my mom, they do everything to win."

"Must make Monopoly a hoot."

"You have no idea," he said.

He caught on quickly. A few customers knew him from morning bread deliveries, and he chatted easily, showing no sign of the nerves I'd detected in his interview.

Back in the shop, my phone buzzed with a pair of texts. From Tariq, the line cook working for Edgar's rival: *Hot on the trail.*

Just what I needed. A hot-headed rogue chef who fancied himself my detective sergeant.

The second came from Tim Peterson. Maddie had been asking for me. Could I come up to the hospital? He couldn't be sure how long she'd be awake and alert enough to talk.

I couldn't possibly go. But I had to.

As luck would have it, that meant Cody and I were headed in the same direction at the same time, on the same bus, me to the hospital, he to hang out with a friend on campus.

"We're hoping to get a place together," he said as we slipped into seats next to the back door. "Maybe next semester. I need to get away from my parents and all the fighting."

"I'm sorry. That's rough." Across the aisle sat the young barista from the Montlake coffeehouse, and the three of us acknowledged each other.

"It's all about money," he said. "She blames him for losing his job—a guy who worked for him got in trouble with the feds and Dad had to shut down his company, even though he hadn't done anything wrong."

Not how I'd heard the story, but it's gotta be hard to confess your screw-ups to your kids.

"So she went back to work, but it's boom and bust, you know? Everybody thinks real estate agents make boatloads of money, especially since the housing market's so hot, but half the time, they work their butts off for nothing."

Though he wanted to get away, he clearly loved both parents and sympathized with their troubles. We were nearing my stop, but I stayed put. Better to give my new employee a sympathetic ear. "Your mom must have been pretty upset when the plans to develop condos on the corner grocery lot fell through."

"Yeah. This other developer, a woman, pulled a fast one and tricked them all. My mom had invested most of their savings into the project and poof! Gone."

As I looked at Cody, I noticed the barista eavesdropping.

"That's the woman who was shot," I said, and Cody nodded.

"I know, man, it was awful," the barista said. "I just came back from the police station. That's why I'm late."

"The police station?" I said.

"Yeah. Last Thursday, when it happened, we'd been swamped. Morning rush was over and I was out in the alley, wiping off tables and cleaning up. It was a pretty day—the rain didn't start until Friday."

"Did you see something?" I asked.

"I heard a loud noise. I thought it was somebody dropping the lid on the metal Dumpster at the end of the alley. I didn't see anybody, so I just kept working. A couple minutes later, I saw movement." He raised a hand and waved it alongside his face. "You know, how you know something is moving, but you can't actually see anything? Anyway, I looked up again and that's when I saw the guy."

"What? You saw the shooter?"

"They think so, the cops, but all I saw was a guy in a dark rain jacket and a ball cap rushing down the alley away from me. Medium height and build—about your size," he said to Cody, and I felt him stiffen. The barista blew out his breath and continued.

"The cops had me look at a bunch of pictures, but I couldn't identify anyone. I didn't even know anything had happened until I heard the ambulance maybe twenty minutes later. They say she's going to be okay, thank God."

No wonder he'd seemed so upset when I stopped in Monday afternoon.

The bus drew into the curb at Broadway and Madison, the corner of the compact Seattle University campus. Cody stood. "Sorry for running my mouth, Pepper. This is my stop. See you next week." Then the door opened and he bounded down the steps and out of sight.

I glanced over at the barista, who'd put in his earbuds and was staring out the window. I got off at the next stop and backtracked the few blocks to the hospital. The barista's description of the man he saw behind the corner grocery was too vague to be useful. But to Cody, upset by his parents' bickering, had it come too close to describing his dad? Without a job to go to, Bruce Ellingson was home during the day and could easily have been in the alley at the time Maddie was shot. And you don't change the locks on a building you plan to tear down. Had Deanna still had keys?

The Ellingsons were grudge holders, and grudges can lead to murder. Bruce's beef was with Patrick Halloran, Deanna's with Maddie Petrosian. Certainly Bruce could have blamed Pat for their current troubles, and Pat's participation in the protests against the Byrd's Nest had benefitted Maddie, at Deanna's expense, but not until long after his death.

I was back where I started, trying to find a connection between a dead man and a woman who could barely talk. An affair? Laurel claimed not to have suspected one until after Pat's death. It gave her a motive to go after Maddie, but she had an alibi. Plus, if she'd tried to kill Maddie, she'd have thrown the lipstick in the trash or off her dock into Lake Union and kept her suspicions to herself.

And if she'd attempted murder on Maddie, who had killed Pat?

Near the hospital, I scanned the crowded for Smoking Man. He was an expert at blending in. I couldn't be sure I'd recognize him.

One of the many things I didn't know—that apparently no one knew yet—was whether Maddie knew who had shot her. Male or female—any detail would help. Though with her injuries and all the drugs, her account might not be totally reliable.

I dodged a puddle on the sidewalk and wondered who else had access to the old grocery besides Maddie and Deanna. Her builder, to figure out how best to demolish the place without damaging the adjacent structures. Jake Byrd. Who else?

A different guard sat outside the ICU today, working a cross-word puzzle. He found my name on the list with no trouble. No sign of Officer Clark.

Maddie was alone, her eyes closed. The curtains had been pulled across both the interior and exterior windows, giving the room an eerie midday darkness, though the door was open. I sat in the chair next to her bed and reached for her hand.

"Maddie, it's me. Pepper."

Her eyes remained closed, but she gripped my hand.

"Between Kristen and me, we've heard from half the girls in our class," I said. "We're all rooting for you. And I see they all sent flowers."

Her mouth twitched, an attempt at a smile. I handed her the big sippy cup.

"Maddie, I know this is hard, but you've never let hard things stop you. Tim said you wanted to talk to me."

"Soccer," she said.

That sent my brain scrambling. What had Kristen said? "The kids are back at practice and doing great. Only a few more weeks in the season. Next spring, you'll be out there cheering louder than ever."

"He—stayed. The building . . ."

I scooted my chair forward, angling so she could see me better. "Are you trying to tell me who you saw in the building? When you were shot?"

"No," she said firmly. "Pat."

That didn't make any sense at all. Pat had been dead for three years. She hadn't seen him in the building.

"What? You saw who shot Pat?"

"No. No."

I heard a soft rap on the doorframe. Tim walked in, a Star-bucks cup in hand. We exchanged air-kisses and chitchat about the kids, careful to include Maddie rather than talk as if she weren't there, though she didn't say anything. She stretched an arm toward the photo albums, now stacked on the deep windowsill, and Tim handed her one absently. She pushed it away and pointed again.

"Grandma," she said.

"You want your grandmother's photo album?" I asked, and she nodded. Tim was closer, so he picked it up.

A nurse walked in. "Time for your pills."

"Time for me to go," I said, and leaned in to kiss Maddie's cheek. "I'll be back in a day or two."

Maddie grabbed my hand. "Tell Laurel—the building worked. Tell her."

"I will," I said, though what she meant, I had no idea.

Twenty-Five

A scent can reduce us to tears in a moment.

—Philippa Stanton, *Conscious Creativity*

"SORRY," Tim said as he walked down the hall with me. "She was talking in full sentences earlier today. It comes and goes."

"No need to apologize. I can only imagine what you're all going through." We pushed through the ICU doors and stopped. The guard stand was empty now. "One thing that's puzzled me, though, is why the Seattle police had a guard on her earlier but not now. They haven't made an arrest, so what's changed?"

"What? No, they haven't been guarding her. Police have been in and out—two detectives, short black guy, kinda grumpy, and a tall thin white guy. And the liaison officer."

"Tracy's the grump. Armstrong's his partner. What about the FBI? Agent Meg Greer, midthirties, always wears black. She might have a male partner. White guy, about your size. Don't know his age."

"Greer, I've seen, once. Early on. No partner. My impression is she's focused on a suspect they'd targeted for Halloran's murder."

"A guy connected to a Chinese import–export firm?"

"Yeah. But I can't see what that might have to do with Maddie. I don't think they do, either."

"Maddie's family owned that corner lot once, didn't they? Decades ago? Why did they sell?"

"They didn't sell it. Some uncle or great-uncle lost it in a bad financial deal, something vaguely criminal. I don't know the details. It kinda tore the family apart."

What had Miriam Petrosian said about her husband's uncle? That he'd been the boy in the photograph of the delivery truck. She'd said his name. Unusual, Armenian, but what was it?

"Just now, Maddie mentioned Pat. He was active in the group that opposed Jake Byrd's development, right? And she went to a few meetings. Is that how she knew him?"

"She knew him before that, from soccer. Pat helped coach the younger kids, including Max."

It hadn't occurred to me that Pat had coached Maddie and Tim's son. "What about Bruce Ellingson? His son Cody played on the same high school team as Gabe Halloran."

"Doesn't ring any bells. I should get back."

"Yeah, yeah." We air-kissed and Tim left, the ICU doors swooshing shut behind him.

So Maddie would have known Pat from the kids' soccer team, which explained why she'd said "soccer." But why say "building"? And why mention him at all?

I glanced at the empty guard stand, then pushed my way back into the ICU. Tim was standing at the nurses' station, talking with the nurse who'd given Maddie her medication. I touched Tim's arm and led him a few feet away.

"Tim, does Maddie know she was shot with the same gun as Pat?"

He ran a hand over what was left of his hair. "It's hard to say what she knows and doesn't. We've tried not to talk about the incident in front of her, but she could have heard us out in the hall."

So why was she talking about Pat? Even scrambled, Maddie's brain had to have its reasons. Laurel's suspicion of an affair was the last thing I wanted to bring up now, but it loomed large.

A strangled gulp caught my attention. Tim had gone wild-eyed and pale, his hand in a fist at his mouth.

"What if I lose her? She's everything, Pepper. I mean, someday something will happen, I know, but not now. Not for decades. We have kids, plans."

I led him to a chair a few feet away and the nurse brought him a cup of water. "It's okay," I said, though it wasn't, and sat next to him, my hand on his arm. "Is Miriam staying with you, or at her own place? Is there someone I can call? Your parents . . ."

"My mother's been ill. My dad can't leave her. My sister's flying up from L.A. this weekend to help with the kids." He swallowed back tears. "The team's been great, giving me time off, sending takeout. A couple of the players came up to visit, though the docs wouldn't let them in to see her. You can bet if they were Seahawks instead of Sounders, the doors would have flown open." He smiled, but without any humor.

I stayed a few more minutes, until Tim had collected himself. "Call me anytime, for any reason. You need anything . . ."

Only then did I notice he was still clutching the photograph album Maddie had pointed to just before we left her room. "Could I borrow that album? I'll bring it back my next visit, I promise."

He handed it over without a word, then turned and strode back to his wife.

I'D MISSED lunch, so I hopped off the bus not far from the scene of last week's crash and headed for Ripe. The aroma of tomato-basil soup nearly knocked me off my feet. Lunch rush was long over, so Laurel sat with me for a quick chat.

"I think Cody is going to work out fine," I said between bites, "but man, tough spot for a kid. He's pretty angry."

"They—Bruce—pushed him too hard. On everything, soccer most of all. He was a decent high school player, but not college level."

One more reason to resent the Hallorans? For an ambitious couple like the Ellingsons, in a bad stretch largely of their own making, the model family next door must have been a constant reminder of their troubles.

Except that no couple, no family is perfect. Part of being an adult is recognizing that. Too often, I failed to remember that about Maddie.

"Tell me about your interview with Detective Tracy."

"He read me the riot act, understandably. As for charges, he can't say that knowing about the lipstick tube three years ago would have solved the crime, especially now, when it's clear that Maddie did not shoot Pat."

"Laurel, what if they weren't having an affair? What if—

what if Maddie went to your house to see Pat about something else?" Was that what she'd been talking about Wednesday, when I thought she was trying to tell me why she went to the old grocery the day she was shot?

"Like what? What would have been important enough for him to skip a soccer tournament? He never skipped a game."

"What if she was consulting him about the development project?"

"That's crazy. He wasn't a real estate lawyer."

"No, but he was deeply committed to making sure that project was something the community could live with. What if he was helping her figure out a way to derail Jake Byrd? He did have a lot of experience dealing with financial transactions." I found the list of Maddie's purchases in my tote and laid it on the table, tapping it with a finger. "She started buying up properties in that block not long after Pat died. Eventually, she bought the corner lot, using an LLC with a name almost identical to Byrd's business name. Her secretary says this is the only time Maddie ever did that. Why? And where did she get the idea?"

"What has gotten into you, Pepper? Suggesting my husband used his knowledge of the law to help Maddie Petrosian perpetrate a fraud."

"Not a fraud. It was all perfectly legal, and perfectly reasonable. Look. Isn't that the kind of methodical planning and creative thinking Pat was known for? Wouldn't you rather believe he was helping her stop Jake Byrd from ruining the neighborhood than believe he was having an affair?"

"But why not tell me?"

The pain in her voice cut my heart. "Maybe Maddie asked him to keep it secret until she could put the plan in place. If it got out, it might not have worked." I hoped we could ask her soon.

"Jake Byrd and Deanna Ellingson," she said. "You don't think they killed him?"

I sat back. "I don't know. Byrd has some kind of alibi—Tracy won't say what."

After a long moment, she raised her eyes to mine. "I'm sorry I snapped at you. You're trying to help my family and that means more to me than I can ever say. I don't know what to think anymore."

"Call Seetha for a massage. Bake cookies for the neighbors. Binge-watch *Buffy*."

That got a smile. We've all got a vampire or two to slay.

I WALKED back to the Market on First, past the Art Museum and the old Lusty Lady building, once home to an infamous adult film and peepshow club. Known for marquee witticisms, when it closed, the final message read "Thanx for the Mammaries." The pink sign now lives on in the Museum of History and Industry.

Had Pat really worked with Maddie to forge a plan to save the block? Who else would know, who could tell me? Jess, her secretary, didn't seem privy to that kind of detail. Maybe Tim. And what was the point of the Bird's Nest deception? Had it been entirely to convince old, ill Emby—Mehmet Barut—to go ahead with the sale despite his prejudices?

No matter. It had worked. The genius of the plan had been to quietly buy up the block to protect it, and improve her chances of acquiring the plum parcel.

If this was true, Maddie had risked a lot to put her plan in place. The original building was an important piece of her family history, but why was reclaiming it worth putting everything she, her father, and her grandfather had built on the line?

What was she trying to prove?

The first person I saw when I walked in the shop was one of the last people I'd expected to see.

"Tariq. What brings you here?"

The young cook stopped pacing. "'Bout time you showed up. I got five minutes before I have to run for the bus. I can't be late for prep."

Lateness, if I recalled correctly, had been a problem when he worked for Alex Howard. Maybe he was finally maturing.

We sat in the nook and Tariq placed a small plastic bag on the table between us. I felt like a rogue drug dealer.

"Where did you get this?"

"Filched it when Chef wasn't looking. It's his version, not Edgar's."

"But how did he get it? Chef, I mean."

Tariq's dark eyes flashed. He swiped the screen on his phone and held out a photo for me to see.

"How do I know that woman?" I asked. "She looks familiar."

"Bartender at my current gig. Fills in at Edgar's place. And guess, what, she's Chef's boo."

"Seriously? How did she get into Edgar's stash? He keeps it in his private office. And how did you figure it out?"

"Heard her bragging to Chef. She pranced into Edgar's office to plead for more hours, then pretended she'd lost an earring and snuck back in to find it while Edgar was tied up during service."

The bag held a reddish-brown mixture dotted with seeds and crystal specks. So much trouble over an innocent blend of sea salts, peppers, and herbs. And the secret ingredient I could never divulge. Such is the history of spice.

"You're a prince, Tariq. And I'll make sure Edgar knows it. Now scoot—I don't want to make you late."

He stood, hitched up his pants, and sashayed over to the side door, then stopped and blew me a kiss.

"I can't even," Sandra said, hands on her hips, staring after him.

I reached for my notebook, a stack of small square plates, and a jar filled with tiny tasting spoons. "Sit." She did and Cayenne joined us. The copycat version looked like the real thing, but how did it taste? We each dipped a spoon in the mixture, sniffed, touched it to our tongues, scribbled notes, compared. Sandra and I had the advantage of having worked with Edgar on the formula; we knew what should have been there. And we both knew right away what was missing.

"It's so close," Sandra said. "But that one thing makes so much difference."

"We split, what—three or four dishes?" I said and she nodded. "They were all like that. Close, but not quite."

Cayenne leaned across the table, reading our notes upside down. "Ohmygosh. And this chef guy tasted Edgar's blend, but he didn't detect that?"

"We went through a dozen versions before we came up with exactly what Edgar had in mind," Sandra said. "You tweak, tweak, and finally, you toss in a pinch of thyme, you switch one salt for another, and voilà!"

I sat back, arms folded. "So now what do I do?"

"Now nothing," Sandra said. "Leave him to his own devices. He'll succeed or fail based on the food and service."

"That won't solve my problem with Edgar."

"How about this?" Cayenne laid out a plan so perfect I instantly wanted to hug her.

There is nothing like the right woman for the job.

Twenty-Six

*Tell me what you eat and I shall tell you
what you are.*

—Jean Anthelme Brillat-Savarin,
French politician and gastronome

THE DOOR TO MY BUILDING WAS FIRMLY LATCHED WHEN ARF
and I reached it. In a day this crazy, that counted as a big relief.

Leftovers for dinner. Fine with me—Nate would be home
tomorrow, and I needed to clean, not spend the evening cooking.
Not that he cared, but I did. Happily, spiffing a place this small
doesn't take long. Airedales don't shed much, thank goodness.

I finished my whirlwind cleaning spree before the first pitch.
The National League team led two games to one, but I was sure my
guys could turn things around, now that they were back in their
home park with a W in their column. Leftover noodles, reheated
broccoli beef, and a light red wine in a clean house.

It was a good life.

During a commercial break, I picked up Maddie's album.
Inside the cover was a name, in thick, old-fashioned script: Tamar
Gregorian. Below that, in a different hand, another name: Rose
Gregorian Petrosian, Maddie's grandmother and, I guessed,
Tamar's daughter. The early pages showed a young woman, dark
hair brushing the collar of her white blouse and dark jacket. At
her somber expression, the phrase "fresh off the boat" leapt into

mind. More photos of the young woman followed, then one of her smiling, next to a handsome, slender man, both in dark suits. I slipped it out and turned it over. "Jacob and Tamar," it read. "March 4, 1924." A courthouse photo of the happy day.

After that came photos of the couple with a small boy. Haig, the mysterious uncle? The back confirmed it. A baby girl followed—Rose.

I flipped forward, one eye on the game. Stopped at a wedding picture, a young man in an Army uniform, dark hair shining, and a woman in a white gown, blond wisps escaping the veil pushed off her face. Next to him stood a stern couple I recognized as Jacob and Tamar. Beside the bride stood her parents, both fair-haired and looking pleased. I slipped it out. "Haig and Elizabeth," it read, in the same script as Rose's signature on the flyleaf.

Then a baby, round-cheeked, smiling, blond. On the back, "Elizabeth, 1946." Two Elizabeths? Mother and daughter; Haig's family.

But no more pictures of the baby or her parents. I flipped through photos of young Rose. Rose and Aram Petrosian on their wedding day in 1947. Their son David through the years, then David with Miriam, and finally, baby Madeleine.

Where had the other family gone? This album had come to Maddie from her grandmother, who would naturally have focused on herself and her husband, their child and grandchild. But had Haig and Elizabeth and the baby never come for Christmas or Easter? Had they not come to the wedding of Miriam and David, the younger Elizabeth's only cousin on the Gregorian side of the family?

Haig had died at some point, but I didn't know when. Or where. Tim had said the loss of the building had torn the family apart. They might have gone anywhere.

The crack of a bat drew my attention back to the game and I realized I'd missed two innings. A line drive took a bad bounce in front of the left fielder. I cheered as the runner beat the throw from left with a slide into second base, and put the album aside. Bottom of the sixth, runners in scoring position with one out. By the time the inning ended, my team had scored three times and led five to two.

After a dash to the bathroom, I sank onto the couch. Heard

a thunk as the forgotten album slid to the floor. Reached down to retrieve it. My fingers grazed a sheet of yellow paper that had fallen out. I picked it up and unfolded it. The handwriting was different from what I'd seen on the back of the photographs. My mind flashed on the legal pad on Maddie's desk. The same writing, and no easier to read.

The pitcher retired the side, and my team came to bat. Yellow sheet in hand, I leaned closer to the floor lamp, squinting. In high school, we'd had to map out our family trees. That's what these notes were, but more recent—this tree included Maddie's marriage to Tim, and the names and birth dates of their two children.

At the top of the tree were names I didn't know, some incomplete, all with a small d. and a date between 1915 and 1918. Killed in Armenia, no doubt. My mother's parents had come from Hungary after World War II, and our family tree, too, showed a rash of deaths in a short time. I traced Maddie's line up to her parents, David and Miriam, bypassing Miriam's family, though I noted those names, too, ended in the telltale Armenian suffix -ian, meaning "son of."

The leadoff hitter reached first, and the second fell behind on the count. David had no siblings; nor had his mother, Rose Gregorian. David's father, Aram Petrosian, had a brother who died in infancy, and a sister who had married and left several children. I glanced up; the hitter was still battling the pitcher. My finger reached Rose's parents, Jacob and Tamar Gregorian, then started down another branch, that of their son, Haig. He'd married Elizabeth in October 1945. After he returned from the war, I guessed. If I was making out the date right, he died in 1952.

1952. He'd been twenty-eight, his daughter six.

What had happened to her? The tree did not tell me.

I turned the pages of the album slowly, looking for more clues. Tucked in the back, in a manila pocket, were three square envelopes, each addressed to Tamar Gregorian, bearing a return address in Oakland, California, but no name, postmarked in December 1952, 1953, and 1954. They'd been slit open, the cards left inside. I slid out the first, but the noise of a TV crowd caught my ear. The second batter had reached first when I wasn't watching, and now a double play ended the inning.

The first envelope held a simple card showing a nativity scene.

Inside, beneath a generic printed message, was the signature "Betty and Lizzie." A small photo showed a smiling blond girl in a plaid jumper. A school uniform? On the back, the same handwriting read "Lizzie, 6, first grade."

The second and third envelopes held the next two years' cards, likewise signed by the mother for herself and the child, a school photo tucked inside.

The eighth inning ended, scoreless, and the opposing team came to bat, trailing by three. I slipped two fingers into the photo sleeve and pulled out one more envelope addressed to Tamar. Same return address and postmark, years later.

The envelope contained a folded card, the cover illustration a drawing of a smiling infant in a sea of blue blankets. I took a deep breath and opened it. Inside was a color snapshot of a sleeping baby, one tiny fist on the pillow beside his head.

I was vaguely aware of the noise of distant cheering as I read the message, in the same hand as the Christmas cards.

"Your first great-grandchild," Betty had written. I turned over the photo, knowing before I read it what Lizzie had named her son.

Jacob.

ARF and I left the building on Western, me checking the door behind us to make sure it latched. We both think better when we're moving. Well, I do; I couldn't speak for my dog.

A light mist hung in the air, mimicking the fog in my brain.

We followed Arf's nose down to Alaskan Way, where the lights of the waterfront glowed like eerie sentinels.

Though Maddie's side of the family tree she'd sketched was current, the Haig branch ended with his marriage to Elizabeth—Betty. Had she found the cards in her grandmother's album, and reached the same conclusion I had, but not yet updated the tree? If Betty had sent Tamar a wedding invitation for Lizzie, neither it or a photo had made it into this album. But despite their apparent estrangement, she'd wanted her mother-in-law to know of Jacob's arrival. There was no hint, on the envelopes, the backs of the photos, or in Maddie's notes, of Lizzie Gregorian's married name.

But I had no doubt that the baby boy born three years before Maddie was Jacob Byrd.

How much had Maddie figured out? Arf's leash in my left hand,

I drew the imaginary family tree in the air with my right. Elizabeth the elder, Betty, had been Haig's wife, making their daughter, Lizzie, cousin to David, Maddie's father. That made Lizzie's child, or children, Maddie's second cousins.

Jake. Jacob, for the great-grandfather he had never known. I'd met a few Jakes in our age range over the years, but it had not been a trendy name back then.

Arf set a good pace, and before I knew it we'd reached our usual turn-around. On the way back, we slowed for cars leaving the ferry terminal. This time of year, tourist traffic wanes, but it was Friday night and people were spilling in and out of the waterfront restaurants. I found the sounds of laughter and footsteps comforting, a reminder that life carried on despite the grim mystery I'd stumbled into. I passed Ye Olde Curiosity Shop, one of Seattle's oldest and oddest businesses, and Elliott's Oyster House, a regular spice customer with crab cakes almost as good as Edgar's, and kept going, north by northwest.

Maddie desperately wanted to regain the property her family had lost—through Haig's shady dealings, if Tim had the story right. To restore the family legacy. Had Jake been trying to get control of it for the same reasons? And yet, his plans differed vastly from hers.

What did that difference tell me?

At Union, I turned away from the waterfront, and crossed the area once covered by the viaduct. Though the shadows were gone and I had left the crowds behind, I had the sense that I was not alone. I paused midstride, listening. Footsteps? Greer again? Or my overactive imagination, spurred by reading too many mysteries? I'd already been too stupid to live once this week. I was not going to be TSTL a second time.

I pulled my keys out of my pocket and found the key for the basement door. (Forget that tired advice to thread the keys between your fingers so you can jab an attacker with the pointy ends. Tag says you can't do any real damage that way, except to your own hand. And you'll probably drop your keys.)

Real or imagined, the sound of footsteps behind me continued, intermingled with the medieval harmonies I sometimes hear at moments of danger. I glanced over my shoulder but saw no one. Moths had weevilled their way into the light fixture by the back door, nearly blackening the glass. Digging out my phone and clicking on the flashlight app, while juggling Arf's leash, would slow me down. I reached the steel door, thrust my key in the lock, and turned it. Yanked the door open and slid my hand around to grab the handle on the inside and shut the door tight.

It didn't budge. Someone had grabbed the edge of the door and held it, sticking a foot out to keep me from closing it.

The light in the garage is one of those sensor things that turn on slowly, giving your eyes time to adjust. By the time it reached full brightness, my mind had considered and discarded a handful of possibilities, including the FBI and Jake Byrd.

But I had not considered Bruce Ellingson. He was roughly the same height and build as Smoking Man, and wore a similar dark rain jacket. A ball cap kept the mist off his face.

"Why are you following me? How did you find out where I live?"

"You're not hard to find—your name is all over the Internet. I followed you home from your shop," he said. "Figured you'd have to take the dog out sooner or later."

The dog's wiry coat brushed my leg, the touch enough to tell me he was on high alert. Me, too.

"You pushed your way into my house," he went on. "Pretending you love roses when you've been a friend of Laurel Halloran for ages."

"You knew we were friends."

"Continuing her family's vendetta against mine. What did we ever do to them? Now you're using my son against us. If hiring him is part of your ploy—"

"That's crazy. Cody heard I needed help with deliveries. He's already working in the Market and wanted more hours, so he can gain some independence." How did he think I was using Cody against them?

"BS," Ellingson replied. "My son would never betray us."

I was trapped in a basement with an angry, unstable man. Did he have a gun? The gun that had killed Pat Halloran and injured my old friend? I couldn't tell, and I couldn't squeeze past him. The Saab was too far away for me to take refuge in it or speed out of the garage to safety, and too old for one of those battery-powered key fobs that sets off an alarm.

"Cody's terrified," I said. "Someone saw the killer in the alley behind the grocery, and he's terrified that it was you." Ellingson's brow furrowed and he started to protest, but I kept going. "He hasn't connected you to Patrick Halloran's murder, but the police will. He doesn't know the truth about your brokerage firm, does he?"

"No, I—" In the distance, something electronic beeped and Ellingson stopped. After a long pause, he went on. "My wife worked her tail off to promote the Byrd's Nest. She sank all our savings into that project, and Pat fought her at every turn. Then Maddie Petrosian conned a sick old man into selling her the property instead, for some pipe dream of restoring the glory days. Do you know how much we lost?"

That stopped me. "You think Deanna shot Maddie. But you don't dare go to the police, so you've come here to stop me from asking questions. Did she shoot Pat, too?"

"I—I don't know. I had some trades pending to look over. My personal finances—my license was already gone."

Thanks to Pat.

Ellingson continued. "She'd gone for a walk. She hadn't said anything about dropping in next door. I noticed a movement outside and saw her leaving the Hallorans' house."

"The hedge didn't block your view?"

"I could see the top of her head. We've let the hedge grow since then. She didn't come straight home—took her walk, I assumed. Then—" He stopped, his eyes briefly unfocused as he shook his head slightly.

"Then what?" I asked, my voice low but urgent. Had the lipstick been Deanna's? I thought I heard another beep, but Ellingson didn't seem to notice.

"Then I went upstairs to my office. Half an hour later, more or less, I heard someone calling. I ignored it—thought it was kids messing around. Finally, I looked out and saw Pat crawling across the little deck outside their back door. Bleeding." Ellingson's face was pale, drained by the memory. "He'd called and called. The words hadn't really registered. When they finally did . . ."

When they did, he'd done everything he could, according to the accounts in the paper, but it was too late. The guilt he felt, if I was sizing things up right, came in triplicate: He'd been slow to grasp his neighbor's distress. He suspected his wife of murder but had kept his mouth shut.

Now, he feared that if she'd been desperate enough to shoot Pat, she must have shot Maddie, too.

He couldn't know that the same gun had been used in both shootings. The police had kept that detail quiet while they tried to trace it. But I understood why he assumed the two crimes were connected, and that the connection was his wife.

And why the tensions between Bruce and Deanna Ellingson were driving their son out of the house, and why Bruce had moved into the room with the pink-and-orange flowered bedspread.

The electronic beep sounded again, followed by the grinding of gears and pulleys as the garage door opened. I heard the rev of a motor as a car pulled in.

Arf began barking. I put a hand out to hush him and saw that he was barking not at the approaching vehicle, but at the outside door as it slammed shut. Ellingson was gone.

I exhaled heavily. The driver parked and shut off the engine. Glenn. A moment later, he climbed out, leather satchel in hand.

"Howdy, neighbors. Answering the canine call of nature?" He ran a hand over Arf's head. I was too rattled to reply. "Late meeting up north. Hey, I've got another issue for the HOA. Took three tries before the garage door opened."

The beeps.

"I've got one, too," I said and told him about the dirty outside light fixture as we climbed the wide stairs.

"That's an easy fix," he said. We reached our floor. "G'night, Paprika. Sleep tight."

Fat chance. Instead of a date with a second glass of pinot and a twisty-turny fictional mystery, I had a telephone date with Detective Michael Tracy.

Twenty-Seven

Researchers say we categorize foods based on experience of past interaction, so we think of pancakes as breakfast food but not Brussels sprouts or spaghetti. Obviously, cold pizza contradicts the theory.

THIS TIME I WAS THE ONE TRUDGING DOWN TO POLICE headquarters for a morning meeting. I swung by the shop first, to help Sandra get ready to open and make sure she was okay keeping the dog for a few hours, then whip up a couple of samples that had been simmering in my brain.

On a Saturday morning, the SPD lobby was eerily silent. Detective Armstrong met me, looking even taller than usual in his skinny jeans, his weekend nod to professional attire a blue-and-white striped dress shirt. Inside a small conference room, Detective Tracy sat at one end of the table, his camel sport coat slung over the back of the chair. Special Agent Greer gave no sign that we'd chatted uncomfortably a few nights ago when she introduced the man at the other end of the table, her partner, Special Agent Javier Navarro.

Who bore absolutely no resemblance to Smoking Man.

"I filled them in," Tracy said. "But we'd all like to hear the whole story in your own words."

"Good morning to you, too, Detective." I pulled out a chair.

Armstrong closed the door and took the seat next to me. Step by step, I relayed my Friday night encounter with Bruce Ellingson, punctuated by sips of hot coffee. Though Tag swears they serve only the good stuff in his precinct, I hadn't trusted the supply here and brought my own. Brother Cadfael might find comfort in an herbal tincture, but dark roast feeds my soul.

I finished. Tracy glared at me. "Your Nancy Drew routine could have gotten you killed."

"Never my favorite fictional detective, though I do love her cars." That blue Mustang. I sure missed mine. My dad's.

"Go back," Agent Navarro said, twirling a finger in the air. "To when you went to his house earlier in the week."

"That hadn't been my plan," I said. "I was just scouting the neighborhood—it's a few blocks from where my family lived, and I hadn't been down that street in ages. Well, since Sunday." I explained about meeting Laurel for breakfast Sunday morning, taking a walk, then going back on Tuesday. "Ellingson assumed I was house-hunting, and I conned him into showing me his rose garden so I could see what he could see from the house, when he saw Pat crawling across the back deck. If you see what I mean."

Navarro looked down the table at Tracy. "We're still scouring the records, but the Ellingsons are in financial straits. The house isn't listed, but they might be thinking of selling."

"His wife would have been furious that he let me see inside," I said. "She's the queen of appearances. Wears fake eyelashes and diamonds to grab coffee on Sunday morning, because you never know who you'll run into. Even if they couldn't afford a major remodel—I'm pretty sure you'll find she sank their savings, including their remodel fund, into the Byrd's Nest project—she would never put their house on the market until it was professionally staged. But how can they be hurting? She's got tons of listings. Condos sell like cupcakes in this city."

"Like you said," Navarro replied. "Appearances. Many of those are colistings with other agents, or proposals for projects that aren't anywhere near shovel-ready. Some will never materialize. She kept her license while he was raking it in, but didn't work much. Now that the burden of earning an income is on her, she's had to rebuild relationships with developers, create new ones, yada yada. It takes years."

"Don't tell me," Tracy said drily. "You were a real estate agent before you became a special agent."

Navarro rolled his eyes. I decided I liked him.

"So, in a nutshell," Armstrong said, "Ellingson believes his wife killed Halloran, because he heard Halloran cry for help and spotted him out back. He called 911"—he paused to check the report—"at five after six, several minutes after he first started hearing something, and roughly half an hour after he saw her leave the Halloran house. And he knew she had motive."

"That's consistent with the physical evidence indicating he was shot in the mudroom, near the back of the house," Greer said.

"But didn't you tell Laurel—Mrs. Halloran—that there was very little evidence of an intruder in the house itself?" I asked Tracy. "If Deanna shot Pat in the mudroom, and then left by the front door, wouldn't she have left some kind of trail?"

"Maybe," he said.

"Laurel cleaned the house Thursday, knowing she was leaving town for the weekend the next morning. Your crew found Maddie's lipstick on the bathroom floor after the murder. What if," I said, "it was Maddie that Bruce Ellingson saw, not Deanna? They're about the same height, and they both have short dark hair. He only caught a glimpse, through the hedge. It would have been easy to mistake them. She could have driven straight to the ferry and made it."

"You're not saying your friend shot Halloran," Tracy said. "Or that she's in cahoots with the killer."

"No. No, I don't have any idea who shot Pat," I said. "Ellingson didn't hear the shot, and he didn't see anyone lurking around. But say Maddie went out the front door. Sometime in the next twenty to thirty minutes, the killer shows up at the back door. Heck, maybe he was watching, waiting for Maddie to leave. That would explain why Pat was shot in the mudroom and crawled out the back."

"Why would Ms. Petrosian have been there?" Greer asked. "Even if they were they having an affair, that wouldn't explain why she became a target three years later. Mrs. Halloran's alibis are solid, for both crimes."

"I think Maddie went to Pat for help." I explained my theory of the plan to buy up the properties, one by one. "Then, when she owned the rest of the block, or most of it, she'd approach Barut with a proposal to buy the corner lot, using a business name similar to the one Jake Byrd and Deanna Ellingson were using. The corner property was her target all along."

"Why was she so hot on that corner lot?" Navarro asked. "If she wanted to run a convenience store, there must be tons of properties available."

"And why the ruse with the business name?" Armstrong said. He leaned toward me, resting his elbows on his knees. He wasn't wearing socks with his boat shoes, and his jeans rode up a few inches, giving me a glimpse of the orca tattooed on his ankle. "From what you've said about her, doesn't sound like her style."

"It isn't," I said. "And any old convenience store wouldn't do. What Maddie wants is to recreate what her family lost. The first business they built in this country, on that very spot. The business and property they lost because of Jake Byrd's grandfather's recklessness."

I dug the album out of my tote and showed them what I'd found: the pictures, the cards, the notes. On the whiteboard on the wall behind us, Armstrong drew a large-scale version of the Gregorian family tree, filling in the names Maddie hadn't added to hers: Elizabeth "Lizzie" married Byrd? followed by a descendant line to Jacob "Jake." Then he drew dotted cousin lines between Lizzie and David, Jake and Maddie.

The detectives and special agents sat around the table, littered with coffee cups and notepads, studying the wall. Tracy reached for the album and flipped back to the photo of the grocery and truck. "Gregorian and Son," he muttered.

"I don't know how Haig Gregorian lost the family grocery," I said. "According to Tim, it was vaguely criminal. Miriam, Maddie's mom, may know more."

"If all that's true, I get why she wanted the building back," Greer said. "But it was Byrd's legacy, too. Didn't he have just as much right to buy it? She sabotaged his dreams to pursue her own."

I had to admit, that bothered me. Was it only in my imagination that Maddie was both successful and perfectly ethical, a woman who took over a business built by men in a field dominated by men, reclaiming rundown buildings and revitalizing neighborhoods without smearing her lipstick? Had I put her on a pedestal unfairly, exposing her to criticism—and worse—for falling off it?

"Why didn't any of this come out three years ago?" Tracy asked. But I knew the answer: Only Maddie could have told them. And she hadn't.

"For fear of jeopardizing the plan," I said. "Which tells us she never imagined it had led to Pat's murder."

"Look at it from her point of view," Armstrong said. "Byrd had no intention of recreating what the family lost. Just the opposite. He meant to poke a great big finger in Maddie Petrosian's eye."

"Wait," I said. "Can't you bring him in for questioning? If the great-grandparents cut his branch of the family off and the Byrd's Nest condos were his revenge, he must have hated Maddie. He had motive up the wazoo."

"And an alibi," Tracy said. "Unless we can break that—and I'm not laying odds, after all this time—we can't tie him to Halloran's murder. In the meantime, we can't risk giving him reason to think we're targeting him. So you"—Tracy gave me the official police officer glare—"say nothing to no one."

I nodded solemnly. Tracy instructed Armstrong to assemble a team to bring in Bruce and Deanna for questioning.

Navarro had not spoken for several minutes. He sat at the end of the table, one arm across his torso, tapping his chin with the fingers of his other hand. "Byrd had motive for both crimes. I'm not convinced that his alibi for the first is all that solid—he bought a ticket to the five o'clock matinee, but that doesn't mean he went in. Or stayed."

"What movie?" I asked.

"*Lady Bird*," Armstrong replied. "And when we talked to him, he knew all about it. But we don't have anything that puts him at the scene of the second crime, either."

"Yes, we do," I said. I looked at Tracy. "I started to tell you this on the phone last night, but you had questions and I forgot. Cody Ellingson works for me—he started this week. His story's been coming out in bits and pieces the last few days. His parents have been fighting for ages, mostly over money, blaming each other for putting them in a tight spot. On the bus yesterday, we ran into the barista who saw the guy in the alley. The guy who might have been the shooter." I stood, pacing in the narrow space between chairs and wall, trying to get it all straight in my mind. "You talked with him—you know he couldn't identify the guy. He'd know Ellingson, though, wouldn't he? Bruce and Deanna are regulars at the coffee shop."

"Depends how good a look he got," Armstrong said. "But the kid's afraid the guy in the alley was his dad." I nodded.

"Going after Ms. Petrosian because he thought his wife had killed Halloran and he was cleaning up after her," Greer said.

"But Ellingson would have known that killing Maddie Petrosian wouldn't put the original project back on track, because her company owned the property," Navarro pointed out. "If Ellingson took a shot at Petrosian, it was purely out of revenge."

"But the barista could easily have seen someone else," I pointed out. "The real killer."

"Bring in the whole family," Tracy ordered. "Separate cars."

And that was my cue to leave.

I NEEDED to get back to work. But solving the problem of Edgar's spice blend was also work. I called an Uber for a ride to the rival chef's joint. Early for lunch, but it was Saturday, the first clear blue day in a week. A few neighborhood types might drift in for crab cakes and a mimosa and call it brunch.

Early also meant I caught the black-coated chef before he was elbow-deep in kitchen chaos.

"Pepper Reece," I said. "I own Seattle Spice. Hoping we can chat."

"You're wasting your time. I've got an excellent supplier for all my herbs and spices."

"I'm sure you do. I'm not here to sell you spice. I'm here to see if we can solve a problem."

Not the response he'd expected. He gestured to a small table near the kitchen and the hostess brought us mineral water. I explained that the spice blend he was using on his crab cakes, among other dishes, bore a remarkable resemblance to Edgar's proprietary blend.

He looked like he wanted to spit in my Pellegrino.

"I created that blend myself. I don't need to steal from other chefs. And if this Eduardo or whatever his name is, is so insecure that he goes around accusing people he doesn't even know, highly respected chefs with years of experience, he won't last long."

"Mmm. Mm-hmm," I said, or something like that. "I don't know whether you sent your girlfriend hunting for Edgar's secret stash, or whether bringing you a sample was her idea. Doesn't matter. Either way, it's theft."

Heat flared off him, like a grease fire on a flaming stove.

"Here's what we can do." I reached into my tote and brought out two small tins, each bearing the Seattle Spice Shop label with our saltshaker logo. I'd labeled them "Sample—Proprietary" followed by #1 and #2. "You stop using the stolen blend or any variation. I will persuade Edgar not to file a complaint for theft against the bartender, your girlfriend. In exchange, I've created two blends specifically for you. You may attempt to recreate them yourself, or order them from me at an excellent introductory price." I slid a quote sheet across the table.

He ignored the quote and grabbed the first tin. Pried off the lid and gave me a dark look before giving a tentative sniff, then a deeper one. Stuck a finger in the mix, touched it to his tongue, and gave me another quick glance. Repeated the process with the second tin. Folded his arms and leaned back in his seat.

"And needless to say," though I said it anyway. "Edgar is no longer in need of your girlfriend's bartending skills."

Twenty-Eight

Once you get a spice in your home, you have it forever. Women never throw out spices. The Egyptians were buried with their spices. I know which one I'm taking with me when I go.

—Erma Bombeck

THE BUS FOR DOWNTOWN WAS JUST LOADING AS I LEFT the restaurant so I hopped on for the long, slow ride. I checked my messages and found one from Glenn saying he'd made contact with the owner of the rental unit. He was thinking of selling; if I wanted to convert two units into one, as Glenn was doing, this was the time to make an offer. *Let me think about it*, I replied, then sent Edgar a text, saying problem solved. Finally, I let Sandra know I was on my way.

We rolled down Madison. On the side of an old brick building, a faded red-and-white Coca-Cola sign, in that familiar script, peeked over the top of an ancient green cigar ad. We passed Seattle University and reached the hospital district.

Wait. At the ATM, head bent, tucking bills in his wallet, was that him? Smoking Man, in his navy rain jacket. The rest of us Seattleites had left ours home. If he wanted to look like every other man, he'd picked the wrong day.

I'd never seen his face up close. An image of the thin file Maddie's assistant had held in her lap flashed into my mind's eye. Flyers for the Byrd's Nest, some with photos. I'd recognized Deanna Ellingson. The other had been Jake Byrd.

It had to be him.

I popped up and waited by the back door, gripping the metal pole. When the doors opened, I jumped off, looking around wildly.

What was Byrd doing here? And where had he gone?

There, striding east on Ninth. Toward Harborview. I waited at the light, giving him a good head start, and pulled out my phone.

Tracy had said earlier that Byrd's alibi couldn't be proved or disproved. Since the alibi was a ticket to a movie, that made sense. Especially if the theater had closed, the staff scattered. Even a team of investigators armed with databases and search warrants might have trouble getting access to security cameras, if there were any, and employee records, then tracking down former employees who might or might not have seen one random moviegoer. And if they had, what would that prove? As Navarro noted, you could easily buy a ticket and slip away. Who would know?

But I had another approach in mind. I might not be able to break Byrd's alibi, but I could put a good dent in it.

There were no movie theaters left on Capitol Hill, not since the Broadway became a Rite-Aid and the Harvard Exit drew its curtains for the last time. But the corner grocery was an easy shot from the University District, over the Montlake Bridge. The Varsity, the Neptune, the Seven Gables.

And one more, west of I-5, on Forty-Fifth Street.

I punched buttons on my phone and silently urged Kristen to pick up. She did and I stepped out of the flow of traffic, keeping my eye on Byrd.

"Do you remember when we saw *Lady Bird*, in the theater?"

"Saoirse Ronan and Laurie Metcalf. It made me terrified of the girls becoming teenagers. I loved it."

"Remind me," I said, and she did, summarizing it in my ear as I trailed after Byrd.

"That was at the Guild, right?" Not one of our usual haunts, but one I remembered fondly, with its bright pink stucco, Deco curves, and classic two-sided marquee.

"Yeah. On Forty-Fifth. Last movie we saw there before it closed, with no notice. That's why we started Flick Chicks a couple months later, remember? Too many theaters were closing, and streaming was filling the gaps."

"Perfect. Thanks. Gotta run. Love you." I clicked off and sped toward the hospital.

One other attractive feature about the Guild was that it was easy to sneak in a side door and watch the movie without buying a ticket. I think we only did it once. We—Maddie had been with us, along with a couple of other girls—were terrified that we'd get caught and they'd throw us in jail. Or worse, call our parents.

If you could sneak in, someone else could sneak out.

In retail and in real life, it's never okay to lie. Pretending you didn't hear when a customer says nobody needs all these fancy salts is good business. Pasting a calm expression on your face when you're strolling past a suspected killer, piece of cake.

Well, I may be puffing on that. But when I saw Byrd in his rain jacket standing twenty-five feet from the hospital door with a cigarette in hand, I tossed him a casual smile and walked on by. Stopped and retraced my steps back to where he stood, next to one of those trash cans encased in concrete, an ash tray on top.

"Hey, I know you, don't I? You're Maddie's cousin Jake, right? Oh, gosh. You must be so relieved that she's finely coming around."

A whirl of panic and confusion crossed his face.

"Oh, my bad. After all that's happened, how could you remember one more name? It's Pepper Reece." What had Ramon the security guard said? They had to be careful of people trying to worm their way in to see patients in the ICU. *Old friends.* That would be me. *Distant cousins.* That would be Jake.

"I hear you two are in business together," I said as he took another puff. "That's great. Must be so satisfying, to picture a building then bring it to life. Like giant Legos."

"You make it sound simple. I worked construction a long time."

"Around here? Oh, silly question. Of course you're from here. You're a Petrosian."

"No, the connection goes back another generation. My grandfather was a Gregorian. His sister, Rose, married Petrosian. They were Maddie's grandparents."

As I well knew. Rose had lived with Maddie's family in her later years. She made the loveliest soft molasses cookies, with sugar sprinkled on top. But she died when we were in the third grade.

"I grew up in Oakland," Byrd said. "Finally made it to Seattle a few years ago."

"In time for the construction boom. Good on you." I shifted my tote on my shoulder. "Well, I better get inside before visiting hours end. It's almost shift change, isn't it? Nice to visit with you."

Inside, I headed not for the elevator, but for the cafeteria, passing visitors and staff, hospital chatter wafting around me as I replayed Kristen's summary of the movie in my head. Bought two large coffees, hot and black. Caught a glimpse of a woman in a navy SPD uniform heading into the restroom.

I made my way back to the front door, hoping my luck had held. It had.

"I was getting coffee," I said, "and figured you could use a cup, too. Hope you don't mind it black." I handed one to Byrd.

"My tastes are simple. Thanks."

I leaned against the wall next to him, in my best best-buddy act. "Quite an ordeal," I said, in a somber tone. "I gather the police are linking her shooting to one that happened years ago. I didn't remember much about it, so I looked it up online. They had a good suspect, but he had an alibi. He was at the movies. *Lady Bird*, the paper said."

The newspaper account had not named the movie, just as it had not named the suspect because he had not been charged. *Yet*. Had Byrd read the accounts? Me, if I'd been a suspect, I'd have practically memorized them. But I was puffing, and praying his memory for movie trivia wasn't as sharp as Kristen's.

"I loved that movie," he said. I was surprised. Classic chick flick.

"The mother–daughter tensions are pretty classic," I said. "She just wants to leave home, spread her wings, but the mom's more worried about money than her daughter's dreams. When she changes her name, the parents are all up in arms. 'What's wrong with Catherine? It's a perfectly fine name.'"

"Christine," he said. "The girl's name was Christine, not Catherine."

Pooh. I'd been hoping he didn't know. "I kinda didn't get the bit about the brother and his girlfriend, though. Did you?"

"Oh, sure. Miguel was adopted. And Shelly had a bad family situation so the parents let her move in."

I could not have remembered those characters' names if you'd paid me a thousand bucks. A thought began to nag me. "What was that bit about the fancy house?"

"Lady Bird is embarrassed about where they live, so she gives her snobby new friend Jenna the address of her old boyfriend's grandmother's house, the boy who turned out to be gay. It's a nice parallel with the scene where Marion invites her to do their favorite thing together, which turns out to be going to open houses in upscale neighborhoods and pretending they live in a fancy house instead of a little sh—" He stopped himself. "Instead of a more modest house."

Marion. The mom's name convinced me.

But knowing the movie so well didn't mean he'd seen it at the Guild three years ago. He could have bought the ticket, gone inside, and slipped out. Sped across Forty-Fifth and over the Montlake Bridge to the Hallorans' house.

I heard a door open to my right and saw Byrd's gaze following someone. I didn't want to seem too obvious, but I managed to sneak a quick glance sideways.

All I saw was the back of security guard, as the man moved in the opposite direction. Ramon?

I turned back to Byrd. He blinked rapidly, the skin on his forehead damp and flush.

"Hey, thanks for the coffee," he said. "I gotta make a quick pit stop inside before I head out." He stubbed out his cigarette in the big ashtray.

I had one shot. The medieval chants began to play in my head. I forged on.

"When you and Maddie decided to do a project together, whose idea was it to buy the property on Twenty-Fourth?"

"You're such a great friend of my dear cousin, and you don't know?"

I'd puzzled it out, but I needed him to say it.

"We weren't in business together. Maddie, the Golden Girl," he said with a sneer that made me shiver. He couldn't possibly know he was using my phrase for her. "All the pictures, all the clippings. Her accomplishments—first in this, first in that, winner of one stupid prize after another."

"How did you know?" I asked. "You're older. You lived in California."

"Her proud grandmother, Rose, sent my grandmother pictures and newspaper clippings of all Maddie's successes. Rubbing it in." Or trying to stay connected to the sister-in-law who'd left the family when Haig died? He was on a roll.

"Making a point that she and her father had picked up the mantle my grandfather dropped. That he nearly destroyed the family fortune, but they built it back up." His voice tightened and he crumpled his cigarette pack, then shoved it into the trash bin beneath the ash tray. "They blamed my grandmother for being a bad influence. Trapping him in a marriage to a non-Armenian who would never understand what land and family meant to people who'd lost everything and everyone at the hands of the Turkish enemy."

His double motive added an element that surprised me. "You wanted that property not just to get what the Petrosians owed you, but also to get the better of a Turk. You'd get the last laugh, turning the corner grocery they all loved into a building they all would have hated."

"If Deanna had done her part, I would have succeeded. She promised me, with her experience and my money, we could make it work."

"The money was all yours?" I asked. "Didn't she chip in?"

"A drop in the bucket." Resentment dripped off his words.

Deanna Ellingson could well have been Jake Byrd's next victim.

"Is this what your grandmother would have wanted?" I asked. It was a shot in the dark, based on the premise that grandmothers want the best for their grandchildren, even if they never say so.

Faulty premise. The shot missed.

"My grandmother was a nasty, bitter woman. She never let me forget that I was the cause of my mother's death. My mother, who had the most beautiful golden hair and the brightest smile." He faltered, then spoke again. "Getting pregnant totally freaked her out. She dumped me with my grandmother and disappeared into Haight-Ashbury."

San Francisco's infamous drug scene.

"When the cops told my grandmother her daughter had died of a drug overdose and asked her to claim the body, she refused.

Her only child, and she refused. Said we didn't have the money for burial, but she could gotten it. She was pure spite."

I was horrified. "But if Rose or David ever knew, surely they would have helped—"

"You think you know them. You saw the side they wanted people to see—the successful business people, the community benefactors. They never forgave my grandmother for taking their son from them. They thought she forced him into the shady deals that cost them their home and business. But they forced him into it, pushing him to make them proud. To replace what was lost in Armenia and build their fortune in America."

I didn't believe that. I trusted what I knew of the Petrosian family. Not that good cookies can only come from a pure heart, but in my heart of hearts, I knew they were good people.

And if Betty's heart had been so hard that she refused to claim her daughter's body, then the source of Jake Byrd's pain was his grandmother's anger, not the Petrosians' success.

"What about your father?" I tried to sip my coffee, acting nonchalant, but it was too hot. I popped the lid to let it cool.

"I have no idea. He gave me his name, and nothing else. It was up to me to reclaim my heritage. As a proud Armenian, who should have grown up with all the money, the fancy schools and trips, my dear cousin got instead."

"So you lured Maddie to the building and shot her. And three years ago, you followed her to Pat Halloran's house, then after she left, you shot him."

"It was all his idea, her buying up the block then buying the corner lot out from under me. I wanted to show them I was just as smart as they were." He glanced at the door again. No doubt he'd noticed, as I had, that the ICU desk was occasionally left unguarded. Ramon would be back any minute. His window of opportunity was closing.

"Show who?" I asked. "Your great-grandparents are long gone. Rose and David are gone. Betty, too, I imagine. I'm not sure Maddie knew what happened to your side of the family."

"Oh, she knew. I've got to go."

Inside and up to the ICU while the guard was away, to finish the job he'd started? "No, stay. We can talk this out, before it gets any worse."

"Why do you care, anyway?"

"Because I care about Maddie, and Pat Halloran even though I never met him, because his wife is one of my dearest friends. Because you've hurt people, but you don't need to hurt anyone else."

"You don't know anything about it. About all the hurt they caused me."

"Jake, don't make this harder on yourself."

"What do you know about hard? You and Maddie, with your easy lives. Your fancy houses and cars. You don't know how real people live."

Clearly he hadn't seen what I drove. He was tarring me with the same brush I'd used on Maddie, and I didn't like the feeling.

"Nobody has it all easy, Jake. I know it looks—"

"She begrudged me everything, my grandmother. I was one of them to her, everything she hated."

"If you'd been willing to work with Maddie—"

I reached for his arm. He put out his hands to push me away. Instinctively, I threw my coffee on him. Hot coffee splashed on his face and dripped down his chin, down that navy jacket. Fury raged in his eyes and he reached for my shoulders with both hands. I dropped the cup, made my hands into fists, and brought them up between his arms. Rammed my arms against his, forcing his arms apart before he could get a decent grip on me.

"You witch," he said, his face a snarl, his feet off balance. I stepped forward and shoved him. He stepped backward, hitting the concrete trash can. He lost his balance and hit the wall, one foot flying up as he tumbled down to the sidewalk. I grabbed his foot and held on. He bent his leg, dragging me toward him, and I crashed onto both knees. As long as I had his foot in my hands, he couldn't get away. I held on, for dear life, yes, but for Maddie, and so much more.

Sounds began to register. Voices. Footsteps. Radios.

Then I found myself face to toe with a pair of sturdy black shoes. Cop shoes. I stared up at Lovely Rita.

"Officer Clark," I said. "Care to give me a hand? And call Detective Tracy ASAP. Tell him he owes me a badge."

Twenty-Nine

*Death leaves a heartache no one can heal; love
leaves a memory no one can steal.*

—Irish saying

"MADDIE! You look like yourself again!" I dropped my tote and
leaned in to hug her. Gently.

"Is it true?" she said. "What the liaison officer just said? They've
arrested Jake for shooting me and killing Patrick Halloran?"

Liaison officer? Between the SPD and crime victim patients, or
their families? So that was why Lovely Rita had been in and out of
the ICU the last week. *Holy saffron.*

I'd waited with Officer Clark until the detectives arrived,
then spent a good hour explaining how I'd fingered Jake Byrd as
both Smoking Man and the two-time shooter. I described how I'd
thought I could trick Byrd into admitting he didn't know much
about the movie he'd bought the ticket for, but then realized he
knew it too well, far better than I did. Tracy and Armstrong
seemed impressed when I suggested they check his streaming
history; I was sure they'd find he'd seen *Lady Bird* twice, shortly
after Pat's murder and again after Maddie's shooting. They were
less impressed at my takedown—what Tracy called my antics—
although Armstrong did give me points for creative use of a cup of
a coffee. The coffee had been too hot to drink, but not hot enough
to hurt Byrd, although he'd been treated for a sprained ankle before

being hauled off to jail. The same nurses who tended him had been concerned about my knees and hands, but while I knew they might sting after the adrenaline wore off, I didn't mind. I'd caught him; what were a few cuts and scrapes?

When Officer Clark returned from the cafeteria with coffee for the detectives and a sandwich for me, she'd given me a nice "atta girl."

"Oh," I said. "You were here today to keep an eye on Jake Byrd." It all made sense. She nodded and slipped upstairs to talk with Maddie and Tim. To liaise.

Finally, Tracy had cut me loose. He offered to have an officer drop me off in the Market. But I'd had another stop to make before getting back to work. Maddie's condition had improved so much that the nurses were getting ready to wheel her to the medical floor when I arrived. Tim had gone ahead with the latest flowers. She asked them to give us a few minutes and close the door behind them.

"That's one thing I hate about this place," she said. "Everyone is so nice and so good at what they do. But unless they're baring your backside, they leave the doors open 24/7, exposing your life to everyone who walks by."

"I'm afraid I've made that worse," I said, perching on the edge of the bed. "Exposing your family secrets."

She exhaled heavily. "Ironic, isn't it? I never would have learned the truth about my family if Jake hadn't been so determined to destroy us. The way he believes my grandmother and great-grand-parents—*our* great-grandparents—destroyed his family."

"Your grandmother's photograph album was the key. Unfortunately, it's now part of the police file. Detective Armstrong—"

"The tall one?"

"The tall one. He says they may be able to make a digital copy for you, since resolving all the criminal charges could take a while." I slipped off the bed and into the chair. "When did you figure out who Byrd was?"

"At the first public meeting he and Deanna Ellingson held, more than three years ago. I wanted to know who'd managed to convince Mr. Barut to sell, and what his plans were. I heard him tell Barut's son that his grandfather had once owned the property and that he wanted to bring it back into the family. It was our *great*-grandfather. His grandfather lost the place. My father had been trying to get it back for years, then I tried, but no luck. Bad timing, I guess."

I had my own theory about that, but no point resurrecting the old Turkish-Armenian tensions.

"I'd always known about Jake," she continued. "Though I never knew his last name or where he was. I pored over those albums with Grandma Rose when I was little, and then again in the last few weeks of her life, when she was looking back. If she knew what had happened to him, she never said."

"It's not a pretty story," I said, but she wanted to hear it, so I recounted what Jake had told me outside the hospital.

"All that anger and bitterness," she said softly. "No wonder he hated us. He was raised to hate us."

"When you couldn't get him to work with you, or to change his plans for the property, you went to Pat Halloran for help. That was kind of brilliant, by the way."

"Other way around. Pat knew my efforts to persuade Byrd to scale back were doomed, and he offered to help. At a soccer practice. I was skeptical at first, because he was part of Neighbors United and they can be pretty outspoken. But he convinced me it would work. That's why I went to his house the day he was killed. I was horrified when I heard what happened, but I never imagined it had any connection to the project. The police said his murder was connected to his work as a prosecutor, and I was sure they were right."

"Byrd figured you and Pat were in cahoots, though why he thought killing Pat would stop you, I can't imagine. Nothing ever stops you."

She smiled wryly. "He almost did."

"But meeting at Pat's house was risky, wasn't it? I mean, he lived next door to Deanna Ellingson."

"We were supposed to meet Saturday at my office. Turned out I'd put the weekend at the island place with Kristen and Eric on my phone for the wrong day. I had to take the chance that Pat would be home, and that the neighbors wouldn't see me."

"Bruce Ellingson did see you, through the hedge. But he thought it was his wife. With all you knew about Byrd, why did you agree to meet him at the building last week?"

"I had no idea he was dangerous. He said he had some sketches he wanted to show us. My builder was supposed to meet me—he didn't know we were meeting Byrd—but he got stuck in traffic on the wrong side of the drawbridge. By the time he got there, Byrd had already left. Thank God, or Byrd would have shot him, too, and we'd both be dead."

With no witnesses, and no chance at justice.

"You are the smartest, bravest woman I have ever known," she said. "How can I ever thank you for figuring all this out?"

"Those are some powerful drugs you're on."

"Pepper, don't joke about this. My whole life, I've admired you, envied you, and I've let it get in the way of our friendship."

I felt like all the air had been sucked out of my lungs. "You admired me? Maddie, that's nuts. I dropped out of college, wasting the internship you wanted. I got divorced. I lost my dream job. You're the one who was the star of every class, married a great guy, took over the family business. Heck, you figured out a way to buy back the family property, something even your dad couldn't do. And don't tell me that was Pat. He may have thought up the plan, but you had the guts to make it happen."

"No." She shook her head, the bandage smaller, the shaved hair turning to stubble. "Maybe it took you a while to figure out what you wanted, but you followed your heart. You made your own life. Me, I was the good girl who followed the path my family laid out."

"And this wasn't it?" I gestured, but I didn't mean the hospital room, the monitors and the beeping machines. I meant what I'd seen as her picture-perfect life.

"I love Tim. I love our kids. I like helping people create the right space to make their dreams come true. Keeping neighborhoods vibrant and alive. It's good work; I know that. It's the work my father raised me to do."

"You wanted a career in social services. I heard you say so."

"I chose my family legacy over my dreams, Pepper. That was my choice, not your fault."

The door opened and a nurse poked his head in. "Five minutes. Then we've got to get you moved."

I reached for her hand. "It's not too late. You can scale back. Sell the company. Hire a manager and work as much or as little as you want. Get that degree in social work. Take up pottery or hothouse yoga. Spend a year in Italy learning to make cheese."

"Petrosian Parmesan," she said. "I know exactly the place to put it in the new corner grocery."

SOME shopkeeper I am, I thought as I angled across the intersection of First and Pike Place. I had missed most of the busiest day of the week.

It's always amazes me how two people can remember the same incident, or the same time in our lives, so differently. Me and Maddie. Me and Tag. Me and Tag and Kimberly Clark. We view what happens through our own lens, and that lens tints our memories as well. Maddie might never be able to fully piece together what happened in her family all those years ago, but she might glean enough facts from Jake Byrd's account, if she could see through the film of his bitterness, to clear the picture.

And that, I hoped, would give her a better vision of what her future could be.

Despite the crowds on the sidewalks, I could see the old lady perched on her stool outside the Asian shop. She wagged her head and Lily came rushing toward me. "Pepper," she said. "We had tea and I helped walk the dog."

"I'm so glad. Arf loves going for walks."

"Guess what else? My daddy's going to stay. He's getting a green car. He and my mama are getting married. On my birthday."

Green car. "Oh. You mean his green card? The paper that means he's a permanent resident of the U.S., even though he isn't a citizen?"

Lily bounced up and down. "Yes! We're going to have a party to celebrate. Will you come? You and Arf."

I glanced at her mother, smiling at us from behind the front counter. "We'd be delighted."

Two blocks down the street, on the corner outside my shop, I spotted a tall, dark, and handsome guy talking to a blond with pink and orange streaks in her hair. By the man's side stood a dog. My guy, my dog.

Nate and I embraced and kissed. I ran my hand through his dark hair. "You're here. You're really here."

He kissed me again.

"I take it you two have met," I said when I came up for air and saw Jamie beaming at us.

"You've been making new friends while I was away," Nate said.

"Plus reconnecting with old ones," I said. "Have I got stories for you."

Nate took Arf home. Inside, in between helping customers, I told my staff what had happened.

"So Cody's parents had nothing to do with it?" Reed asked.

"Looks that way," I said, though it would be a long time before the Ellingsons' family life returned to anything like normal.

Minutes before closing, the two detectives arrived.

"You look like you could use a pick-me-up," I said, and poured cups of spice tea. We sat in the nook.

"Byrd confessed to both crimes," Tracy said. "It would have taken us a lot longer to nail him without you."

A weight I hadn't known I was carrying slipped off my shoulders.

"He was waiting for an opportunity to get into the ICU, wasn't he, to take another shot? When the guard took his afternoon break."

"Looks that way," Tracy said. "He was armed, and we're pretty sure it was the same gun that shot both Mr. Halloran and Ms. Petrosian. We also found a burner phone, probably the one he used to set up the meeting with Ms. Petrosian."

Making sure no one could track him.

"We've informed Mrs. Halloran," Armstrong said, "of the arrest and confession. We've also made sure she knows Ms. Petrosian confirmed your theory about Pat Halloran's role devising her property buy-out scheme."

I hoped this put an end to Laurel's nightmares.

"What about the Ellingsons?" I asked.

"We were wrapping up our interviews with them when Officer Clark called," Tracy said. "For three years, he feared she'd killed Halloran. Turns out she thought he'd done it."

What a tangled web.

"I ran into a very happy little girl down the street. I take it Special Agent Greer's investigation lets Joe Huang off the hook."

"Not completely, not yet," Tracy said. "But it appears to be headed that way. Seems her birthday explains the timing of his presence in the country. He's cooperating with the feds and has implicated his boss and others in the organization. Something to do with imported goods and trade secrets—that's about all we know at this point."

So all suspects were present and accounted for. All was right with the world.

Or would be. Shortly.

THE fragrance of a deep simmer, of fish and stock and bay leaves, greeted me when I unlocked the front door to my building.

And a fuzzy dog and a gorgeous man greeted me at the front door of the loft. From the living room came the sounds of Diane Schuur singing Cole Porter. "So nice to come home to."

Nate took my face in his hands and kissed me. Then he took my red, scraped hands and kissed my palms.

"Can you stand one more bowl of soup?" he asked. "All that soup talk early this week got me in the mood."

"When it smells this good, you bet."

I was halfway to the bathroom when I stopped and turned around. "By the way, Mr. Fisher Man, I don't think I've told you lately that I'm madly in love with you."

"It goes both ways, Spice Girl." A slow sweet smile crossed his face. "It goes both ways."

I took a quick shower to rinse off the remains of the day. In the bedroom, I put on a clean T-shirt and glanced around. Two walls redbrick, two painted a soft caramel. The bed covered with the black-and-white antique quilt Kristen and I had found in a shop up near the Canadian border. The rolling doors, the *tansu*, the neon lips on the wall. Nate's sweater tossed over the wooden chair.

I didn't need to expand into the unit beneath this one. Maybe Glenn and his Nate could rent it during their construction project. My loft was perfect just the way it was. I'd rather leave it alone and gain a new neighbor. Throw more potlucks and cocktail parties for the building. Start working on that rooftop garden.

Then the music stopped and the broadcasters started their World Series pregame chatter. I stepped into a fresh pair of yoga pants and smiled.

Everything I wanted, everything I loved and needed, was safe and warm and dry, right here, between these four walls.

Thirty

Our house is a very, very, very fine house . . .
Now everything is easy 'cause of you.

— Graham Nash, "Our House"

.

A WEEK HAD PASSED SINCE WHAT MY NEAREST AND DEAREST were calling the Great Sidewalk Coffee Caper. The newspaper had run lengthy articles discussing virtually every aspect of Patrick Halloran's career, the twists and turns the investigation had taken over the years, and the unexpected link to Maddie's shooting. A series of stories covered the Petrosian family, the properties they'd saved from the wrecking ball, and their good deeds. At my request, the detectives had referred to my role only as "assistance from a citizen." If the charges against Byrd went to trial, I'd have to testify and my identity would be made public. But I didn't want reporters and camera crews following me through the Market or camping on my doorstep. I had a business to run, and a party to throw.

All the staff were on hand, including Cody Ellingson, whose main job today was to help Matt keep the pseudo-samovar full of tea and sweep up cookie crumbs and dropped napkins.

The heads of the Public Development Authority and the Market Merchants Association had both dropped by to offer congratulations and enjoy lemon thyme shortbread and ginger-snaps. Friends and suppliers had sent flowers and other gifts.

Market neighbors, including Misty the Baker, Vinnie the Wine Merchant, and my new pals, Jamie the Painter and Lily and her mother, had come by.

Edgar arrived with a shopping bag. "For you and your sweetheart. Hide it so your employees won't be tempted."

I peered in at the brown paper "to go" boxes. "What is it?"

"The best crab cakes in the city. And bones for your dog."

Treats for the entire family. "I have to confess, I didn't solve your stolen spice problem all by myself. Sandra helped, and so did Tariq."

Edgar's eyebrows rose, but I had a feeling that if Tariq came looking for a job, Edgar might give him a chance.

"Good," he said. "Good. But now I need a new bartender."

I glanced at Cody. I knew from his job application that he'd turned twenty-one a few weeks ago. "Will you train?"

"Si, si, yeees!" Edgar said.

My good deed might cost me my new deliveryman. No matter. At that age, I hadn't had a clue what I wanted to do with my life, but eventually I'd found the right path. Restaurant work might be Cody's path or not, but I was happy to give him all the help I could.

I left the two men talking and greeted Jamie, who held out a small flat package. "Special delivery."

I unwrapped it and turned the canvas over. Then I gasped, and I swear, my hand flew to my heart.

"It's—it's spectacular. The colors. The flowers. The joy."

"I call it 'The Dance of the Dahlias,'" she said. "It's a thank you gift, for making me feel so welcome in the Market."

In a day crazier than any day in ages, tears streaming down my hot, sweaty cheeks, nothing could have made me happier.

Except the next arrivals: Tim, Maddie, and the kids, each in new Sounders jerseys, along with Miriam and Tim's sister.

"You came." I took Maddie's hands in mine. Seeing her wearing lipstick again almost made me cry.

"I wouldn't have missed it," she replied. "Life's too short to let anything stand in the way of friendship, as I have just been reminded."

I led her to the nook where she could sit while her family got snacks and explored the shop. "So what's next?"

"Rehab, PT. And I've got a construction project to oversee, though my project manager will be stepping up his role in the company. In fact, we started demolition earlier this week, and I wanted you to see what we found." She held out her phone and showed me a picture of the side of the insurance agency building, the name "GREGORIAN & SON, GROCERS" visible in faint white paint.

"A ghost sign," I said.

"I asked my architect to see if we can reconfigure the building plans to show it off. She thinks we can create a rooftop deck below the sign, so it will be visible from the deck and the street. My gift to the neighborhood."

"That's a terrific idea. See, I told you—you always find a way to do what you want."

"No more pedestals, Pepper. Please. It's lonely up there."

"I promise," I said, and drew an X across my heart.

"And I'd like to spend more time with you and Kristen. Go antiquing, catch a movie."

I nodded. Maybe, now that Laurel's suspicions had been allayed, we could invite Maddie to join Flick Chicks.

"Bay leaves?" I heard a customer say. "I didn't think anyone used them anymore."

"The soup cook's best friend," Sandra replied.

Between the friends and the customers, old and new, I almost didn't notice the arrival of three Seattle police officers—two detectives and a uniformed bicycle cop.

"Quite a shindig," Detective Tracy said, surveying the scene.

"My second anniversary as the Mistress of Spice," I said. "Worth celebrating. Care for a cookie?"

"In a minute," he said. "First, I have a bit of official business to conduct. Well, semi-official."

For half a second, I panicked. When a cop says he's got business to conduct and he's staring right at you, panic seems like a reasonable response. Especially when he turns down a cookie.

And then I saw the grin on Tag's face, and another on Armstrong's.

Tracy drew a flat, faux leather box out of his sport coat pocket and held it out.

Inside, on a blue velvet bed, lay a shiny gold shield. "Seattle Police Department," it read. "Honorary Member."

My badge. Honorary, maybe; but a badge.

I pinned it on my apron, just above the saltshaker logo. Heaven knows, I'd earned it.

Recipes and Spice Notes

The Seattle Spice Shop Recommends . . .

The Spice Shop stop on the Market Food Tour includes a few favorites from the Spice Shop collection, featured in earlier books:

Spiced Glazed Nuts and Pretzel Mix—*Assault and Pepper*
Lemon Thyme Cookies and Pepper's Gingersnaps—*Killing Thyme*
Edgar's Baked Paprika Cheese—*Chai Another Day*
Grape, Prosciutto, and Mozzarella Skewers—*Chai Another Day*, using Pepper's Italian Herb Blend from *Assault and Pepper*

And you'll find recipes for chai for baking and sipping in *Chai Another Day*.

LAVENDER-BAY SALT

While Pepper can't tell you every ingredient in the blend she created for Edgar, she loves encouraging customers to try an herbed salt or two. Herbed salts are an easy way to add flavor without spending a lot of time in the kitchen. Lavender-bay is particularly tasty with eggs, potatoes, and sautéed veggies. Remember, bay needs a little heat to release its full flavor.

> 1½ teaspoon dried bay leaves, dried lavender buds, or a 50/50 mix
> 2 tablespoons kosher salt

Strip 8 to 10 bay leaves into a spice grinder. (Tip: Fold the dried leaf in half along the spine and break off each half; discard the spine.) Pulse until finely ground. If you're using lavender, coarsely grind the buds.

The crystal structure of kosher salt makes a great base for flavored salts. Coarse, flaky salts like Maldon are a better choice if you're using the salt on top, as a finishing salt, rather than as an ingredient.

Keep in mind Pepper's advice that blends are best after they've had a few hours to meld, marry, or mellow, as the case may be.

A Classic Cookie from Ripe

ALMOND BISCOTTI

Biscotti have a reputation for being a major kitchen project, but Laurel's version of the classic Italian dipping cookie is as easy as it is tasty, crunchy on the outside and chewy inside. For an extra treat, dip a few in melted chocolate, or paint chocolate on one side.

2 cups unbleached, all-purpose flour, plus more for the work surface
1 cup plus 1 tablespoon sugar
½ teaspoon baking powder
¼ teaspoon sea salt
1 cup slivered almonds, lightly toasted (see below)
3 large eggs (one separated)
1 teaspoon almond extract
1 teaspoon vanilla extract

Heat the oven to 350 degrees.

Toast the nuts on a rimmed baking sheet for 7 to 10 minutes, or until they just begin to change color. Remember that nuts continue to cook as they cool. Cool completely before using.

Line a large rimmed baking sheet with parchment paper or a silicon sheet.

In the bowl of your mixer, combine the flour, 1 cup sugar, baking powder, and salt. Add the almonds and beat on low to blend well. Add 2 whole eggs, the yolk of the third egg, and the extracts. Beat on medium until a sticky dough forms. (If your flour is quite dry, you may need to add a teaspoon of milk.)

Lightly flour a cutting board. Turn the dough onto the board and shape it into a disk. Cut the disk into four equal quarters. Lightly moisten your hands, then roll each quarter into a log, about 1 1/2 inches wide and 9 inches long. Place logs on the baking sheet, at least 2 inches apart. Press the tops gently to make sure they are even.

Lightly beat the remaining egg white; brush it on the tops of the logs, then sprinkle them evenly with the remaining tablespoon of sugar.

Bake 20 to 25 minutes, or until the logs are lightly browned and just set; there will be cracks on the surface. Transfer the baking sheet to a wire cooling rack; let the logs rest for 5 minutes, then carefully peel them off the parchment—they will be hot—and place them directly on the rack to cool for 10 minutes. Discard the parchment.

Reduce oven temperature to 300 degrees. Use a chef's knife to trim the end of each log. Then cut each log on the diagonal into 10 equal slices. (Press down into the log, rather than sawing, to prevent breaking.) Place the slices on the baking sheet, with a cut side facing up. Bake 10 minutes, then turn each slice over. Bake an additional 10 minutes or until the slices are lightly golden. Cool on a rack before dipping in chocolate, if you'd like.

Makes about 40 cookies. The biscotti will keep in an airtight container at room temperature for up to 2 weeks.

Spice Up Your Life with Pepper and the Flick Chicks

CARROT SOUP WITH TOASTED SPICES AND PECANS

Who doesn't love soup? The ultimate comfort food on a chill, dreary day, soup appears in almost every culture and cuisine. To host a soup exchange, keep the numbers small. Each guest brings enough soup for the others to enjoy a cup and take home a few servings. Guests bring their own to-go containers. The hostess provides salad, bread, and a light dessert.

2 tablespoons unsalted butter
½ medium onion
2 cloves garlic
¾ teaspoon kosher salt
1 pound carrots
½ cup canned coconut milk
3 cups water
½ cup pecan halves
1 teaspoon ground cumin or coriander
1 teaspoon celery seed
½ teaspoon red pepper flakes
½ teaspoon whole black peppercorns or coarsely ground black
    pepper
Sour cream or plain Greek yogurt, for serving

Chop the onion and mince the garlic.

Melt the butter in a stockpot over medium-low heat. Stir in the onion, garlic and ½ teaspoon salt; cover and cook for 6 to 8 minutes, until the onion has softened, stirring occasionally.

While the onion mixture sautées, scrub and trim the carrots, then slice into thin rounds.

Increase the heat to medium; stir in the carrots, coconut milk, and water. When the mixture begins to bubble at the edges, cover and cook 15 to 20 minutes, until the carrots become tender.

Meanwhile, toast the pecans in a small dry skillet over medium-low heat for 3 to 4 minutes, until fragrant and lightly browned; remember that nuts will continue to brown and crisp as they cool. Transfer to a cutting board to cool; coarsely chop. Add the cumin, celery seed, red pepper flakes, and black peppercorns to the skillet; toast 3 to 4 minutes until fragrant, then crush and blend in a spice grinder or with mortar and pestle. Don't skip this step, as crushing the spices together helps to blend the flavors.

Test the carrots for doneness; when soft, remove from heat and allow to cool about 5 minutes. Add all but a pinch of the toasted, crushed spices and stir well. Then use your immersion blender or regular blender to puree; leave some chunks, if you prefer. Stir in the remaining ¼ teaspoon salt.

Divide among individual bowls. Garnish with the remaining toasted spices, a dollop of sour cream or yogurt, and the toasted pecans.

Serves 4.

A favorite at Ripe, easy to recreate at home.

LAUREL'S TOMATO-BASIL SOUP

4 large tomatoes, cored, seeded, and coarsely chopped
4 cups tomato juice
12–14 small to medium basil leaves
½ cup heavy cream
⅓ cup butter
kosher salt and fresh ground black pepper, to taste
Basil leaves or edible flowers for garnish

Place chopped tomatoes and juice in a stockpot, on medium heat. Simmer about 30 minutes.

Add the basil leaves. Remove from heat and use a blender or immersion blender to puree, leaving some chunks.

Return puree to stockpot. Add cream and butter; stir well. Season to taste. Reheat, but don't boil, stirring until the butter is melted.

Serve and garnish.

Serves 4.

BLACK BEAN CHILI

Although this version is vegetarian, you can easily add ground beef, browned separately or with the onions. The spicing is flavorful, but not hot.

1 pound dried black beans
4 cups water
1 bay leaf
1 tablespoon olive oil
1 large onion, chopped
4 cloves garlic, chopped
1 red bell pepper, diced
1 28-ounce can chopped tomatoes, with juice
2 tablespoons tomato paste
1½ teaspoons ground cumin
2 teaspoons Hungarian paprika
½ teaspoon cayenne
2 teaspoons chili powder
1 teaspoon dried oregano
1½ teaspoon kosher salt
Fresh ground black pepper
1 tablespoon brown sugar
Monterey Jack cheese, grated, for topping (optional)

Soak beans overnight in enough water to keep them covered as they expand; drain and place in large stockpot with 4 cups water and bay leaf. Simmer 25 to 30 minutes, until tender but still slightly chewy.

While the beans are cooking, add the olive oil to a large sauté pan. Sauté the onion, garlic, and bell pepper until soft, 12 to 15 minutes. When the beans are cooked, add the onion mixture to the pot and stir well. Add the tomatoes, tomato paste, herbs and spices, and brown sugar. Simmer, covered, about 1 hour. Serve sprinkled with cheese, if you'd like.

Serves 6 to 8.

MISTY'S ROSEMARY FOCACCIA

With so much great bread available in the Market, Pepper rarely bakes bread, but Misty generously shared her recipe. This version is topped with rosemary and coarse salt, a classic combo.

Don't be intimidated by bread baking! It seems mysterious, but is really quite easy. This recipe makes one 8 to 9-inch-round loaf, plus dough for a second loaf. Use instant yeast rather than active. Pepper mixes the dough in a stockpot rather than a bowl, so it can easily be covered.

1½ cups plus 2 tablespoons lukewarm water
¼ cup olive oil
1½ teaspoons dried instant yeast
2¼ teaspoons kosher salt
1 tablespoon sugar
3¾ cups unbleached all-purpose flour, plus more for dusting
1 teaspoon finely chopped rosemary (1 to 2 stems)
Coarse or flaky salt, for sprinkling

In a stockpot or large bowl, mix the water, half the oil, yeast, salt, sugar, and flour until it forms a rough dough. Cover and let rest for about 2 hours on the counter. Chill dough about half an hour to make it easier to handle.

Place a baking stone or heavy baking sheet on the middle rack of your oven. Heat oven to 425 degrees. Pour the remaining oil into a 9-inch cake pan and evenly coat the bottom of the pan.

On a cutting board or work surface, dust the surface of the chilled dough lightly with flour, then pull off half, about one pound. Dust with more flour and shape into a ball by stretching the surface of the dough around to the bottom on all four sides, rotating the ball a quarter-turn as you go. (See note below about refrigerating or freezing.)

Use your hands to flatten the dough into a round about 1/2 an inch thick and 6 to 7 inches across. Place dough top side down in the cake pan, moving it around to coat it with the oil. It will not fill the pan. Turn the dough over, cover the pan with plastic wrap, and let dough rest for 10 to 15 minutes.

Use your hands to gently push the dough to the edges of the cake pan. Sprinkle with the rosemary and coarse or flaky salt, as needed.

Cover with plastic wrap, and allow the dough to rest and rise for 20 minutes.

Place the cake pan on the heated baking stone in the oven. Bake for 20 to 25 minutes, or until the crust is medium brown and feels dry and firm on the surface. The baking time will vary depending on the focaccia's thickness.

Use a rounded knife to loosen the loaf from the edges of the pan, then transfer the focaccia to a cutting board. Cut into wedges and serve warm.

The remaining half of the dough can be tightly wrapped and frozen, or refrigerated and kept up to a week. Remove dough from freezer or refrigerator; thaw if frozen. Shape and bake as above.

At Home with Pepper

COLD SESAME NOODLES

A terrific addition to a weeknight dinner—despite the name, no need to chill them!

¼ cup chopped peanuts, toasted
10–16 ounces Chinese egg noodles (1/8-inch thick; often sold as Lo Mein noodles)
2 tablespoons sesame oil for the sauce, plus a splash for the cooked noodles
3½ tablespoons soy sauce
2 tablespoons Chinese rice vinegar
2 tablespoons Chinese sesame paste or tahini, well-mixed
1 tablespoon peanut butter (smooth or chunky)
1 tablespoon sugar
1 tablespoon finely grated ginger (fresh or jarred)
2 teaspoons minced garlic
2 teaspoons chili-garlic paste
Half a cucumber, peeled, seeded, and diced or julienned, or a few scallions (green onions), chopped

Heat oven to 300 degrees. Toast the peanuts 10 minutes and remove from oven. Remember that they will continue to brown as they cool.

Bring a large pot of water to a boil. Add noodles and cook until barely tender, about 5 minutes; they should be al dente, with a touch of chewiness. Drain, rinse with cold water, drain again and toss with a splash of sesame oil.

In a medium bowl, whisk together the remaining 2 tablespoons of sesame oil, the soy sauce, rice vinegar, sesame paste or tahini, peanut butter, sugar, ginger, garlic, and chili-garlic paste.

Place the noodles in your serving bowl. Pour the sauce over the noodles and toss. Garnish with cucumber or scallions and peanuts.

Serves 6 to 8.

BROCCOLI BEEF STIR FRY

Classic and easy, a great weeknight meal, especially when paired with Cold Sesame Noodles and baseball.

3 ounces dry sherry
3 tablespoons soy sauce
1 tablespoon finely chopped ginger
1 tablespoon finely chopped garlic
1 teaspoon sesame oil (raw, toasted, or a mix)
½ teaspoon red pepper flakes
10 ounces flank steak, cut into thin strips
1 teaspoon corn starch
1 tablespoon canola oil (or other neutral vegetable oil)
4 cups broccoli, flowers and stems, cut into bite-sized pieces
    (trim stems and peel if tough)
¼ cup thinly sliced scallions (green onions)
¼ cup sesame seeds, toasted (optional)

Prepare marinade in a bowl or a large sealable plastic or silicone bag. Combine sherry, soy sauce, ginger, garlic, sesame oil, and red pepper flakes. Add beef and stir, or if you're using a bag, squeeze out the air, seal, and turn to coat beef. Marinade 30 minutes to an hour.

Toast the sesame seeds, if you're using them. Heat oven to 300 degrees. Spread seeds in a shallow baking pan and bake about 10 minutes, stirring occasionally. Don't overcook; they will continue to brown as they cool.

Strain marinade into a small saucepan and bring to a boil. Remove from heat and add enough water to make ⅓ cup liquid. Stir in corn-starch until dissolved.

Heat a wok or large nonstick skillet over medium-high. Add the oil and beef; fry, stirring, until the beef loses its red color, about 2 minutes. Use a slotted spoon to transfer the beef to another dish. Add broccoli and stir-fry about 3 minutes, then cover and allow to steam a minute. Add the beef and boiled marinade; increase heat and stir-fry until the sauce thickens, 2 to 3 minutes. Sprinkle with scallions. Serve with optional toasted sesame seeds.

Serves 4.

Readers, it's a thrill to hear from you. Drop me a line at Leslie@ LeslieBudewitz.com, connect with me on Facebook at LeslieBudewitzAuthor, or join my seasonal mailing list for book news and more. (Sign up on my website, www.LeslieBudewitz.com.) Reader reviews and recommendations are a big boost to authors; if you've enjoyed my books, please tell your friends, in person and online. A book is but marks on paper until you read these pages and make the story yours.

Thank you.

Acknowledgments

IN OCTOBER 2001, ASSISTANT U.S. ATTORNEY THOMAS C. Wales was shot and killed outside his Seattle home, the first known murder of a federal prosecutor. The case has never been solved, although it remains open and at this writing, news accounts indicate that investigators have identified a suspect. Law enforcement officers and the Department of Justice believe Mr. Wales's murder was related to his work. It's a terrifying and haunting prospect. Although Patrick Halloran is not Tom Wales, and I have no insights into the case, I have borrowed some details from the investigation that have been made public. The tragedy inspired me to highlight the impact of murder on the family and on the wider circle that surrounds each of us.

The dispute over the Gregorian & Son site is fictional, although loosely inspired by real-life concerns over the potential loss of a beloved grocery in Seattle's Montlake neighborhood to highway expansion, and by similar tensions in communities everywhere.

Although the real-life block featured here does include both a coffeehouse and a salon, mine are completely invented.

I have attempted to be accurate in my brief recount of the Armenian genocide and continuing tensions between the Turkish and Armenian communities. The book Pepper mentions, *Passage to Ararat* by Michael Arlen, originally published in 1975, is a highly respected account of the Armenian experience; there are other accounts, both fiction and nonfiction, about this tragic period in history, and I encourage modern readers to learn more about it.

Die-hard movie buffs in Seattle may realize I've fudged the date the Guild 45th closed by a few months. Rumors of a reopening are circulating; it would be great to see a classic theater given new life, in one form or another.

My thanks to Lita and Celia Artis for exploring Montlake with me, and drinking way too much coffee. Thanks to Debbie Burke for brainstorming, even if the final product took a different path. Amanda Bevill of World Spice Merchants and her staff in Seattle and in Montana could not be more supportive; thank you for the stories, for the cookies and chai, and for letting me eavesdrop on your lives. Although Jamie Ackerman is fictional, her paintings are inspired by those of Market artist Sally Simmons.

Thanks, too, to independent editor Ramona DeFelice Long for diving into an incomplete manuscript; my agent, John Talbot; my editor, Dan Mayer, along with the designers, production staff, and other booklovers at Seventh Street Books; and Dana Kaye, Samantha Lien, and Hailey Dezort at Kaye Publicity.

While writing this book I was constantly amazed by the appearance of exactly the right reader note, via email, my Facebook page, or other channels, at exactly the right time. Thank you, readers, for letting me know you like what I do. It helps; oh, my goodness gravy, as Pepper would say, how it helps.

I am blessed with a group of women friends who continually inspire and encourage me, through their words and examples, to fully live the creative life. Deep gratitude to Jordonna Dores, Jules Howard, Marsha Sultz, Rebecca Bauder, Nancy Rose, Sue Phillipson, Maggie Logan, and Carla Hannaford.

And always, thanks to my Mr. Right, Don Beans, for the male perspective, the ready ear, and the willingness to eat almost anything.

About the Author

LESLIE BUDEWITZ IS PASSIONATE ABOUT FOOD, GREAT mysteries, and the Northwest, the setting for her national-best-selling Spice Shop Mysteries and Food Lovers' Village Mysteries. Leslie is a three-time Agatha Award winner—2011 Best Nonfiction for *Books, Crooks & Counselors: How to Write Accurately About Criminal Law and Courtroom Procedure* (Linden/Quill Driver Books); 2013 Best First Novel for *Death al Dente* (Berkley Prime Crime), first in the Food Lovers' Village Mysteries; and 2018 Best Short Story for "All God's Sparrows" (Alfred Hitchcock Mystery Magazine). Her books and stories have also won or been nominated for Derringer, Anthony, and Macavity awards. A practicing lawyer, she served as president of Sisters in Crime in 2015–16 and currently serves on the board of Mystery Writers of America.

Leslie loves to cook, eat, hike, travel, garden, and paint—not necessarily in that order. She lives in Northwest Montana with her husband, Don Beans, a musician and doctor of natural medicine, and their cat, an avid bird-watcher.

Visit her online at www.LeslieBudewitz.com, where you'll find maps, recipes, discussion questions, links to her short stories, and more.